The Astronaut's Son

A Novel

TOM SEIGEL

woodhall press
NORWALK, CONNECTICUT

Isaac Bashevis Singer quote copyright © Nobel Foundation 1978. Used by permission.

"Pedro Navaja." Words and music by Ruben Blades. Copyright © 1990 Ruben Blades Publishing. All rights administered for the world, excluding Panama, by Kobalt Songs Music Publishing. All rights reserved. Used by permission. Reprinted by permission of Hal Leonard LLC.

"It's Only A Paper Moon." Words by Billy Rose and E.Y. Harburg. Music by Harold Arlen. Copyright © 1933 (Renewed) Chappell & Co., Inc., Glocca Morra Music, and SA Music. All rights reserved. Used by permission of Alfred Music.

"The Yachts" by Williams Carlos Willams, from *The Collected Poems:* Vol I, 1909-39, copyright © 1938 by New Directions Publishing Corp. Reprinted by permission of New Directions Publishing Corp. and Carcanet Press.

"You're" from *The Collected Poems Of Sylvia Plath,* Edited By Ted Hughes. Copyright © 1960, 1965, 1971, 1981 by the Estate of Sylvia Plath. Editorial material copyright 1981 by Ted Hughes. Reprinted by permission of HarperCollins Publishers and Faber & Faber Ltd.

"Too Tough to Die." Words and Music by Dee Dee Ramone, Joey Ramone, and Johnny Ramone. Copyright © 1984 Taco Tunes, Inc. Administered by WB Music Corp. All rights reserved. Used by permission of Alfred Music.

Hermann Hesse quote used by permission of the Estate of Hermann Hesse.

Copyright © 2018 Tom Seigel

Library of Congress Cataloging-in-Publication Data available
ISBN (hardcover) 978-0-9975437-8-0
ISBN (e-book) 978-0-9975437-9-7

Cover Design: LJ Mucci
Interior Design: Casey Shain
Copy editor: Tracy Salcedo

Woodhall Press, 81 Old Saugatuck Road, Norwalk, CT 06855
Woodhallpress.com
Distributed by INGRAM

*To my wife
and daughters*

The Astronaut's Son is a work of pure fiction, not a history book. No novel should ever be considered a source of facts, and this one is no different. While this made-up story may appear to bear some resemblance to events and persons of the past, it is a product of the author's imagination and no more real than your dreams.

There must be a way for man to attain all possible pleasures, all the powers and knowledge that nature can grant him, and still serve God—a God who speaks in deeds, not in words, and whose vocabulary is the Cosmos.

ISAAC BASHEVIS SINGER
Nobel Lecture

1

November 19, 2004

10:27AM

Jonathan Stein reread the angry letter he'd written to Neil Armstrong at 3 a.m. and put it, signed and sealed, into the inside pocket of his suit coat. He promised himself it would be the last one. He pulled out his mobile phone and listened to the voicemail again.

"Jon, it's Dr. Charnas. It's not a serious condition. Your primary was absolutely right. I'm not surprised the prolapse didn't show up on earlier EKGs. Sure, it might, *might* be inherited . . . but it might not. And it almost never produces that kind of event. We'll just keep an eye on it. Deke Slayton's problem was an arrhythmia, more severe, and he made it to outer space. So don't worry. Good luck with the big announcement."

Each replay—five in the last two days—only diluted the message. He stood near a vintage lunar globe next to a wall of windows overlooking Biscayne Bay. The midmorning sun flooded his top-floor office. With eyes closed tight, he spun the moon that had once belonged to his father, playing a secret game he'd invented as a boy, a peculiar form of astrology. He counted—One . . . Two . . . Three . . . Four—and, like always, placed his index finger on the sphere's polished wooden surface to stop its rotation. Would it be the Sea of Tranquility or the Sea of Crises? The Bay of Rainbows or the Bay of Roughness? He found himself in the southern Sea of Clouds. He drew a long, deliberate breath and checked his watch. Time to go.

He hit redial on his desk phone.

"Security."

"Any sign?"

"No, sir. My guys haven't seen him. You want me to check again?"

"I'll be down in five."

As he walked to the elevator, he made sure to touch each of the pictures lining the corridor—a sepia-toned photograph of the Wright brothers at Kitty Hawk, a black-and-white of Lindbergh at Le Bourget, a lithograph of Miró's *Dog Barking at the Moon*, an original poster from *2001: A Space Odyssey*, and a glossy color print of the Apollo 11 crew dressed in space suits, Neil Armstrong, Buzz Aldrin, and Michael Collins grinning in front of an image of a full moon in the background, its top half arcing over their heads like a halo. The photograph had been signed by Collins and Aldrin. Jonathan streaked a pair of fingerprints across the glass cover.

He tried to check his appearance in the bronze-plated elevator doors, but their brushed finish blurred his reflection. Before entering the company auditorium, he tossed the envelope into a lobby mail drop and made a quick detour to the first-floor men's room, patting his cowlick, checking for unplucked gray hairs, listening to the voice-mail once more.

The public relations director delivered the introduction Jonathan had scripted. Hundreds of his employees and members of the local and national media welcomed him with crackling applause and a volley of camera flashes. He approached the podium, lowered the microphone, and waited for the noise to subside.

"Thank you all for coming today." His voice quivered. He cleared his throat and continued. "Our Moon is unique in the nighttime sky. We gaze at the pale, quiet lunar surface in the late hours of the evening and go to sleep peacefully, assured by its reflective glow that the Sun has not abandoned us. Though the stars may be legion and luminous, they are simply too distant to soothe. The Moon encircles us and makes us feel safe. As God is said to have created the first woman from Adam's rib, a rogue planet, Theia, long ago struck the newly formed Earth, breaking off a chunk of rock that would later become the reliable companion who would never turn her back on us, or let us see her dark side. More than mere pacifier, the Moon attracts us. She has been patiently and persistently pulling at us, tempting us to climb up and touch her shining face."

Jonathan's senior management, seated in the first few rows, wore bright but bewildered smiles. He shot a perplexed look at his wife, Susana, seated right behind them and next to his mother, Eva. Susana's wide eyes and encouraging nod told him everything was fine, that he should keep going. He resumed, hoping the glance at her for reassurance had appeared as nothing more than a pause for dramatic effect.

"Ladies and gentlemen, today I am proud to announce, as chairman and CEO of Apollo Aeronautics, that after years of planning and preparation, we are ready to embark upon a great journey—the first manned mission to the Moon in over three decades."

The cameras flashed like strobe lights. The reporters perched on the edge of their seats. The cheering partisan crowd must have read Jonathan's predawn e-mail about showing team spirit.

"We have been away far too many years. The scouts came home long ago. The age of the pioneers is now." More applause. "The Moon was once just a destination, but now it will be a stepping stone to a larger existence. From the surface of the Moon, we will take a giant leap forward into outer space for the benefit of ourselves and our posterity.

"I'm honored that our private venture to return to the Moon and establish a permanent presence has the support of my good friend, the President of the United States. I am equally pleased that a man who has been a part of my family since I was a boy, Dale Lunden, the last man to walk on the Moon, has returned to Florida to take charge of mission operations."

Jonathan gestured to the front row. Lunden turned to face the crowd, waving both hands above his head, the Medal of Freedom pinned to his lapel glittering at the end of a shiny blue ribbon.

"This expedition will lead to both unprecedented scientific discovery and unlimited commercial opportunity." Jonathan paused and looked at his mother. "And finally, on a personal note, I'm making good on a promise I made to my father on a rainy afternoon thirty years ago." He clicked a remote and looked over his shoulder. A wall of projection screens formed a virtual mosaic, displaying side-by-side pictures of his father, Avi Stein—an official portrait in dress uniform, ramrod straight next to an Israeli flag, and a candid Kodachrome in a sky-blue jumpsuit at the Kennedy Space Center, the Apollo 18 rocket poised in the background.

"My father may have died of a heart attack before launch, but his dream of going to the Moon lives on in all of us." He put his hand over his heart. "Thank you all for coming, and in twelve months, we'll see you on the Moon."

A second click fired a whirling collage of iconic photographs from the greatest achievements in space exploration. The stirring, muscular theme from *Star Trek: The Motion Picture* blared from ceiling speakers. The whoops and whistles of junior employees accentuated a persistent ovation. Jonathan stepped away from the podium toward the very front of the stage, smiling, clapping, acknowledging his senior staff with open palms like a Broadway performer thanking musicians in the pit.

He enjoyed the warm glow of the stage lights, waving to enthusiastic spectators, posing for photographers. He even pointed to a stranger like the man was his long-lost best friend. He'd seen veteran politicians execute that exaggerated pandering gesture at the end of campaign rallies and had always wanted to try it. With a pressed-lip grin, he glanced at Susana, who flashed a discreet thumbs-up, and Eva, who blew a kiss—their eyes twinkling with pride, both unaware a valve in his heart had sprung a leak. He gave the crowd a final wave, crisp and military, as if he were about to board a Marine helicopter on the White House lawn. He left the stage, the phone pressed against his ribcage, and vowed to keep its message secret.

2

November 19, 2004

11:56PM

The gala at the Four Seasons following announcement of the lunar mission had been a great success. After a three-course meal and a "Godspeed" toast from John Glenn, via satellite, the ballroom roared at a blooper reel of Jonathan's early training exercises—the conquering hero banging his head against the fuselage of a NASA jet diving to simulate weightlessness, spraying a sneeze against his visor while being fitted for a space suit, and slipping off the pool deck at the underwater simulation facility in Houston. At the end of the night, each guest went home with a gift bag stuffed with Tang packets and three flavors of freeze-dried ice cream. Jonathan and Susana lingered in the lobby, shaking hands and posing for photographs until the last well-wisher had left. Near the parking garage elevators, Susana glanced over her shoulder and whispered, "How many TV interviews did Dale give? Like twenty? I don't think I saw him without a microphone in his face."

Jonathan waited for the elevator doors to shut. "All that camera time only bumps up the rates he can charge for those commercials he does. Give him a break. It had to be rough."

"Why?"

"Because after thirty years he's about to become the penultimate man on the Moon. Everybody knows Ted Williams was the last man to bat .400, but nobody knows who was second to last."

The elevator doors opened. "Didn't Williams have his head frozen?" she asked.

"Exactly my point. And nobody knows the second most famous person to get his head frozen, either. Fame's a hard drug to give up.

Dale loves it. Today had to be bittersweet." Dale Lunden never turned down the chance to be in a parade. He had the keys to so many different cities that Jonathan had nicknamed him "America's locksmith." Susana's clicking heels, like a ping-pong ball in a championship match, echoed through the empty garage. "So which one cost me more?" Jonathan said. "That outfit or the new car?"

"If you have to ask, *mi amor.*"

Susana Azevedo, the chair of planetary sciences at the University of Miami, played against type at social events. Making the most of a dancer's physique, she shopped at the chic boutiques of South Beach and spent a small fortune on hair, makeup, and jewelry. On rare occasions, like this one, she wore a choker with flawless oval emeralds set in platinum, a gift from their tenth anniversary. He had said the stones matched her eyes.

Jonathan, tipsy from too many toasts to the success of his mission, recoiled at the thought of the sobriety lecture Susana would deliver if he asked her to drive—and she didn't even know the new reason for him to cut down on his drinking. Deke Slayton had quit cold turkey after NASA grounded him. Jonathan loosened his tie and started the engine.

"I don't feel so well," she said. She rubbed her face with both hands.

"What is it?"

"New car smell."

"You always liked that."

"Smells are different now. Packed away all my Chanel last week." Susana was seventeen weeks pregnant, a planned conception delayed for years by their professional ambitions.

"This audio interface makes absolutely no sense." Jonathan stabbed at the dashboard of a black SUV fresh off the boat from Bremerhaven. "It's categorically unintuitive. I told you we should've bought the Volvo."

"Watch out, Jon."

He drove over the edge of a concrete median as they left the garage. "It's this stupid stereo system."

"Did you just slur? How much did you drink?"

"No. Nothing. Like two glasses, stopped an hour before we left."

"Put on your wipers. It's starting to rain again."

"So, what did you think about the speech, really?"

"I already told you it was good."

"But why did the guys have those goofy smiles and frozen deer eyes?" He activated the left blinker instead. "Damn it. Did they say anything?" He worried his employees might have realized he'd lifted some of his better lines from old speeches given by NASA officials. Had there been something on his face? In his hair? He discreetly checked his zipper.

"I need some fresh air," Susana said. Jonathan offered to crack the back windows. When each window went up and down at least twice, she reached for the glove compartment. "Want me to get the manual, Mr. Goodwrench?" He ignored her good-natured dig, determined to master the controls. When he finally had the wipers going, the back windows cracked, and a news station tuned in, a traffic and weather update had begun. A multicar accident blocked Bayshore Drive, the quickest route home to Coral Gables. After the report, Susana changed the radio station to 95.7, El Zol, salsa and merengue. Jonathan tapped a random sequence of buttons to silence Celia Cruz, tripping past an evangelical preacher predicting the end of days on the AM band before shutting off the radio.

"Put it back on."

"You haven't answered me yet. Accounting looked like a bunch of parents smiling at a hokey grade school play."

"They were caught off guard, Jon. They don't know you like I do."

"I've worked with some of those people for years."

"But they don't *know* you. They only know the Bill Gates of aerospace—brilliant, driven, uncompromising, the consummate MIT geek. Today you showed them a glimpse of your heart." She reset the radio to another salsa station. "Don't touch it. Ruben Blades, one of my favorites." She sang along with the infectious refrain. "*La vida te da sorpresas, sorpresas te da la vida, ay Díos . . .*"

He felt doubly relieved—no wardrobe malfunction and even his wife was unaware of his petty plagiarism. "If you thought my speech was so moving, did I have any luck persuading you?"

"No, *por favor,* I still think it's a bad idea . . . at least the scientist in me does. Too much to do before retracing old steps."

"Like Europa," he said.

"Exactly." Susana led a NASA team that had sent an unmanned probe to Europa, one of Jupiter's moons, to look for life in the ocean beneath its frozen surface. The first data was expected by mid-December. "You know I would never say that in public," she said. "I've always understood. When you were on stage, your mom squeezed my arm so tight my fingers went numb. I'm sure your dad would have been so proud." She shed her stilettos and begin to rub a foot.

"Didn't I warn you about those heels?"

"The baby's only the size of a nectarine, please. I'm not giving them up yet." The sound of an approaching siren interrupted their conversation. Jonathan checked the speedometer to make sure he wasn't the cause. A state patrol sedan raced past. Susana stashed a pair of two-carat earrings in her clutch purse.

Fifteen minutes from home and just off the highway, they heard a hissing sound coming from the engine. Twin columns of steam, wispy and white like spider's silk, shot up from the narrow strip of space between the front of the hood and the frame.

"You broke something over that curb."

"No, I didn't. Engine must be overheating. It wasn't me." He parked on the side of an unfamiliar road. The raindrops had shrunk to a fine mist. Dim street lamps, spaced far apart, provided sketchy light. On the near side, a chain-link fence ran the length of the block, enclosing a grassy yard.

"We should try to keep driving," she said.

"No need to risk it. It's not North Miami." After he called the auto club for a tow truck, he got out, leaving the door open, and paced alongside the SUV. Two cars raced by without slowing down. "No one stops anymore. They just assume you'll make a call." He pressed his hand against his jacket to feel the contours of his phone.

"Jon, I have to pee."

He peered over the honeycombed fence. Three low shadows darted back and forth at the far end of the yard. He leaned farther over the top and jumped back as a trio of enormous Dobermans barreled toward him. His slick Gucci soles proved a bad match for the slippery grass. He hovered in the air for an instant and crashed down on his ass. The dogs lunged at him, barking ferociously. The alpha reared up and stuck its snarling snout over the fence. Globs of slobber flew from both sides of its mouth.

"You OK?" Susana yelled.

"I'm fine." He stumbled back to his seat. "Just caught off guard. Stupid fucking animals." She handed him a wad of tissues. He patted the bottom of his wet wool pants. "Nothing out there unless you want to knock on doors."

Susana brought her legs onto the seat and folded them under her body. "I can hold it." She blew hot breath onto the cold passenger window and in the short-lived fog wrote "$DS \geq 0$," an equation representing the gloomy second law of thermodynamics.

"Entropy?"

"What do you expect?" she said. "It's starting to rain harder, and I'm freezing." She rubbed the moisture from her fingertips. "Remember when the first woman went into orbit?"

"Of course. Valentina Tereshkova, 1963. Three-day solo flight."

"No, no, not the Russian. The first American on the shuttle. The first time men and a woman had room to move around. Maybe they took Sally for a 'ride,' so to speak? For science, of course."

"Are you serious?"

"Yeah, what do you think?"

"I think you're nuts." He hit SCAN on the radio console. The tuner stopped on a country and western station playing "Dueling Banjos." "Jon Voight was so good in *Deliverance*. He had that intense panicky glare."

"Intercourse wouldn't really be of much significance," she continued. "What about fertilization? Mitosis? You could do that *in vitro*. I bet you NASA's done it, but kept that little experiment top secret to avoid pissing off the red states. What do you think, Jonny?" He didn't respond. "Jon? Hello?" She knocked on his thigh.

"Sorry, just thinking about how my all-natural hydraulic lift might function in the absence of gravity." She snapped a right cross to the body, while he laughed at his own joke, as usual.

Headlights filled the inside of the SUV as the tow truck pulled to a stop. In the rearview mirror, Jonathan studied the silhouette of a man, backlit by high beams, walking toward them. A scene from *Close Encounters of the Third Kind*, when the aliens first emerged from their ship, flashed in his mind. The faceless figure's slight limp sent a shiver down Jonathan's spine.

"Jon, stay in the car." Susana watched the approaching man over her shoulder. "He's like a zombie."

"He's fine, but put the necklace away."

When the tow truck driver reached them, Jonathan lowered his window, halfway, to explain the problem in layman's shorthand. The mechanic banged a fist on top of the hood for Jonathan to pop the latch. Despite a nagging drizzle and Susana's concern, Jonathan got out, as if he could be a useful consultant. He leaned back into car. "Call 911 if this guy hits me with a tire iron." He flipped the double thumbs-up sign.

"Shut the door," she said, her finger on the power lock button.

The sound of the tow truck had stirred up the dogs. Their high-pitched barks mixed with low growls. The driver approached them and tossed something over the fence.

"What are you doing?" Jonathan asked.

The man answered with a backhanded "it's under control" wave. He appeared to slip treats through the fence. "Them hellhounds should quiet down in a minute," he said, returning to the street.

"You carry kibble just in case?"

"Be prepared and all that. I do some repo work on the side. Dog bones soaked in codeine. Works real good."

"Wyatt" was embroidered on the oval patch sewn on the breast pocket of a forest-green work shirt. The thin, angular man of about fifty, with short, silver hair and a long, clean-shaven face. He looked surprisingly neat, like it was his first day on the job. He wore an efficiently organized and well-stocked tool belt. No grease stains anywhere. Even more unexpected were the latex gloves he wore. Jonathan had no intention of asking why. He pretended to study the engine over the mechanic's shoulder. With only a cursory check, good Dr. Wyatt diagnosed the problem as a coolant leak, likely a faulty hose. He pulled off his gloves with a dramatic snap after completing the exam. Wyatt had an odd manner of speech. He spoke without contractions and with a deliberate, almost Stephen Hawking-like rhythm. He said he would tow the SUV back to the garage, but they wouldn't be able to replace the hose until morning. He repositioned the truck, directed the couple to get into the cab, and asked for Jonathan's auto club card. "Are you Jonathan Stein, the aerospace executive?"

"Yes."

"We have got a lot to talk about."

Susana, heels back on, followed her husband into the truck while Wyatt hooked up the disabled vehicle. "What the fuck?" The interior of the white Ford reeked of artificial pine scent. A dense coniferous forest of miniature green air fresheners hung from the rearview mirror, and a clear plastic slipcover wrapped the beige vinyl bench seat like 1950s living room furniture. "This guy's like a total psychopath. What if—"

"Relax, at least your dress won't get stained. It's fine. Probably just OCD." Jonathan's phone vibrated inside his pocket. He checked the caller ID before answering. "It's Zubin."

"Answer it. Tell him about what's going on, in case—"

"In case what? Wyatt drives us down some deserted dirt road? Zudu's in Shanghai anyway." Jonathan met Zubin Dukkash at NASA's space camp. They reunited as roommates at MIT and, after graduation, formed a venture capital technology fund with deep-pocketed alumni in New York City. Zubin took over management of the fund after Jonathan moved to Miami to run Apollo. "Where the hell are you?" Jonathan asked. He raised his voice to compete with the looping house music blaring out of his phone's receiver. "Isn't it lunchtime?"

"Nightlife in the new Shanghai, Jon-o. 24/7, baby. Communist party is over, but the new party never stops. How'd it go?"

"Good. Great. Massive coverage."

"Sorry I couldn't be there, but one more bottle of Cristal should do it."

"The search engine?" Jonathan asked.

"The potential ad revenue is huge," Zubin said.

"Walk somewhere else. I can barely hear you."

Susana thumped Jonathan's forearm and told him to say something about Wyatt. He held up his index finger to silence her. The driving techno music rose and fell as Zubin passed booming speakers and a Frenchman shouting a drunken request for two gin and tonics in broken English. After a blast from one last speaker, the music was muffled behind a creaking door.

"Zudu, where'd you go?"

Before Zubin could answer, Jonathan heard the gurgle and whoosh of a toilet flush. "You couldn't go outside?"

"All that champagne, dude. I had to take a leak."

Jonathan heard him streaming into a pool of water. "Did you meet with my vendor?" Susana reached for the phone, but he switched ears and hunched toward the steering wheel.

"Your friend said they met with the regional authority last week, worked out the environmental issues. That thing, and three Yao Ming jerseys. Nice to have contacts in Houston."

"What does that mean, 'worked out'?"

"Did you really want me to ask? It's done. The components should start shipping in three weeks."

"Perfect."

"Jon-o, I came up with an incredible idea on the flight over. We've got to do this. Vegetarian submarine sandwich shops in India. I've already got the slogan: 'India: the SUB continent.' Get it?"

"Very funny."

"I'm dead serious. We'll talk when I get back. You on your way to an after-party?"

Jonathan made saucer eyes at Susana and explained his car

trouble, giving a detailed description of the spick-and-span mechanic. Zubin, laughing through his words, said he got all the "deets" scribbled onto a paper towel.

"There," Jonathan said, after dropping the phone into his pocket. "Happy?"

Susana peeled her hands off the clingy slipcover and looked out the rear window. "What the hell does this Wyatt want with you?"

"Money. What else? Probably a gun freak who wants a donation to his 'Guardians of the Second Amendment' club. Thinks because I'm a Republican I must believe every American has a constitutional right to keep an AK-47 under his pillow . . . like I really want this prince carrying an assault rifle."

Susana deforested the mirror in one fell swoop, stuffing a handful of overly scented pines into the glove compartment. "No guns in there. Probably got an arsenal in the toolshed behind his double-wide."

"He fits right in," Jonathan said. "Florida's motto should be 'Welcome snowbirds, drug lords, and carnies. Anything goes here.' It's no wonder they put the Dalí Museum in Tampa."

Wyatt opened the driver's side door and scooted next to Jonathan, who had taken the middle seat to serve as a buffer. Suburban chivalry. For three to fit, Jonathan had to straddle a long, uncomfortably close gear stick rising up from the floorboard. "I heard your announcement on the radio. Going up to the Moon yourself, are you?"

"That's the plan."

Susana rolled her lips inside her mouth as Wyatt reached between her husband's legs to shift into gear. Jonathan braced against the seatback.

"My deodorizers?"

"Wife's pregnant. Strong smells. They're in the glove box."

Wyatt glanced at Susana, whose hand, now covering her mouth, looked as if it were cradling a CB radio transmitter. Jonathan couldn't tell if she was laughing or about to vomit. Apparently, neither could Wyatt. He reached into the storage tray of his door and handed Jonathan an Eastern Airlines airsick bag. "You can find anything at

liquidation auctions down here. Wait a minute. Have you been training in one of them weightless airplanes? The vomit comet."

"Of course."

"I could give you a whole box of these, *gratis,* for you and your
crew. I got hundreds."

"Haven't needed them yet, but thanks anyway. One's good for
now."

"All right, but if you get splashed in the face by some dude's floating puke—"

"I'll take my chances."

"You do know, Mr. Stein, what really happened at NASA back in
the 1960s?"

Jonathan sighed, fearing he might need another airsick bag after
all.

"I am sure, Mr. Stein, you will think I am some unbalanced trek-
ker who still lives in my mom's cellar, collecting and indexing old
comic books, but I have read a lot of articles by serious scientists.
There is no way we went to the Moon in 1969. We did not possess
the technology."

Wyatt was worse than a disgruntled former employee or even a
gun freak. He was a moon conspiracy nut, a so-called hoax believer,
one of those cluttered basement troglodytes who think NASA never
landed men on the Moon.

Susana put her hand on Jonathan's thigh and leaned toward
Wyatt. "What about that picture from the Moon's surface that has
a rock with a letter painted on it? That tells you they planted it on
a movie set. They can't explain that one." She seemed to enjoy the
lunar yahoos and occasionally forwarded Jonathan hyperlinks to the
most outlandish hoax reports she could find. He once nearly choked
on his lunch after she sent him a clip of Buzz Aldrin landing a solid
right cross to the face of a particularly persistent hoaxer. Their ensuing e-mail banter—light and playful, sprinkled with puns and double
entendre—diverted Jonathan from intense work days, but at times
he thought she did it to remind him of her opposition to manned
spaceflight.

"I would have never thought the wife of an astronaut's son would be a Lunatic like me, but she is right on the money. That's why we call ourselves 'Lunatics'—get it? Being ironical. Look at the lunar photographs and those grainy home movies. Obviously fakes. Why are there not any stars in the sky? Supposed to be outer space, right? And the lunar lander did not stir up even one speck of dust. Seriously?" Wyatt's head swiveled back and forth in quarter turns as he spoke, his voice rising higher as he made his case. "And how did the American flag wave in that video with no air up there? I bet you never noticed that one." He jammed his palm on the horn to ward off an encroaching white BMW convertible. "Keep to your lane, you dingbat." He turned to his passengers. "Probably some smart-ass lady divorce lawyer drunk on cutesy umbrella drinks. I guarantee it." He tapped Jonathan's knee with a stiff pointer. "And there's more, a lot more. What about the radiation from the Van Allen belt? From what I heard tell, those astronauts would have been fried."

Jonathan rolled his eyes at Susana. This would be an easy battle to win. "The stars are not visible, Wyatt, for the same reason we can't see them in the daytime. Sunlight blocks them out. The flag waved in the film because an astronaut moved the flagpole. The lander disturbed very little moon dust because, as you said yourself, there's 'no air up there.' And the Apollo astronauts were protected from radiation by specially treated heat shields. By the way, I'm pretty confident my father was going to the Moon, and not to some Hollywood soundstage."

Wyatt made a sharp turn onto a road running behind a high school, said it was a shortcut to the garage. Jonathan's body leaned into Susana's, pressing her against the passenger door. "No doubt your dad believed it. So did his replacement, Lunden. They trained them up good, mind-fucked them all, pardon my French. That was part of the con job. In 1969 everybody I knew still had black-and-white televisions and party-line telephones. Opened garage doors and car windows with nothing but elbow grease." Wyatt threw back a shot of orange Tic Tacs. His offer to share was waved off. "How could we possibly have sent a spaceship 238,000 miles to the Moon, gone into orbit, dropped a lander to the lunar surface, walked around, launched back from the surface to rendezvous with the command module, and then safely splashed down to Earth? Plumb makes no sense. Not a whit. Atari did not even invent *Pong* until 1972. I am sorry, Mr. Stein, but that dog most definitely will not hunt."

Jonathan reoriented himself, sat up taller, his hands cupped defensively at his inseam. "Technological innovation trickles down from the military. It takes decades. NASA could've easily built you a remote-controlled garage door opener back in 1969, but it wouldn't have done much good on the carport you probably grew up with."

"True enough," Wyatt admitted. "But what about the lettered rock photograph your wife brought up?"

"That mark was made in the film developing process, but I'll grant you it looks like a C."

"Mind if I put on some tunes?" Wyatt asked. "Nothing too loud." Without waiting for a reply, he popped in a CD. The cab filled with easy acoustic riffs rotating around major chords and the tinny twang of a steel guitar.

"Sounds like Jimmy Buffett," Susana said. She leaned forward and squeezed her knees together.

"You got that one right too: 'Trip Around the Sun' with my girl Martina McBride. There are many more questions that NASA, or as we like to call them, Never A Straight Answer, refuses to confront. What about Armstrong? Why is he so cagey, avoiding the public eye like a possum? They say he is practically a shut-in. Did you know he will not even sign autographs anymore?"

"Actually, I've heard that," Jonathan said.

"You think he is bonkers too, do you not?"

Jonathan wondered if Wyatt had read a tell in his body language, like a good poker player. Despite what his posture may have revealed, he had no intention of telling the man that since childhood he had been asking himself the very same questions about his unresponsive astronaut pen pal. He'd zealously guarded the history of his unrequited correspondence with Armstrong for decades, sharing it only with his wife, his mother, and Zubin, his oldest and best friend. He couldn't even tell Lunden, his surrogate uncle. That would have been weak, embarrassing.

"Did you folks hear the latest, the one about his barber?"

Jonathan nodded, his lips pressed together, eyes half-closed. "My wife forwarded me an article from some website."

Armstrong had recently threatened to sue his long-time barber. The man, a committed eBayer, had gathered up the clippings surrounding the barber chair after Armstrong left and posted them on the Internet auction website for sale. The frenzied online bidders drove the sale price to $3,000. Infuriated, Armstrong hired a lawyer and demanded the immediate return of his hair. It struck Jonathan as bizarre, but consistent with Armstrong's idiosyncratic nature.

"Do you know why he wanted that hair back?" Wyatt asked.

"I'm sure you'll tell me."

Wyatt shut off the music. "I heard it was really about something called *mee-tah-kon-drel* DNA," he said, attempting to pronounce the polysyllabic name for the microscopic powerhouses located in every cell of the body.

"Oh, I haven't seen that one yet," Susana said. She took Jonathan's hand and squeezed it twice. He got the message: Play along. He obliged, curious to learn the secret details of Armstrong's purpose.

"Since you are a scientific type, Mr. Stein, I am sure you will appreciate this. All of the DNA in Armstrong's body would have gone through a powerful change if he was exposed to that Van Allen radiation belt. All his cells, including hair follicles, would have been mutated, permanently. You know, like the Fantastic Four, or the way Charlton Heston looked different when his hair got all white after seeing the burning bush. Armstrong was shitting that somebody might have been sharp enough to have them clippings tested. That for sure would have exposed that he were not ever exposed. No burning bush. You get me? That there would be the real reason he wanted that hair back." Wyatt lowered his window to hack and spit. "My buddies and I actually bid on it, you know, just for fun. Only went up to three hundred. We had no idea it had real hoax value. Some guy with the screen name 'HirsutePursuit' won the auction." Slipping into a thicker

North Florida drawl and more colloquial speech, Wyatt said, "I don't even wanna know what that joker's gonna do with Armstrong's hair."

While Jonathan bit down on his tongue until it nearly bled, Susana stepped in to save him. "Really interesting. I don't think I saw that in the latest issue of *Scientific American*."

"No ma'am. My buddy Russell is a short-wave freak. Heard it from a ham operator up in Sitka."

Jonathan did his best to muffle the laughter he let escape.

"If you do not mind me asking, Mrs. Stein, what was the name of the website where you found that article? The one about Armstrong's hair. Russell is an avid collector of anything on strange astronaut behavior. Got an overstuffed drawer file on Neil."

"I don't remember. It must have been more than a month ago. How soon will we be there? What time is it?" She put her hand on her stomach. "I don't so feel well."

"What's wrong?" Jonathan asked.

"That pine tree smell."

"Just a few more minutes, ma'am. Hold on." Wyatt drove faster. "Here, take this." He reached across Jonathan's chest to hand her another airsick bag. It was covered in Chinese characters. "Was it houstonistheproblem.com?"

"I really don't remember."

"Wasn't there something in the URL about an eclipse?" Jonathan asked.

"No, I don't think so." She cracked the window and pressed her cheek against the glass. "How much longer? I can't take it."

"Almost there. I think your husband is on the right track. Russell reads one called eclipsedtruth.com."

"That was it," Jonathan said. "Are you going to make it, honey?"

"Is that the garage on the right?" Susana coughed into the bag.

"Yes, ma'am, it is. Hang in there. That site is Russell's new favorite, said it has got some of the best graphics he has ever seen. Apparently has got loads of stuff on Armstrong. Russell called me at 3 a.m. a couple weeks back—I was out on a repo anyhow—all revved up about how NASA drugged the astronauts, planted fake memories, but apparently it did not work on Armstrong. He figured it out. The government forced him to keep his mouth shut, threatening him and all, Russell said. That could make any man cuckoo for Cocoa Puffs. I have been meaning to check it out for myself, soon as I am paid up on my cable bill."

When they reached the garage's parking lot, Susana grabbed her husband's forearm and yanked him close to whisper. "Over there," she said, tilting her head in the direction of an IHOP. "I have got to pee. Now."

"The truck should be good to go by ten o'clock, but call the garage first. Would you like a lift home?"

"Let's go," Susana said, pulling at her husband.

"No, thanks," Jonathan replied. "I want to get a cup of coffee." He pointed to the restaurant. "We'll call a taxi."

Susana shot out of the truck. Jonathan was about to step out when he felt a hand on his shoulder. "Could I trouble you for an auto-graph first?" Wyatt said, smiling and offering a pen.

Jonathan snatched it from him and scribbled on an unused airsick bag. "No eBay?"

Wyatt made an X over his chest. "Cross my heart."

Susana ran in short strides, her heels skittering across the wet pavement. Jonathan matched her pace, his arm around her waist.

"Are you all right?"

"Better now, just really have to go. I don't know what was worse, those goddamned air fresheners or that *pendejo's* bullshit."

"He was harmless. That other stuff on Armstrong. Why didn't you tell me?"

"I thought you were finally done with him. That's what you said. Hurry, I'm seriously about to burst."

3

November 20, 2004

1:54AM

After paying the cab fare, Jonathan followed Susana through a side door leading to their recently remodeled kitchen. He brushed his fingertips over the custom-cut black granite surface of an island so large he had nicknamed it "Madagascar." Two circular skylights looked like a pair of dilated black eyes beneath the overcast night sky. A bowl of fresh fruit next to a commercial-grade sink gave the air a tropical scent.

"That guy was categorically nuts," Jonathan said, referring to Wyatt.

"Jon, I swear if he'd put on another pair of latex gloves in the truck, I would have peed myself. Downshift or hernia check." She held onto his shoulder and took off her heels. They kissed.

"I love you this way," he said.

"I love you too, but what do you mean 'this way'?"

"Barefoot, pregnant, and in the kitchen."

She thrust her hand toward his crotch, a mock hernia check to make him flinch. He jumped back and wagged his finger. She opened the vault-like steel door of a refrigerator big enough to serve as a small-town morgue and pulled out a bottle of vitamin-infused water. He grabbed a bowl of leftover spaghetti. Jonathan always came home hungry from social events. No eating meant no sauce-blotted shirts and no errant parsley between incisors. Susana called it his fast of advancement.

"I'm going to check out that website before bed." He sat at the kitchen table, opposite his wife, who pulled bobby pins from her hair and lined them up in a row.

"Why waste your time? It's stupid, like the rest of them. Let's go to sleep."

He stabbed a fork into a mound of spaghetti. "It's ridiculous, totally. But the idea that Armstrong was *forced* to keep quiet, that's a new one."

"He's just an introvert who hates the spotlight." She swept the bobby pins into her purse and stood up. "We've been over this *ad nauseam*. SETI has a better chance of getting a response. Don't you have an early spin class tomorrow?"

"Just a few minutes. But I've written my last letter. I promise you that." He stuffed two tight knots of pasta into his mouth and pushed his bowl aside. "I'll be right down." He moved toward a spiral staircase leading to his office.

"Jon, wait. Sit down. Please." She returned to the table and folded her arms like he'd called her bluff.

He stopped on the first step. "What is it?"

"I went back to that site a couple of weeks ago, my regular survey of hoaxer bullshit. There were some new postings, insensitive, mean-spirited crap about the Apollo 1 astronauts, and about your dad too. I didn't want to upset you."

"Anti-Semitic stuff?" His words sounded brittle and scratchy, as if they'd been freeze-dried in his throat.

"This idiot claims they were all killed."

"The Apollo 1 crew? Because of the hoax?"

"Yes."

"What's it say about my dad?"

She shook her head. "Why would anyone listen to people who call themselves Lunatics?"

"What the hell does it say?" He had recovered his voice, which now echoed off the cavernous kitchen's stainless-steel surfaces.

"I didn't even read all of it, complete nonsense, something about the German rocket engineers at NASA not wanting an Israeli astronaut. Total bullshit. There was no reason to bother you with *esa pura mierda*, especially before your speech."

"You mean it says they killed him?" Jonathan sat on the step, hands on his thighs, arms flared out. Even though Jonathan was more certain than ever that he shared a terminal heart with his father, the old questions bubbled back to the surface. Avi had been a legendary athlete, bench pressed twice his weight, ran the 100 meters in under twelve seconds at age thirty-three. How could there have been no warning signs? How did the NASA doctors miss it? The cardiologist's voicemail replayed in Jonathan's head. "So what happened?" he asked.

Susana, elbows splayed on the table, sliced knifed fingers through her hair as if she were shearing it off. "The website says they drugged him, or something. Jesus, I wish I'd never sent you that stupid article about Armstrong."

"I've got to see it now," he said, one hand clutching a banister to pull himself up, the other rubbing the back of his neck.

She slouched back in her chair. "Please. *Olvídalo.* Forget it, it's not worth your time. These hoax people are *cra-zy.*" She bugged out her eyes and shook jazz hands by her ears. "Even the UFO nuts make fun of them. Think about it, Jon. Nobody mocks the Sasquatch-Elvis-Loch Ness spotters more than you do. This is no different. Don't let it get to you."

"This is worse than the other stuff . . . it's personal . . . fucking intolerable. Fucking assholes." He returned to the table and grabbed his fork. "You know I could probably sue. Bury that motherfucker in legal fees and judgments." He shoved a wormy nest of noodles into his mouth.

"Sue? What sue? You mean like Armstrong and his barber? Because some inbred idiot dumped a load of garbage on the Internet? So what? You don't really want to go to court. You hate lawyers. Why are you so worked up? Is this even about the website?"

He stared at the bowl, afraid eye contact might reveal his secret condition, and twirled a loose clump of spaghetti into a stringy ball. "What's it about then?"

Susana moved next to him to take his hand. She waited for eye contact and softened her tone. "Resolution. Closure."

"Not this again, please." He yanked out of her loose grip. "I've dealt with what happened to my dad. OK? Believe me. I know. That's why these schmucks make my blood boil." He pushed the gnawing questions back down. A halogen bulb from an Italian chandelier flickered and sizzled. "Didn't we just replace that one? Shit, we should have ordered more. Fuck." He imagined Dr. Charnas in the kitchen wearing a white lab coat, nodding with a broad smile, saying it was nothing to worry about.

"Don't blow another gasket," Susana said. "I'll order more tomorrow. No parent's death is ever easy. Remember how I was at my parents' funerals? The timing, his good health, his country, that's enough to sow some pretty deep doubt . . . and distress, especially in a thirteen-year-old. And now you're about to go to the Moon, and become a father."

Guarded adolescent memories, the first seeds of suspicion, added unspoken weight to her argument: a warning from the Mississippi Jew he'd met on the bus to space camp, about the ex-Nazis still working for NASA at the Marshall Space Flight Center in Huntsville, Alabama ("You surely know that back in nineteen hundred and forty-five, many proud members of the SS jumped right into striped pajamas to keep from getting shot on the spot by them Russians. If they'll dress like that, like *us*, to save their hides, you think they got any problem with a double-breasted suit and a shiny Old Glory pin?"); his Indian bunkmate's indiscreet curiosity ("Did anyone suspect foul play? Not everybody loves you Jews, especially Israeli soldiers."); and an unnerving encounter with a pair of German engineers on the Huntsville campus.

Jonathan tossed his fork in the bowl. "Dad never smoked, ever, and everybody smoked in Israel." Preparing for his own mission, Jonathan had spent hours in the gym, reduced his body fat to sixteen percent. He'd been surprised each time his annual EKG was pronounced normal. Even before his recent diagnosis, he was determined to overcome his father's fate.

"I know he's been on your mind lately," Susana said, "more than usual. If you want to feel at peace, go at it the way you would anything else. Get answers. Get the facts."

"What, like read the autopsy?" A noodle dangled from the corner of his mouth, twitching when he spoke. "My mom told me what happened. I know what happened. And please don't say it again. I don't need any more closure." He went back to the Sub-Zero, took out a pint of Susana's double chocolate Häagen-Dazs, and headed for the stairs.

"But how did your mother know?"

"Dale must've told her. Christ, got any more questions? I feel like I'm on the witness stand. We all know what happened. Everybody does."

She backhanded the table top. Her engagement ring sounded a sharp crack. Jonathan froze halfway up the staircase. "You're not going to get any answers from the hoaxers," she said. She stood to clear the table. "Your good friends at the RNC could slice through the red tape, get you whatever you want to see. You're not going to find any understanding on some *cabron's* website. Listen to me, it might actually be good for you . . . since you won't go to real therapy."

Jonathan stomped down the stairs. "Is that why you send me those hoax links? Some kind of shock treatment? I don't have abandonment issues." He hated being manipulated, analyzed like a mental patient. "You might have a PhD, but it's not in psychology."

"I thought those links were funny, the ones I sent you." She put his bowl in the sink and let the water run. "And I thought the one about Armstrong's hair might remind you that he's just an eccentric weirdo, that his silence has nothing to do with you."

"This isn't about Armstrong. I'm going on that *fercockt* website to see what this guy says because I don't want some libelous fuck turning my father into a pseudo-martyr for a band of crackpots. Why am I even explaining this? I have every right to be angry." He spun around and marched back up the staircase.

In the hallway outside his study hung Susana's most prized possession—a framed handwritten letter scratched on the back of a restaurant placemat and flecked with grease stains highlighting random words. It was from Professor Richard Feynman, the legendary physicist and one of her mentors at Caltech. Written shortly before he died, Feynman apologized for failing to name her as a coauthor on an important paper about variational perturbation. Jonathan reread the heartfelt acknowledgement of her contribution.

Before sitting down to scrutinize eclipsedtruth.com, he pivoted in the center of his home office, sizing up a wall covered with degrees and awards and a framed front page from the *Jerusalem Post* with a banner headline announcing his father's special selection for the Apollo program. Armstrong could have papered his own study from floor to ceiling with the ream of unanswered letters Jonathan had sent. His thirty-year, one-way correspondence covered a cosmic spectrum of topics, attitudes, and emotions. There were youthful ramblings about waiting in line in the pouring rain to see *Star Wars* for the twelfth time, planning and executing clandestine model rocket launches on the beach, and counting cards for beer money with Zubin and a pair of fake IDs in Atlantic City. There were serious requests for guidance: whether Jonathan should enlist in the Israel Defense Forces against his mother's wishes; when to begin flying lessons; whether to mount a takeover bid for Apollo Aeronautics. In the eighties and nineties, Jonathan wrote frequent critiques of the misguided shuttle program, referring to NASA as "a bunch of glorified teamsters." When Armstrong had agreed to join the Rogers Commission to investigate the *Challenger* disaster, Jonathan volunteered to help him, offering to write software to aid in the forensic analysis. When *Columbia* exploded in 2003 and the Concorde went into mothballs eight months later, Jonathan wrote to him from the last supersonic flight, lamenting humanity's retreat from the heavens as "the satanic sound of my favorite record playing in reverse."

There were also countless, silently spurned invitations: graduations, the wedding, a seat on the board of Apollo and, most recently, the announcement of the lunar mission. None of his letters, not even the modest plea with which Jonathan began his efforts to make contact, received a single word of reply. The silence in response to that first letter still stung the most.

November 17, 1974

Dear Astronaut Neil Armstrong,
My name is Jonathan Stein. You probably know my
dad, Captain Avraham Stein. He was going to be

Commander of Apollo 18, but he died of a heart attack in September. The launch of his mission is tomorrow. I'm supposed to go watch it with my mom. Captain Lunden is a good friend of my father. A lot of astronauts came to the funeral, even a few who didn't know him. I know it's a long trip to Israel.

I was eight years old when you landed on the Moon, but I'm thirteen now. I remember watching you on television when we lived in Tel Aviv. Mom, Dad, and I got up really early to see it. When you took your first steps on the surface, we clinked glasses of Tang and said L'Chaim *(to life). We were all so excited. I read everything I can about space, and I'm learning all about rocketry. I've even shot a few off in our backyard. I want to be a pilot like my dad, and maybe an astronaut, like you.*

On the news yesterday, they said that the first radio message to the stars, called the Arecibo message, was just sent from an observatory in Puerto Rico to a star cluster 25,000 light years away. The message was a series of numbers. They interviewed an astronomer named Carl Sagan who helped write it. He said that they used only numbers because math is the one true universal language. I'm really good at math. I even go to the high school twice a week to work on more advanced problems. Maybe I'll communicate with the aliens one day.

I hope whoever is out there started looking for us a really long time ago. That astronomer said we won't know if our message will reach anybody for at least 50,000 years because that's how long it will take for the message, traveling at light speed, to get there, plus the time it takes for an answer to get to back. I know I'm only a kid, but I can't wait that long.

Since my dad's funeral, I've started a collection of autographed astronaut photos. My mom says that

*you're a very busy man, but I'd really appreciate it if I
could get one from you.*

Sincerely,
Jonathan Stein

The screen saver on Jonathan's home computer looped through a
series of vacation pictures while he shoveled spoonfuls of soupy ice
cream. A favorite shot from the Netherlands dropped from the top of
the screen, bouncing like a rubber ball. Jonathan, in a chrome-plated
conquistador helmet, held a bright red tulip in his teeth (at Susana's
insistence) and thrust a snub-nosed lance into the whitewashed body
of a windmill. He licked the spoon clean and tossed the empty carton
to the trash. Next up, rising from the bottom of the screen, a picture
of Susana, dressed head to toe in khaki safari wear, posing alongside
the Great Sphinx at Giza. They had staged the shot with Jonathan, the
photographer, lying on the sand to make it appear she was whispering a secret into the ear of the silent stone sentinel.

He moved the mouse and the image vanished from the screen.
He typed in the website address: eclipsedtruth.com. The screen went
black. A full moon appeared, moving in a slow arc from the bottom left to the middle of the screen. At center it stopped, and music
began to play, Ella Fitzgerald's classic version of *It's Only a Paper
Moon.* Jonathan searched for a way to skip the introduction, but visitors were apparently required to listen to the whole song because the
escape and *enter* keys afforded no shortcut. When Ella reached the
final verse, the lyrics faded into focus, black letters against the background of the snow-white lunar circle:

It's a Barnum and Bailey world
Just as phony as it can be
But it wouldn't be make-believe
If you believed in me.

Next, in white letters below the moon, more words appeared as
if typed at that moment, accompanied by the staccato machine-gun
bursts of a midcentury newsroom typewriter:

Don't be a sucker in Barnum's world. Learn the truth that the

> government ringmasters have been hiding for years. NASA is the greatest show ON EARTH (not the Moon). Click here and let Cassandra expose the hoax.

Jonathan hesitated before activating the hyperlink. The homepage hi-res graphics and apt use of a vintage recording were impressive, even inspired—a surprising improvement on the crude text and dated site design of the moon conspiracy nuts who filled the Internet with a maddening lot of cyberspace junk. He felt certain the creator of the website, using the name "Cassandra" for the mythological reference, was a young male—like nearly all hoax believers, science fiction fans, pranksters, fraudsters, and mass murderers.

When he clicked the link, a new image appeared—a screenshot of O. J. Simpson in a scene from *Capricorn One*, the mildly entertaining adaptation of Ray Bradbury's story about the government's use of a Hollywood soundstage to fake a Martian landing. *Capricorn One* was to lunar conspiracy theorists what *Catcher in the Rye* seemed to be to deranged assassins like Hinckley and Chapman. A caption bubble appeared next to Simpson's face: "See folks, I even went to Mars to look for the real killers." Words again appeared as if being typed at the bottom of the screen.

> If Johnnie Cochran can brainwash twelve people (and thousands of supporters!) into believing the Juice was innocent, how many people can be fooled by NASA and the United States military into thinking that we actually landed on the Moon in 1969?

A left-hand column listed hyperlink choices with titles like "photographic anomalies," "lunar atmospheric discontinuities," "Van Allen Belt radiation," "Armstrong's silence," and, preceded by a flashing "New Posting" heading, a link called "NASAssassins."

Jonathan moved cautiously through the website, reluctant to start with the undoubtedly sensationalized account of his father's death. He chose the Armstrong link because he often enjoyed the hoaxers' hyperbolic rants about the world's most famous and most enigmatic astronaut. The theories covered the entire delusional spectrum. Armstrong was a KGB agent. Armstrong was a robot. Armstrong became a Muslim on the Moon. Armstrong was a CIA agent. Armstrong was an alien.

Having just heard Wyatt's vivid description, Jonathan skipped an updated account of the auctioned hair clippings and selected a hyperlink entitled "Downloaded Dreams." In the section's preamble, Cassandra claimed to have gained access to top secret government files, including reels of 8mm films detailing the extent of the lunar conspiracy. What followed, Cassandra averred, was an account assembled directly from "unimpeachable NASA sources."

> No one disputes the ability of NASA to achieve low earth orbit in the 1960s. But we never left it. The astronauts were put on a regular schedule of sleep during their missions, and that's when the mischief took place. Tiny holes in the interior lining of the capsules secreted an odorless combination of chemicals that put the astronauts to sleep. The potent mixture of gases also made their minds more malleable, ready to accept the messages radioed into their heads. The capsules' instruments were adjusted to conform to the vivid hallucinations implanted in their brains. In their minds, the Apollo astronauts followed the intricate procedures of a lunar landing, surface exploration, and docking with the capsule for the return trip. None of it happened. They were the victims of secret government mind control. We all were. The radio and television broadcasts were faked but carefully synchronized to the virtual experience of the unwitting astronauts. They were awakened only on splashdown, at which point their elaborate dreams merged with reality.

Jonathan immediately saw the gaping holes in Cassandra's theory—spontaneous radio communications, frequent midmission malfunctions, like Apollo 13, simple bodily needs and functions. Still, he couldn't help wondering whether Cassandra's shadowy government scientists had used too many drugs on Armstrong.

> The ruse started out as an interim measure. NASA intended to send a manned mission to the Moon, but they couldn't do it in time to fulfill Kennedy's promise. Technical setbacks and budget cuts ultimately made this impossible. NASA ran out

of time, and Washington ended the lunar program—its successes consisting of implanted memories in a handful of unsuspecting space travelers—and the largest manipulation of mass perception in history.

But something went "wrong" with Armstrong. He became convinced that none of it was real.

"Not enough drugs," Jonathan whispered.

During classified post-mission debriefings, Armstrong claimed that he did not land on the Moon but instead had a "remarkably vivid" dream. Government psychiatrists tried to convince him that his "delusions" were simply the overwhelming stress and elation of the experience. Secret CIA footage viewed by Cassandra shows Armstrong in a windowless room at a Naval facility in Hawaii. A man in a white lab coat entered. With an accent of unknown origin, he said, "So now you know the truth. Announce it to the world and you will be branded a madman by your government, the press, and the public. People believe what they see, not what they're told, especially when they see the lie and hear the truth. Live the life we have chosen for you. No one will ever believe your story."

Armstrong capitulated. He agreed to toe the NASA party line, to fly in formation. Some believe he must have received handsome payoffs for his silence. Others say the government threatened him and keeps him under surveillance. Whatever the incentive, Armstrong has kept NASA's secrets buried all these years. The truth, however, has gnawed at him, eating away from the inside, driving him into deeper exile, and provoking increasingly bizarre behavior.

So now you know why Armstrong retreats from public life. Cassandra urges him to come forward and confirm the arrogant duplicity of our so-called democracy.

Jonathan reread the passage like a rubbernecker taking one last look at a car accident. Cassandra had an undeniable talent for pulp fiction. Was it nothing more than a clever mishmash of the plots of *Capricorn One* and *The Manchurian Candidate*? Could any of it be true? Jonathan almost pitied Armstrong, suffering for so many years in compelled silence. Though he put no faith in the author's wild fantasy, he wondered whether Armstrong's isolation might be some form of self-sacrifice.

He clicked the link for "NASAssassins" and found a choice of two pages—one on the deaths of Gus Grissom, Ed White, and Roger Chaffee as a result of the launchpad fire of Apollo 1, and the other titled "The Question of the Jewish Astronaut." Still leery, he chose the Apollo 1 link. According to Cassandra, the Apollo 1 fire ignited because of a malfunction in the delivery system for the hallucinogenic cocktail. The sleep-inducing agents were released prematurely during a prelaunch rehearsal one month before liftoff. A short in the system also set off a minor but controllable fire. The NASA director in charge of ruse operation protocol immediately flooded the capsule with highly flammable pure oxygen, pursuant to emergency concealment procedures, to prevent detection of the highly classified system during the ensuing forensic investigation. The secret was covered, wrote Cassandra, "by a murderous smoke screen."

Jonathan rubbed his forehead as he read, shocked by the insensitivity and awed by a paranoia capable of such fantastic tales of covert government schemes. Cassandra's whoppers made his occasional brushes with neurosis seem trifling. Jonathan no longer wanted to know what this degenerate had said about his father. Susana had been right. The hoaxers were the fringe of the fringe. He contemplated crashing Cassandra's site but that would only legitimize the cause, spawning even more elaborate conspiracy theories. He had allowed his emotions to lead him down a virtual back alley to a rendezvous with a toxic link. He needed to get away.

He abandoned eclipsedtruth.com, deleting the browsing history, cookies, and temporary Internet files, making the severance complete, the encounter untraceable. There would be no record that he'd ever visited the site. He would lie to Susana. He'd apologize, tell her that he should've listened. It wasn't worth his time. He had surfed the net for cribs instead. Case closed.

He hated covering his tracks like a truant teenager, keeping secrets, but it had become a necessary black art. He swore each time would be the last. His guilty mind went to a dark place. Camouflaged but not discarded, a glob of gray matter, like a cockpit data recorder, preserved the details of his most shameful crashes, the handful of instances when he had veered recklessly off course.

It had happened only a few times, always when Susana was away. After she finished her doctorate, Susana took a position as an assistant professor at Columbia and moved into Jonathan's Upper West Side apartment. During the early 1990s, coordinating their schedules proved a constant challenge. She traveled frequently, giving guest lectures and attending conferences around the country. He circled the globe with Zubin in search of investment opportunities. As he once told Susana, "Right now, too much time together would only produce friction, not bonding." She didn't laugh, but didn't disagree.

His misadventures typically began in a law firm conference room, past midnight. A bright young associate from the mergers and acquisitions team would agree to join him for a celebratory drink. They would compare notes about their favorite sushi restaurants and the worst European airports. She would talk about her crazy hours, the semester she had studied in Italy or France, her law school friend who worked in the White House, the diplomatic attaché she had dated during a summer internship. They would laugh about her fridge, barren except for its curdled milk and bricks of white rice in red-and-white Chinese takeout cartons. With his vodka tonic inches from his lips, he'd joke that there were enough rice bricks in Manhattan refrigerators to construct a replica of the Great Wall around Chinatown. He always found a way to work in the same joke. It sounded smart and smooth, like a pickup line Dale Lunden might have used. They would stay longer and drink more than they should have—Manhattanites unrestrained by car keys. They would share a taxi, its backseat licentious as a hot tub.

He would wake up the next morning, staring at the sorority sisters on her nightstand, eyes doubly red from too much flash and too much drink, fighting against the weight of heavy eyelids and a king's ransom in Mardi Gras beads. He could hear the gaggle of Thetas or Kappas mocking him. "We just had a night to remember. Looks like you just had one to forget. Like, what are you trying to prove anyway?

Aren't you too old for this? Dude, time to grow up already."

Bathed in a ghostly white glow by the monitor, Jonathan leaned back in his chair and rubbed the stubble on his cheeks. His occasional dalliances had stopped after they'd moved to Miami, but there were a couple of times, in Europe or San Francisco, when he had relapsed, always blaming it on alcohol. He couldn't be like that anymore. He had more reasons than ever to change. Paparazzi after the mission. The risk of tell-all blackmail. A heart attack under twisted hotel sheets. Impending fatherhood. And Susana, of course, who deserved a husband without secrets. He wondered if his wife had ever been unfaithful. She stood out in any crowd, and exponentially more so at astrophysics conferences. Knowing her finely tuned moral compass, he felt it unlikely that they shared that denominator in common. He shut off the computer and went to bed.

He slipped under the covers next to Susana, asleep as usual on her side, and ran his hand from her left shoulder down her arm. Unable to sleep and impatient to demonstrate his renewed commitment to monogamy, he inched his body closer and softly kissed her neck. He used the same technique each time he woke her for sex.

"I'm not in the mood," she mumbled without moving.

He wasn't surprised. It was past 3 a.m. He felt his pulse, elevated from arousal but strong and steady. His dad couldn't see it coming either. He rolled away from Susana, his pillow in a headlock, trying to distract himself. He thought about how women in 1970s sitcoms always said "I have a headache," which got such big, undeserved laughs. Applause signs. How can a person be told when to laugh or when to clap? Maybe Cassandra was right. Audiences were told how to feel and react and took no offense.

The clock on his night table read 3:24 a.m. Instinctively, he played "Make Ten," a game with clocks for sleepless nights he'd invented at the age of eight. 3:24 → 3 × 4 = 12 − 2 = 10. The next minute worked too. 3:25 → 3 + 2 + 5 = 10. He stared at the flickering cool green light cast by the clock's numerals through the whirring blades of a ceiling fan. Back, side, stomach, nothing worked. He imagined each contortion traced by detective's chalk. After what seemed a very long time, he looked at the clock again. Only seven minutes later, 3:32 a.m. No way to make ten. His efforts to fall asleep useless, he hopped to his feet and returned to the office.

He tapped his finger on the mouse, unwilling to click. He feared what Cassandra had written about his father, how it might affect him. Until he opened that webpage, her screed could follow a dozen different paths—absurd, ominous, pernicious, laughable, credible—like the infinite avenues of an unobserved subatomic particle in quantum mechanics. Schrödinger's cat isn't dead if you never open the box. He considered returning to bed, or getting a drink, but his constitutional reluctance to confront couldn't restrain his restless curiosity. He needed to open the box. He clicked on the hyperlink about his father.

Avi Stein was a Jew. This presented a particular problem at NASA.

Though the public had a general awareness that, after World War II, our government had imported a few German scientists and engineers who were able to advance the state of our rocket program, the involvement of Nazis was even greater than NASA ever admitted. Dozens of German experts were quickly and quietly brought to the United States. Their knowledge of rocketry and other scientific fields related to space travel far exceeded that of our best scientists, and for this reason, not only their presence but their predilections and criminal pasts were tolerated. Though our government has attempted to portray the "defectors" as highly skilled and innocent men of science forced to work for the Third Reich, many were ardent fascists and loyal to Hitler until the very end.

Most were kept isolated on military bases, handsomely paid, and even allowed to display memorabilia from the "old days" in their quarters. Some even celebrated the Führer's birthday with an annual Riefenstahl film festival, courtesy of Uncle Sam. (These indulgences also helped buy their complicity in the "temporary" lunar ruse.)

Wernher von Braun, head of the Marshall Space Flight Center for over a decade, was in the SS; so was Kurt Debus, head of the Kennedy Space Center until 1974. Arthur Rudolph, project director for NASA's Saturn V rocket, the rocket that launched Apollo 11, was in the SA, a "brownshirt."

Because of the need for productivity from the Germans and the convenient prevalence of anti-Semitism among our top military commanders (don't forget Patton kept the Jews locked up in Morocco *after* its liberation), NASA stayed an overwhelmingly gentile outfit. The astronauts and flight controllers had names like Krantz, Kraft, Cooper, Slayton, Glenn, Collins, and Armstrong. There were few, if any, Rothsteins or Greenbergs, and that was no accident.

NASA's German contingent was less than thrilled that a Jew would be piloting one of their rockets. They could accept the fair-haired Midwestern boys, like Lunden, shooting off into orbit (even if the lunar landings were faked), just as they could accept defeat at the hands of other Germanic types, like Eisenhower and Roosevelt, but a Hebrew astronaut before a German was unacceptable. It was even worse than Jesse Owens and the embarrassment of 1936. In an effort to derail the mission, the Aryan brain-trust told their NASA superiors that Avi Stein was most certainly a spy for *Mossad*— that he would surely steal as many military and technological secrets as his hidden spy cameras could carry. The NASA brass wouldn't listen. They took their orders from a cadre of powerful congressmen who insisted on having an Israeli pilot in the space program after the massacre of athletes at the Munich Olympics. But Stein's involvement was too much for the Germans to bear. Determined to stop him, they secretly poisoned his food with an untraceable chemical, making his death seem like simple cardiac arrest. (Some of the Nazis were experts in biochemical warfare. Sarin gas was named for the German scientists who invented it in 1938.) There would be no Luz Long, the friendly German Olympian who helped Jesse Owens avoid a disqualifying long jump fault, to intervene and save Stein from permanent elimination.

NASA officials suspected foul play but knew that an earnest and successful investigation would trigger a diplomatic disaster no matter the culprits—Germans, Arabs, or some other international anti-Semites. So, the investigation had a preordained, expedient result: Natural causes. "A real tragedy." **N**ever **A S**traight **A**nswer strikes again, and the truth has remained untold—until now.

Jonathan sat paralyzed by an anger that welled up from his toes. He sensed the twinge he had always felt in his chest whenever someone said "natural causes" or "God's will." Cassandra's rancid tripe was pure rubbish. He knew it. But he couldn't stop the darker thoughts from emerging—NASA's sanitized German rocket men, like the celebrated von Braun, whose service as an SS officer had been scrubbed out of his official government biography, America's puzzling thirty-year absence from the Moon, his father's peerless fitness, and Armstrong's inexplicable silence.

His heart pounded through his rib cage, living proof of what really happened to his father, conclusive forensic evidence embedded in an unexploded time bomb. Each syncopated beat sounded the same message, the same truth. Though burning to prove Cassandra wrong, he wouldn't dare reveal his trump card, and he hoped that destiny wouldn't force his hand. He would search for another way. Fate could not possibly be so cruel, allowing Avi to escape the Holocaust in his fleeing mother's womb only to become its last victim forty years later. Jonathan slammed his palms against the armrests. That would be cosmically unjust, unfathomable. He squeezed his eyes shut and bit his tongue until the pain overwhelmed his thoughts.

The screen saver resumed its automatic slide show. Jonathan, with locks of wavy, dark hair flowing out from underneath a mortar board, stood between his mother and Dale Lunden. His new girlfriend, Susana, had made a surprise appearance at college graduation and snapped the shot. No one at NASA had been closer to his father than Lunden. Jonathan needed to go back in time, retrace his father's final days. Lunden—the man who taught him how to drive a stick shift, who took him to Dolphins games, who helped pay for space camp, a man who had also made a promise to Avi Stein—would be the first step.

4

October 22, 1975

10:25AM

Jonathan, age fourteen, and his mother returned to Tel Aviv a year after the funeral for the dedication of his father's headstone. The unveiling took place at the Old Cemetery in Tel Aviv, under a low roof of dingy clouds trickling a steady rain. The cemetery looked like a giant board game covered in granite, gray-scale dominoes.

"Mom, you think I'll have something when we get back?"

"Don't get your hopes up, Jon."

"You forwarded the mail to our new address, right?" Two months earlier they had moved from Cape Canaveral to Hollywood, Florida, where Eva, an American, had found a job as a high school art teacher. Jonathan wanted to move back to Israel, to serve his time in the military, but his mother refused. Eva told him she'd already lost one soldier too many.

"You asked me about the mail yesterday, Jon. Come, we're ready to start."

The rabbi, Eva, and Jonathan stood next to his father's grave. Avi's mother was buried just behind him. A semicircle of mourners—a few close friends, a small number of government and military officials, and a handful of cousins—huddled around. Eva rejected the rabbi's umbrella before beginning her remarks. "Avi has been, and will continue to be, an inspiration to his son and the sons of Israel," she said. "Moses led our people to the promised land, but remained behind as they crossed the River Jordan. Avi showed us the way to a new frontier, and though he did not reach the stars, his courage and his belief in exploration remain a limitless source of strength as we stretch to touch the heavens."

She had wrapped one arm around her son as she spoke. When she finished, Jonathan looked up at her. She squeezed him tighter and kissed his forehead. He reached inside a clear plastic rain poncho to pull a folded sheet of wide-ruled notebook paper from his pocket and stepped forward. "In the last months, Dad took me fishing whenever he could. He loved to be out in the sun, floating on the water, just the two of us."

"A little louder, sweetheart," Eva said, leaning close to his ear.

"He told me stories about the family he'd lost during the Shoah. Sometimes they were just pieces of stories he'd heard about relatives who didn't make it out. The butcher, a great-uncle, with a magic scale that could make the thinnest cut of meat weigh at least a pound. A clarinet-playing second cousin, a girl, who they said could play better than Benny Goodman, whoever he was. And there was my grandfather Jacob, a pharmacist's apprentice, who would always try to sneak caramels to little children when his boss wasn't looking and who spent every last cent he had on travel papers for my grandma. Dad told me to always remember them. Whenever I do that now, I remember him too." Jonathan sniffled and dragged the back of a hand across his runny nose. Raindrops blurred the blue ink of his block letters. He kept his eyes locked on the disintegrating paper. "On the last day we went out to fish, Dad talked to me about two different kinds of flight, the escaping kind and the exploring kind. He told me that we didn't have to flee anymore, like my grandmother did," he glanced back at her marker, "because we were here and finally free to fly, to do that second kind of flight. And in my eyes, my dad soared higher than all of us." Jonathan returned to his mother's side, put a waterlogged wad of paper into her hand, and stared at his shoes.

At the conclusion of the unveiling, the rabbi led the group in *kaddish*. After Avi's death, each time Jonathan recited the plaintive mourner's prayer, he raised his voice for the final lines because he felt they were particularly appropriate for his father and because he believed that his recitation of those ancient words had the special power to secure his father's place in heaven. This time was no different.

Oseh shalom bim'romav hu ya'aseh shalom
Aleinu v'al kol Yis'ra'eil.

He who makes peace in his celestial heights,
May he make peace upon us and all Israel.

As the rain subsided, Dale Lunden closed his umbrella and shook off the water, holding it at arm's length to keep his dress uniform dry. When his eyes met Jonathan's, he jerked his head to summon the boy. Once a star defenseman for the West Point hockey team, Lunden— tall, muscular and square-jawed, with a permanent crew cut—looked like he could start a cascade of falling tombstones with a solid hip check.

"Let's talk for a minute."

The crowd separated into two groups, one comprised of Eva, friends, and family and the other made up of Israel Defense Forces officers. Some of the mourners, but none of the military contingent, looked up in response to the roar of three Israeli Air Force jets streak- ing across the sky in tight formation toward the Golan Heights. Eva glared at Lunden, her head cocked. He waved her off as if to reas- sure and led Jonathan to a cement bench that looked like a miniature Stonehenge trilithon.

"F-4 Phantoms," Jonathan said.

"One of the best designs we ever had," Lunden said. "Loved fly- ing her."

"So did my dad."

Jonathan sat on the bench. Lunden squatted on the stone path, eye-to-eye. "Chip off the old block, kiddo. He'd be damn proud. I know Mom is." His thick-fingered hand rested on Jonathan's slight shoulder. "Dad's passing was like the loss of a brother. I'm not just saying that. When they told me I would replace him, I couldn't do it . . . couldn't, you know, take his spot. I knew somebody had to, but for me it was too much." Lunden exhaled as if reliving the inten- sity of a fresh wound. He swallowed hard and continued in a shaky voice. "But a few days after I declined the mission, your mother called me. She'd heard about my decision, said Avi wouldn't have wanted anybody else. I resisted at first, but she can be pretty stubborn some-times, can't she?" Lunden leaned in. Jonathan shrugged. "In the end, she convinced me to go. I tried my darndest best to live up to your dad's example. But you were right, what you said. He flew a little bit higher."

"Everybody at NASA liked my dad, right?"

"Never heard an unkind word. Not one." He rested both hands on Jonathan's shoulders and stared him straight in the eye, as if his gaze had the power to steel the boy for what was to come. "There's one more thing you should know. While we were in training, your dad and I talked about what would happen if he didn't come back from the Moon, and I promised that I would look out for you and your mom . . . and you can count on that. I should have told you at the funeral, but I was too choked up, after your mom read that poem, the one about packing up the Moon. I'm sorry."

"It's OK. I understand. Good thing you decided to go."

"No idea it would be the last one, eh? I feel bad for the two guys supposed to go with me on Nineteen. They might make it up on the shuttle one day, I guess. Not the same." Lunden reached into his inside breast pocket as he stood up. Four more silver Phantoms thun-dered through the air, disappearing into the clouds. "I know you've become an expert on the Moon and everything astronauts do. So you must know that all of the moon rocks we collected, down to the smallest ones, were carefully catalogued and secured inside vaults at NASA laboratories." He continued in a hushed voice as he gestured skyward. "When I was up there, I did something your dad would've never done." His voice got even softer. "I broke the rules." After look-ing both ways, he pulled his hand out and gave Jonathan a milky white stone, slightly larger than a marble, with an imperfect oval shape and a rough surface.

"You took this from the Moon for me?"

"Yep . . . been saving it for today," Lunden said, with his neigh-borly Minnesota inflections. "I don't think they'll miss it, eh, but don't tell 'em or I might lose my job." He gave Jonathan a cockeyed wink and mussed his hair.

"It's amazing, but . . . I don't want to keep it."

"What?"

"Every night before bed, I promise my dad that I'll get there and walk on the Moon for him. I want a moon rock more than almost anything, but what I want most is to show him I can get it myself."

Lunden remained silent, apparently stunned by the rejection of his gift. Jonathan rolled the stone between his thumb and forefinger.

"What do you want to do with it?" Lunden asked.

"Let's give it to my dad." Lunden looked confused, as if the boy were speaking in Hebrew. "It's what we do."

Jonathan approached his father's headstone. Moving his fingers from right to left, he traced the engraved letters of his father's name, *Avraham ben Yaakov,* and below that, a verse from the Book of Psalms in both Hebrew and English: "The heavens declare the glory of God, and the sky above proclaims his handiwork." Jonathan mouthed the biblical passage and then whispered so that no one else could hear him. "I don't understand why you're here. I'm supposed to be looking up, not down. It doesn't make any sense."

He placed the moon rock on top of the tombstone.

"I promise I'll bring you another."

5

December 6, 2004

8:02AM

Jonathan sat on a bench outside the Arcadia Diner in downtown Miami. He had wanted to meet ever since visiting eclipsedtruth .com, but Lunden had gone to Vancouver to shoot more commercials. He cringed whenever those late-night advertisements came on, a former astronaut and Vietnam veteran peddling reverse mortgages and guaranteed death benefits on basic cable at 2 a.m., like so many faded TV stars clinging to the final flickers of their afterglow. Lunden couldn't possibly have needed the extra money.

A shiny Corvette convertible raced into an open slot near the entrance. "That's really red," Jonathan said.

"Picked it up yesterday. Sorry I'm late. Still getting astronaut deals up in Melbourne after all these years. Can you believe it? Factory calls it 'Victory Red.'"

"Little cool to have the top down, isn't it?"

"I like to feel the breeze in my hair." Lunden rubbed his buzz cut.

Jonathan suggested they grab a corner booth to avoid being interrupted by "any pesky autograph hounds." He slid into a bench seat against the wall so that Lunden would have to sit with his back to the crowd. "This place hasn't changed in thirty years," Jonathan said. "Look at that menu font, like the Chance cards in Monopoly."

Lunden studied the breakfast pages without responding.

"Not too loud in here for you, is it?" Jonathan asked. Feverish busboys tossed clattering plates into plastic trays while shrill servers called out orders in kitchen pidgin.

"Hearing's not gone yet," Lunden said. He flagged a nearby waitress and ordered a stack of pancakes with a side of bacon and two eggs over easy. He'd come from his usual early morning workout. His dress shirt collar was unbuttoned, and the navy-blue tie he insisted on wearing, despite Jonathan's casual dress decree, hung untied around his neck. Though sixty-nine, he smelled alive and fresh, like baby powder.

Jonathan wore the unofficial company uniform, khaki pants and a sky-blue golf shirt that felt too big on him. "How can you still eat like that?"

"You mean clogging up the arteries? Hell, good genes will outdo Lipitor any day. My pop left the dock in Two Harbors every day at 0600 until he was eighty-five. Lived another ten years after that. Died in his sleep. Ate three eggs for breakfast every blessed morning. Never sick a day in his life. Of course, he'd never have let on if he was. Didn't believe in making excuses. Typical Swede."

"The odds might be in your favor," Jonathan said. "But why risk it?" He wanted to curse the unfairness, the fragility of his own genetic inheritance.

The two men discussed various goals and deadlines for the lunar mission. Jonathan reported gradual improvement in landing simulator exercises. Lunden confirmed all project teams were on schedule— a fact Jonathan had already known. The job was largely ceremonial. Lunden had been retired from defense industry consulting for three years when Jonathan plucked him out of a hammock on Coronado Island. They reviewed the difficulties of satellite coordination with NASA and the European Space Agency and the details for an upcoming visit of a Russian delegation from Roscosmos. Jonathan slurped an occasional spoonful from the bowl of corn flakes he regretted ordering as soon as the waitress had left the table. "A few days ago I stumbled onto a new website run by one of those lunar landing conspiracy nuts. I know you're going to think this is ridiculous, but I can't stop thinking about it."

Lunden let loose his silverware to clank on his plate. "Nothing shuts up those fucking cockroaches. Why in the world waste your time with that baloney?" His voice steadily crescendoed. "You'd never give a second look at the tabloid rags in the checkout line, barking nonsense about flying saucers in the desert. You, of all people."

Jonathan leaned over the table to speak. "I know, but let me—"

Lunden, knife back in hand, shushed Jonathan's response with a fencer's thrust. "Memorized the crew of every Apollo mission before you popped your first pimple. I walked on the Moon myself for God's sake. What better proof do you want than that?" He stabbed his fork through a chunk of pancake four layers thick and huffed.

"It's not that this kook believes we never went to the Moon," Jonathan said. "He does, of course. But what really got me is this claim that my dad didn't die of a heart attack, that he was murdered. At first, I wanted to kill this guy, calls himself 'Cassandra,' but I've barely been able to sleep since I read it." Jonathan cradled his face. "Crazy, right?"

Lunden stopped eating and grasped the edge of the table with both hands. He spoke with a fixed jaw, radiating the restrained heat of a drill sergeant about to explode. "This is precisely why I despise the Internet and our precious Age of Entitlement. Every little snot-nosed scrub gets a participation trophy, 'nice effort, Billy,' and every nincompoop with a computer thinks he's got something important to say." Lunden turned around as if he expected to see the other patrons staring at Jonathan, nodding their support in unison. "Arpanet was never meant for the masses."

"I know, it's absurd, but just humor me for a minute."

"Humor you? I can't believe we're even having this conversation. For Pete's sake, after all these years, you know what happened. It was too late when they found him. I can tell you, from firsthand, eyewitness knowledge, if that still counts for anything, that your father's death was not the result of foul play. Plain tragedy, that's what it was. You know that, Jonathan." Lunden resumed eating, eyes fixed on his plate.

Jonathan felt like a teenage boy rebuked for merely suggesting he might not join the family business. He knew it was a heart attack better than any eyewitness. He could feel it.

Without looking up, Lunden asked, "What's this freak's story? Let me guess. Russians? No, that almost makes too much sense. Martians? That's it, isn't it?"

Jonathan shook his head. "Cassandra says my dad was killed because some former Nazi engineers at NASA were upset a Jew was going to be an astronaut. Once their efforts to keep him out of the program failed" —Jonathan paused and surreptitiously lifted his eyes to study Lunden, who was chewing his food— "they supposedly poisoned him in a way that made it appear he had suffered a heart attack. It's outrageous, totally, I know, but it's like this bad song I can't shake out of my head. There wasn't anything weird, right? Before launch?"

"Of course not." Lunden wiped a strip of syrup from his lip. "Any moron can invent whatever fantastic yarn he wants, and the Internet, unfortunately, gives it global reach. 'All the News That's Fit to Print' is all but forgotten. Today, it's just 'All the News.' You don't disagree with that, do you?"

"I don't, absolutely."

"So why in the hell have you got this rotten slice of malarkey stuck in your craw? The imbecile who posted this nonsense is no different than the bum with a picket sign saying the world is going to end tomorrow. You'd walk right past that idiot." His voice grew sharper, and he spoke faster, his gestures swift and pronounced. "Ex-Nazis killed your father? What bull crap! I'd like to see this worm crawl out of his hole and say that to my face." His cheeks flushed. "They didn't call me 'Penalty Box' Lunden for nothing, you know. I still got a few good swings left."

"Calm down, Dale. I didn't mean to get you upset. I'm sorry."

Lunden's eyes bulged as his tirade intensified. "It's insulting, to both of us. I guarantee this guy's a little puny shrimp too. They always are. It's the psychos who think they're Jesus who are the big ones. That David Koresh, from down in Waco, the guy the ATF barbecued. Remember him? He was six-foot four. But this Internet twerp, I'm telling you, is a five-foot nothing, needle-dicked bug-fucker." He pounded a fist on the table, rattling their plates and finally drawing the attention of fellow diners.

Jonathan raised fingers spread wide in defense. "I understand why you're upset. I do. Nobody was angrier than me when I first read it. Believe me." He finished a full glass of water in two gulps. "I'm not saying this guy is right about anything. I'm sure he isn't. But I want to understand more about what happened, even if it was just awful timing and natural causes. That's what Susana thinks anyway. I didn't really ask a lot of questions back then. She says it's part of getting ready."

"For what? Launch?"

"And fatherhood."

The ruddy swell cresting on Lunden's cheeks began to recede. He leaned back against the booth and exhaled. "Jonathan, there were no unusual circumstances. Everything, every log, every checklist—and there were lots of them—was in perfect order. I spoke to your dad daily when he was in prelaunch quarantine, up to the day he passed. He was the same old Avi, eager to go and overprepared. He worried about you and your mom, of course. The launchpad, like the guillotine, tends to focus a man's mind on what's important. You and I talked about what he said, remember?"

Jonathan nodded with his eyes closed to blot out the image of his father being beheaded. "What about his drinking?"

"What drinking?"

"What you told me at that hotel bar in Arecibo." After his junior year at MIT, Jonathan interned at the Arecibo Observatory in Puerto Rico. Lunden had visited after a defense contractor conference in San Juan. "You were hitting the Cuba libres pretty hard; said my dad could outdrink all the other astronauts, even Aldrin." Jonathan thought about how he minimized his own intake and worried that he might be doubly cursed by genetics. "Did my dad have, you know . . . a problem?"

Lunden blew a short burst of air through vibrating lips, like an exhaling stallion. "Heck, no," he said, his eyes half-shut, waving a dismissive hand. "People drank harder in those days is all, and your dad could hold his liquor, especially for his size." He smiled and slid a hand across his face. "We had some times out there, I'll tell you, at the Beach House. NASA was a different place back then." Lunden screwed his eyes up. "Ann-Margret even showed up once, wanted to meet some real astronauts. Shooting a movie near the Cape or something. I broke out the ten Swedish words I could remember from my pops. Must've been 0300. She wants to see a launchpad. We grab a bottle of tequila and go for a hike." He scraped together the last bits of pancake into a scrap heap and forked it into his mouth. "Don't think NASA lets people stay at the house overnight any more. Too bad, eh, those sunrises out there, open ocean, they were something." He sat up and tapped his finger on the table. "Avi's got an empty bottle in the liquor cabinet, like the rest of us, autographed."

Jonathan stared out the window. A scrawny kid in a "Canes" hat straddled a bicycle while he inspected the new Corvette. "NASA will probably have to auction off the whole collection to pay for the next shuttle mission. They're even trying to shake me down for a bigger launchpad fee."

"You been out there lately, the Beach House?" Lunden asked. "Heard they spruced it up."

"Never went back. It's where we said goodbye to Dad before he went into quarantine."

Lunden cleared his throat. "The main thing is that your father wasn't ever out of control. He was no kind of lush."

"What about the Germans we brought over? It's not exactly a secret anymore that at least some of them were Nazis."

"What about them? A few were forced to join the party as I recall, wear the uniform, give the salute. So what? Simple self-preservation from what I understood. Trust me, those guys were all eggheads— slide rules, chalkboards, and gyroscopes. Not one tough in the bunch. Plus, the feds made sure they didn't have any skeletons in their closets."

Jonathan tilted his head and squinted, his mouth half-open, his jaw shifted.

"Poor choice of words," Lunden said. He slid his lower lip up like he intended to button it. "You know what I mean. Those jokers were all checked out. The old-timers in our day were strictly rocket men. Those geriatric Krauts couldn't possibly have gotten near Avi, even if they wanted to—which they didn't."

"What about Kurt Debus? He was at Kennedy until November '74, right after my dad."

"Debus loved being top banana. We saw him at press conferences, but that's about it. He didn't get down in the nitty-gritty with the mission crews, especially by the time Avi showed up. Never heard anything bad about him, other than he was arrogant as hell like his old boss, von Braun. He used to walk around with this stopwatch, obsessed with efficiency. They say he timed every goddamned meeting. No barrel of laughs, I'll give you that, but I'm telling you there is no great mystery to solve here. It was natural causes."

Jonathan felt the twinge. "What did my dad know about the Germans?"

"Why are we rehashing ancient history?" Lunden threw a crumpled napkin onto his plate. "You been watching reruns of *Colombo* or something? *Kojak?* It was launch first and ask questions later in those days. Sure everybody heard whispers in the hallways. Dad must've heard them too. But we never discussed it." Lunden slipped his hand under the table to pat Jonathan on the knee. "I understand why you'd like to find an enemy, but you can't fight bad luck. There is no earthly reason to let this cheap Internet slander get you riled. Forget it. It's not worth your time."

"Believe me," Jonathan said, "nobody understands how precious my time is." He reached for the check, edging out Lunden. "I know how Dad died, but I was just a kid. I swallowed my questions instead of asking them." He opened his wallet and thumbed through a stack of plastic-sleeved pictures—his parents riding a camel in the Negev, Lunden and his father pretending to tackle a Larry Csonka cutout at the Orange Bowl, Avi holding a planked, ten-year-old Jonathan over his head on Gordon Beach in Tel Aviv. "Maybe this scumbag did me a favor. I need to deal with this as an adult, the way I would now. It feels like unfinished business."

"Do whatever you need to do, Jonathan, but you're going to find the same answers that this eyewitness just gave you." Lunden stabbed his finger into Jonathan's chest. "At some point, you've got to let things be. If you let yourself get distracted, looking back too long, you'll crash—just like in the cockpit. I never once made a landing—here, or on the Moon—by peeking over my shoulder."

6

December 10, 2004

11:19AM

Jonathan made it to Susana's obstetrician appointment with a minute to spare. He'd been stuck on the phone with a junior White House staffer, trying to find the right contact at the National Archives. He couldn't be late. He'd missed the fifteen-week amniocentesis because of a critical meeting with a guidance system subcontractor in Orange County. Susana only forgave him after the tests came back negative and he promised to be at the twenty-week ultrasound.

They were definitely having a boy. Before it had only been hearsay. Today he saw it with his own eyes, a living, swimming creature. He heard its heart, thumping away like a metronome set on *vivace*. Maybe the curse hadn't been passed. He'd told himself dozens of times—every time Susana dragged him to the fertility clinic—that he should want to be a father. But he couldn't escape an occasional sense of diminishment. There had always been one Jonathan Stein—brilliant, indivisible. He loved the Spanish phrase for an only child: *hijo único*. Unique child. Now, there would be a halfling, maybe more. The thought that he would no longer be the *ne plus ultra*, that he would become a mere step and not a destination, made him shudder. It was like being dethroned. The ticking inside him grew louder.

Fathers die. That's what they do.

He'd searched on the wrong level of the parking structure for at least fifteen minutes before finding his Jag. He loved to drive the XK8, blaring classic rock, Springsteen or CCR, or sometimes contemporary Russian masters, Stravinsky or Prokofiev. And on special occasions, the Third Movement of Beethoven's Fifth Symphony. When the horns joined in, near the beginning, in resolute three-four time, it sounded like they were trumpeting his name. "Jon-a-than Stein, Jon-a-than Stein . . ." He wore black leather gloves and gunned the engine whenever he cruised the service roads near the Miami Executive Airport, where he kept his latest plane, a Cessna Skylane. With two doors and tight space in the back, the Jag had no place for a car seat. He had planned a midday getaway before going back to work, an hour of uninterrupted silence ten thousand feet above Miami.

Before leaving the garage, Jonathan checked his Blackberry. He did a double take when he saw the subject line of his latest e-mail: "A Note from Cassandra." He tried to open the unexpected e-mail, but the device failed to recognize the format. He could only read the "re" line. The sender's e-mail address had been blocked. Jonathan tried turning it on and off. Nothing worked. He abandoned his flight plan and sped instead to his office to get to a desktop. Had Cassandra used some sort of spyware, when he had visited eclipsedtruth.com, to snatch his company e-mail address? There were other possibilities. Maybe the timing of the e-mail was a coincidence. Cassandra was obviously obsessed, probably spent hours online scavenging for hidden "truths" about his father's death. He could have easily tracked down Jonathan's corporate e-mail address with elementary detective work. That less intrusive possibility provided Jonathan with little relief.

How contact was made soon gave way to the more worrisome question of why Cassandra sought to communicate. He obviously knew about the upcoming lunar mission. Was that the reason? Was it a warning? A rebuke? A threat? Back at work, Jonathan threw himself into his chair, spinning to the keyboard. After a flurry of keystrokes, he managed to open Cassandra's message.

> So, Mr. Stein, you've been to my little website. Does it sound hopelessly trite to say I have been expecting you? I assure you I am no spider. I am part of a growing cyber-movement intent upon exposing the treachery of a government far less democratic than its claims.
>
> They treated that Nazi von Braun and his crew like Kris Kringle and his *Elfen*. Not just all the tools and workshops they wanted, but medals, money, and fame. They even got to swap out your father for a bona fide

nordische mensch. And then NASA buried the truth, but you will uncover it.

Avi Stein's murder was covered by a thick blanket of realpolitik. The American government employs tactics that would make Machiavelli blush. Those politicians happily plant banal stories about $500 hammers sold to the Pentagon by price-gouging defense contractors. A little outrage among the masses inoculates them against full-blown rebellion. We don't live in a two-party system. We live in a two-port system. Take your pick. Hyannis Port or Kennebunkport. The lobster tastes good in both places. Their public fights are mostly for show. That's how the racket works. When subtle manipulation does not suffice, however, they will do whatever it takes to preserve their institutions. With Vietnam and Watergate boiling over, the power structure was in a state of panic, afraid that a revolt might bring about true and fundamental reform. Your father's assassination could well have been the tipping point. At least that's what they feared, and at that time, they were at DEFCON 1. Nixon, Haldeman, Ehrlichman, Liddy—it was the golden age of treachery. So I am sorry to say that what the Germans did was covered up, or should I say, never uncovered.

The investigation was a complete sham, a whitewashed inquest with a made-to-order conclusion. "Natural causes." Case closed.

Jonathan made sure no one was watching through the half-open door. He slid his fingers between the buttons of his shirt and pressed them against his chest. He downed a full glass of water. He rolled up the mouse, letting the blinking cursor hover over the red X, trigger finger at the ready. Just two quick clicks, close and delete, and it would snap out of existence. He knew he should be outraged and offended, but a potent rush of compulsion and apprehension dowsed any competing emotions. The message was pure delusion, but it possessed the inextricable grip of revelation. Jonathan kept reading.

I hope your visit means you are in pursuit of the real truth. You see, Mr. Stein, you were becoming one of them already. It's not easy to open your eyes when you don't know you're dreaming. Armstrong was an exception.

By the way, have you seen *The Matrix*? Did you get the point? The people in the pods? It's the working class. They live in towers of cubed apartments wired with electricity, seven hundred channels of television, and the Internet. Isn't it obvious that Marx's chains have been replaced by coaxial cables? Those helpless beasts of burden are just as plugged in as the unconscious bodies in that film. The government and the corporations (like there's a difference) keep the masses sustained, complacent, and weak. The poor fools don't realize how controlled they are. They cry square tears and keep their ideas in neat rows. If the elite know one thing, it's the parable of Pandora. The powerful want stability. Don't let the people out of their boxes.

And the title of *The Matrix* was no accident, by the way. Did you figure it out? Its letters have a secret meaning. **M**ilit**A**ry indus**TRI**al comple**X**. But that's not all. The main character's name, *Neo*, was no random selection. Say it fast and you know whose first name it sounds like. I'm not the only one who knows about Neil Armstrong, but you are the one with the power and the prestige to bring the truth to light.

Conceal your true objective from as many as you can. Be most wary of those who appear to want to help. Assistance is the most powerful form of control. Get to Armstrong. He knows all the secrets—about the Moon, the Nazis, and your father. Persuade him to speak out.

I leave you with one final thought. Read it forward or backward. It tells the same undeniable truth, a truth no longer eclipsed.

A SANTA LIVED AS A DEVIL AT NASA.

Good luck, Mr. Stein.

As he reread the e-mail, Jonathan imagined Cassandra's voice sounding like the disembodied man from the tape recordings on *Mission Impossible*. Lunden had been right. This troll was a paranoid, unhinged maniac with a technicolor imagination.

Jonathan made several unsuccessful efforts to discover Cassandra's hidden e-mail address. He pictured his pathetic nemesis with a beer gut and three-day stubble writing unpublished graphic novels about children committing random acts of ineffectual rebellion against a futuristic police state, or about demented old men spewing gibberish about invasive alien visitations. Cassandra had probably committed to memory the entire screenplays of *Rollerball* and *Logan's Run*, and marched around his shabby apartment all day on a heroic mission, like some catcher in the rye, even though he never got out of his grungy bathrobe or bothered to empty the stale bread crusts from its pockets.

Jonathan swiveled, pausing to study a photograph on the acrylic credenza behind his desk, a treasured old Polaroid snapped on a father-and-son fishing trip. He hated the dime-store frame, its imitation wood betrayed by a glossy, plastic shine, but he was stuck with it. The photo paper had long ago fused to the inside surface of the glass cover—a singular moment twice frozen.

Wearing whitewall shorts, tight and high-cut, and braces glinting in the sun, Jonathan—dark tan, curly hair, and obsidian eyes—stood on the threshold of puberty. His radiant image was outshone by the shimmering tarpon hanging, tailfin up, between father and son on a boat dock jutting into the Gulf of Mexico. He could feel the warmth of the Florida sun, sense the gentle rocking of the boat as it floated through the flats, hear the rhythmic splashes of water displaced by the bobbing hull, and smell the oddly pleasing potpourri of seaweed, baitfish, and suntan lotion. Fixing his hands in his lap, fist over fist, he turned his chair from left to right and back again, mimicking the erratic movements made on the back of the fishing boat during that epic battle. His eyes welled as he remembered the strength of his father's burly embrace—those thick, sturdy arms wrapped around him from behind, helping to haul in their whiplashing prey. That idyllic Sunday afternoon in the Gulf was the last day he'd spent with his dad.

Jonathan turned back to his desk and saw a yellow Post-It—apparently placed there by his assistant while he was out—with the number for an administrator at the National Archives. He passed it from fingertip to fingertip along the adhesive strip, like spider legs scaling a wall. He stared at the DC area code ($20 \div 2 = 10$), thinking about palindromes and how he'd read in both directions his whole life.

"I'm doing this for the right reasons."

One . . . Two . . . Three . . . Four.

He reached for the telephone.

7

January 12, 2005

8:31AM

Jonathan was eager to pilot the Skylane to DC, but Reagan National had been closed to private aircraft since 9/11. He took a commercial flight instead, en route to the National Archives and Records Administration (NARA) facility in College Park. Even with his connections, he couldn't get an appointment until after the holidays. He sat in a first-class window seat. The woman next to him had been struggling with the *Herald*'s crossword. He focused on the puzzle to keep from looking at her too long. She was in her late twenties, straight ginger hair, and blue-green eyes like the flats in Biscayne Bay. A cartilage hoop dangled from the top of her left ear. The inside of her wrists bore blue-black Chinese characters. She had managed to complete about one quarter of the grid.

"I think it's justice," Jonathan said.

"Excuse me."

"Eight down: 'What Rehnquist orders with his Glenfiddich.' 'Just ice.'"

Her eyes went catatonic.

"William Rehnquist. He's the Chief Justice, *just ice*, of the Supreme Court."

"Oh, you're right. That works. Thanks."

He'd guessed she wouldn't mind the help. It was the *Herald*, after all. Helping her was like giving advice to a gambler at a five-dollar blackjack table. Mouths only need to stay shut in the high stakes rooms. During the bicoastal phase of his relationship with Susana, the late 1980s, he'd often worked crossword puzzles with her over the telephone. Sometimes they would cut out the clues from the *New*

York Times and throw away the grid. They would recreate it by taking turns without knowing how many letters were needed, or how the other words intersected. She called it "phone sex for nerds."

"It's my New Year's resolution to get better at these," the young woman said. "Preventative medicine for Alzheimer's. Runs in the family. Happy New Year, by the way."

"Same to you. I'm Jon."

"Cassie." She reached across the seat to shake his hand.

"That's some grip you've got there," he said.

"People are always saying that. My job, I guess. I'm a massage therapist and acupuncturist. Always using my hands." She flexed her fingers. "Hey, what about thirty-nine across? 'Rage of a Romanian harlot.'" She pronounced "harlot" as if it rhymed with "car lot."

"Vamp-ire," Jonathan said. He stared out the window, wondering why it had to be a wooden stake in the heart.

"I didn't even tell you how many letters yet."

"Does it fit?"

"Wow, you're really good at these."

"It's a hobby." He kept his eyes on the puffy cloud tops, a model of practiced insouciance, like a muscle-bound lifeguard strolling the beach in Malibu. He knew she had turned her head sideways to look at him, like he was someone consequential.

"You going home or traveling?" she asked.

"Business. I live in Miami."

"How long you in town?"

"Just one night. How about you? Meeting in the Oval Office?" The blank stare returned. "Sorry, stupid joke."

"I'm coming back from visiting my ex-boyfriend."

"That doesn't sound like an ex."

"No, it's over. Believe you me. He wants me back, crying his eyes out like a baby when I left, but I've made that mistake for the last time. No, sir." She reached up to twist the air conditioning knob. "It's always so freaking hot on these planes." She unzipped her pink hooded sweatshirt, reveling a form-fitting athletic tank top. Jonathan turned back to the clouds. "He's in prison, my ex. We own a couple of juice bars outside of Baltimore, where he's from. Only assets the feds couldn't get their hands on. He owes me, big time."

That explained the first-class seat. "White collar then? I heard those low security camps aren't too bad."

"No, he didn't qualify." She touched her nose and sniffed. "DEA," she whispered.

"I see. What do those characters mean?" He touched the tattoo on her left wrist.

"That's 'forgiveness,' the right one's 'destiny.'"

Jonathan couldn't think of any remotely hip comment. "They're really well done."

"Thanks." She returned to the crossword puzzle, and he pulled a SkyMall catalog from the seat pocket, flipping through the pages without looking at them.

"You probably don't have any ink, do you?" she asked.

Jonathan replaced the catalog, looked at her pen, and reached for his briefcase.

She laughed. "No, silly, I mean any tattoos. Well that answers that, doesn't it?"

"No, I don't. Sorry." He thought about the Torah's prohibition and how a tattoo could keep him out of the family plot.

"You like massages?"

"Not particularly."

"You just never had a good one. You'd think different if I got my hands on you. House calls only. I'm so booked I don't even take on new clients. Lots of stressed-out politicians and all."

"I'm sure."

"Don't get the wrong idea." A plastic water bottle crackled as she pulled it from the seat back. "It's all straight up, legit. None of that frip crap. I'm a certified holistic practitioner. Jacksonville School of Massage."

"Frip?"

"Yeah, you know, what those fresh-off-the-boat Korean girls say before giving some John a happy ending."

"Got it. I didn't think that you—"

"Your name's John too, that's funny, isn't it?" She touched his fore-arm. "Could I ask you one more?"

"Go for it." While she searched the grid, he struggled to pull his Blackberry out of his pants pocket and scrolled through e-mail messages.

"I don't think you're supposed to do that up here. Doesn't that mess up the telekinetics and whatnot?"

"No, no. It's totally safe. Trust me, I build, I mean, I'm a pilot. The electrical systems in here are all shielded. Running this handheld is like firing a pea shooter at a tank. Don't worry. You found a clue yet, Cassie? That short for anything?"

"Why would it be? How about forty-two down: 'Going concern?'" She sat up and held her pen like she was taking dictation.

"Destination."

"So quick. You sure?"

"There's a question mark at the end of the clue, right?"

"Yeah."

He put his Blackberry away and leaned back against the fuselage, gesturing like a professor giving a lecture. "The question mark is the key. It means 'don't assume the most *obvious* reading.' The puz-zle editor isn't suggesting some corporate entity. The question mark means the word is something less colloquial, more literal—something you're concerned with that's associated with the act of going. *Where* you're going is the concern, and *that* is your destination."

"That's like, genius. Thanks. I got to remember it, long as the Alzheimer's doesn't get me." She tapped her temple. "So what do I owe you?"

"No charge," he said.

"You really could use a good massage. I'll make an exception. Give me your hand."

"What?"

"Come on, don't be shy. This won't hurt a bit."

He offered his hand, expecting a free sample. She bent back his fingers and began to write a phone number on his palm. "What are you doing?" He felt a sensation in his groin.

"Don't worry. It's not permanent. Call me before it wears off."

Trying to play it cool, Jonathan forced a smile and a shallow laugh. "My first tattoo."

They said good-bye in the concourse. He waved with his inscribed hand. Standing at a men's room urinal, he studied her writing—acute, energetic, different. He closed his eyes to remember the pressure of the pen tip. As he zipped up, a hulking young man in sandstone fatigues stood next to him, dropped a rucksack on the floor, and pulled out an unavoidable, uncircumcised penis. Jonathan averted his eyes and closed his hand. The air reeked of ammonia. At a row of sinks, he pushed his sleeves back and scrubbed his palm. "What the hell am I doing with numbers on my skin?"

A herd of limousine and livery cab drivers crowded the baggage claim area, elbowing each other for position and holding up signs for their customers. Before finding his own name, Jonathan saw "Armstrong" floating in the middle of the surname alphabet soup. He scanned the flow of arriving passengers for a glimpse of his low-profile hero. New Yorkers barged in from the latest shuttle, jostling him, obscuring his view. Once the fog of frenzied travelers lifted, he reoriented himself and looked back toward the exit. The sign was gone. Frustrated but not surprised, he searched again for his own chauffeur, finally finding "Stein." He approached the rail-thin driver, who seemed very old, even in a profession with no shortage of balding, gray-haired men.

"Excuse me," Jonathan said. "I'm Jonathan Stein. You here for me?"

The old man seemed startled by the routine question. "No, can't be for you. They told me to pick up a Mr. Stein at 8 a.m., but he must've missed his flight because I'm still here waiting."

"I *am* Stein, Jonathan Stein. Maybe you got the wrong itinerary? I bet you're supposed to be here for me, coming from Miami. Check in with your dispatcher. I'm in a hurry, and I don't see any other drivers looking for me."

"Calm down, young fella. No need to shout. Don't have a phone, just the two-way in the car." The man continued to hold up his placard during their conversation, staring at the steady stream of arriving passengers. "You're not the only Stein in the world, you know."

"How can you be a driver in 2005 without a phone? Here, you can borrow mine." When Jonathan reached into his jacket, he grabbed his digital mini-recorder instead. While he probed the rest of his pockets for his phone, a short, stocky man in his late forties with Brezhnev eyebrows and a cigar in the breast pocket of a tight-fitting navy blazer pushed the old driver aside and said, in a gruff Eastern European accent, "Are you Stein, Jonathan Stein, to College Park?"

"How did you know?"

"The sign." The driver pointed to the old man, still looking for his absent fare.

In the livery cab, Jonathan found his Blackberry in his briefcase and typed a message to Zubin Dukkash, who was back in China on new business. "Call me if you're awake." Minutes later the screen shook with a familiar number.

"*Ni-hao*, my nizzle. Where you at?"

"On my way to College Park."

"What the fuck is in College Park? No, wait. I'll tell you exactly what. A quadrangle full of barely legal temptation, that's what. 'Abandon hope all ye who enter—'"

"Calm down, Zudu. I'm going to the National Archives. Doing some research on my dad."

"Because of that whacked-out web link you sent?"

"Yeah . . .well . . . no, actually. It got me started, but I've got my own reasons."

"You don't honestly believe that Cassandra bitch was on to something with that hackneyed Nazi-scientist-murder-plot bullshit? You think life is like that dumb movie with that Holocaust-and-Vatican II-denying asshole, Mel Gibson . . . *Conspiracy Theory*? It's because of what happened when we were at space camp, in the gym, isn't it?"

"No, this is about me and my dad, not the Germans. I'm trying to work out things for myself. Susana calls it 'closure.' God, I hate that word. Closure. I don't want to close anything. I'm trying to be methodical about this, doing research, getting information. Right now I'm trying to reserve judgment, keep an open mind."

"Just be careful. People can pour a lot of shit into an open mind."

The gym incident had occurred on a rainy Saturday morning at space camp. Jonathan, age sixteen, woke up early and decided to use the free time to exercise. Zubin slept in after a marathon night of backgammon and contraband Budweiser. The field house, built when the Huntsville complex was still the Redstone Arsenal, had an indoor track encircling side-by-side basketball courts. After a few laps, Jonathan noticed a pair of older men in gray, loose-fitting sweat suits and white sneakers lifting dumbbells and tossing a medicine ball near the exit. Their voices echoed in the hangar-size building, as did their language—German. Every few minutes they would break into an upbeat marching tune but never finish, each song interrupted by laughter, or a competing melody. After jogging what he calculated to be about three miles, Jonathan took off his soaked terry-cloth headband and walked toward them, sucking in air.

The taller of the two, a sturdy man with an athletic frame, spoke in clear but accented English. "Are you here for the space camp?"

"Yes, sir."

"Excellent. You are wise to spend your free time doing exercises. You must be of sound mind and body. *Sehr gesund.* What's your name, my boy?"

"Jonathan."

"Jonathan Swift, perhaps? You seem to be fleet of foot." The man's companion jeered at his feeble attempt at humor. "Come now, Jonathan who?"

He wanted to lie, give himself an astronaut-sounding name like "Albright" or "Tomlinson," but he couldn't. They were obviously NASA. At least one of them might have been a camp instructor. "Stein. Jonathan Stein."

The man's smile vanished. "How far did you run?"

"Four miles."

"Maybe you can answer a question that my friend and I were just considering. You're Jewish I presume?" The men's eyes widened in anticipation of the answer.

"Yeah, yes." Jonathan wondered if they had already known who he was.

"Why are there so few Jewish athletes?"

"There are more than you think." Jonathan searched in vain for a sympathetic nod. "But there aren't very many of us to begin with, statistically speaking." He squirmed against the doorjamb.

"True. A pity. But there used to be more." The man's tone was bone dry.

Jonathan felt baited and mocked more than pitied. "Mark Spitz won seven gold medals in Munich. He's Jewish."

"Probably of mixed blood," the man said. He murmured something in German that received nods and laughter from his cohort. "Don't you know, young man, that you shouldn't even be here on Saturday morning? It's strictly *verboten*." The gratuitous German word seemed chosen to intimidate.

"I thought we could use the gym whenever it's open."

The man clicked his tongue. "But isn't today supposed to be your day of rest?" His friend laughed openly.

Jonathan bowed his head and bit his lower lip. Grasping the metal bar on the door, he looked over his shoulder at the man. "I guess you're right . . . see you at temple."

The rain still pouring, Jonathan zigzagged, hopping to avoid puddles as if he were in a minefield. He recalled his bus ride to space camp and the Jewish man's warning about the double-breasted Nazi turncoats. Why hadn't his dad mentioned any of the Germans? Had Avi been shielded, or was he doing the shielding? Until that moment, Jonathan had assumed that before Avi's sudden death, his experience at NASA had been a nonstop amusement park ride. But now he imagined his father as an unwelcome guest, an outsider enduring cold shoulders and icy stares. Jonathan stopped in the gym parking lot next to a black sedan, the only car there. "Heart of Dixie" license plate, 20-14900 ($9 + 4 = 13 - 2 = 11 - 1 = 10 - 000 = 10$). He pulled his room key from his pocket, squeezing it in his hand until its jagged teeth left red bite marks in his palm. He knew what he wanted to do. Slow and deep, all the way around. Or a Star of David on the hood. No, a swastika. Much better. "So what if they kick me out?"

One . . . Two . . . Three . . . Four.

Jonathan touched the tip of his key against the driver's side door. His right hand shook. He hadn't inherited Avi's hair-trigger temper. He knew his father would have knocked out the imperious German with one punch, taken them both on if he had to. His parents had prepared their son for the hateful epithets and caricatures—the greedy, conniving Jew, the blood-sucking bankers, the "Christ-killers." His mother had preached nonviolence, fighting bigotry by example. "Pick your battles," she had said. "Jews don't have to wear a yellow star on their chests seven days a week anymore." His father hadn't disagreed but secretly taught Jonathan how an undersized kid could hold his own in a scuffle.

Even using two hands and holding his breath, Jonathan couldn't steady the tremor. He couldn't do it. He sprinted to the far side of his dormitory, sloshing thoughtlessly through ankle-deep water, and sat cross-legged in the wet grass, leaning against the building, rivulets streaming down his face making the raindrops and his tears indistinguishable.

8

January 12, 2005

10:33AM

In a khaki trench coat, charcoal gray suit, white button-down shirt and red tie, Jonathan felt like an FBI agent in a big-budget movie. He approached the mammoth steel and glass government records facility, his gait brisk and confident. He put on his metal-framed sunglasses, despite an overcast sky, to complete the look. He told himself that visiting the National Archives had nothing to do with Cassandra, that he had merely wanted to learn the details of his father's death, to ready himself for the Moon, to become a father, to cope with the twinge. It was a reasonable desire, a healthy one. If, as a result, he could disprove the lunatic ravings of an anonymous menace, so much the better.

Through his White House contact, he had arranged for an archivist to act as a personal guide. A man in his early sixties, coke-bottle glasses, bald except for a few stubborn wisps of gray on the sides, elbow-patched sweater, met Jonathan in the lobby. "Greetings, I'm Cecil Frutiger." They shook hands. "I must tell you it's so nice to have a unique project to work on. With most VIP requests, I end up spending the whole day with a bushy-tailed White House aide sent by the new president to find out what *really* happened to JFK, or Jimmy Hoffa. They always leave disappointed."

Jonathan obliged with a courteous smile. They descended four levels in silence, except for the chime that signaled each floor. The elevator doors opened to endless aisles of identical shelves filled with brown banker's boxes labeled with unfamiliar codes—countless combinations of letters, numbers, and different colored dots. Frutiger moved through the underground labyrinth as if he were its creator.

He positioned a step ladder and, with Jonathan's help, removed six boxes of material from a shelf. The two men loaded them onto hand trucks and headed to a glass-enclosed "fishbowl" research room in the middle of the floor.

"What do all these codes mean?"

"Just what you'd expect. They identify the agency, the time period, the location of the originating office, and the type of files. The colored dots indicate whether there are any original audio or video records associated with the files in a particular box."

"Why's that done?"

"I suppose you don't know too much about archiving materials, do you? Old audio tape and film reels have to be stored in special, climate-controlled rooms to prevent degradation. We have a room on each floor, northeast corner, for the associated boxes on the same level."

"Just digitize the records and throw out the old copies. Wouldn't that save space, and money?"

"You're preaching to the choir. But it costs a lot to do that conversion. Not a big issue for the hometown constituents. We've done some of that with the oldest material in the worst shape, but Congress hasn't given us the funds to do all the work we should be doing." He tapped Jonathan on the elbow. "Maybe you can put in a good word with your friends up on Capitol Hill? If a box has got no dots, there's no av material. If it has a red dot, it has audio tapes, and if it has a blue dot, it has videotape or film. I'm the only person with a key to the av room on this floor. We try to limit access to protect the physical integrity of the old records as much as possible."

Jonathan felt relieved to reach the research room. Its furniture—two long, midcentury conference tables and metal-framed chairs with black plastic seats and backs—and its distinctive smell—a blend of old paper and commercial floor cleaner—took him back to long undergraduate nights with Zubin in the Hayden Library at MIT. It was as if his nostrils sniffed through an olfactory wormhole leading right back to Cambridge, 1979. Those had been heady times filled with possibility and little need of sleep. Though the opposite of cozy, the barren room made him feel at home, relaxed. He conducted an initial survey of the boxes. No dots. He frowned, annoyed with himself for thinking there might be anything other than yellowing documents and some stray desiccated microfiche. "Is this everything on my father?"

"You can bet on that. Those NASA guys were great at filing paperwork. Their documentation was impeccable. Indices for indices, all perfectly typed. On the other hand, you should see the mess we get from the Bureau of Indian Affairs. Those characters are really off the reservation, if you know what I mean."

"I guess I'll take it from here," Jonathan said, eager to get to his search.

"Oh, no, you've got me the whole day. These records are still classified. I can't leave anyone alone with them. Didn't they tell you? The documents may be viewed only under restricted conditions?"

"So why do I get to see them?"

"You've got top secret clearance, don't you?"

Jonathan had needed the clearance to work on military projects with the Department of Defense. "How'd you know? Nobody asked me when I set this up."

"As you might expect, Mr. Stein, we're pretty handy with government databases."

"Why's it all classified?"

"'Why' is a question above my pay grade, I'm afraid. You'll have to ask NASA that one." The man seem perfectly content to sit for hours in silence, and Jonathan made no further efforts to dispatch him. He tried to recruit Frutiger to make copies, but the mannerly archivist said the records could not be photocopied. Only handwritten notes were permitted.

The first few boxes contained Avi's personnel file—records of his security clearance background check (intermittently redacted with streaks of thick black ink), aptitude tests, training reports, routine medical examinations, and expenditures related to his special enrollment in the Apollo program. The documents—mostly translucent onionskin carbon copies—smelled like the 1958 edition of *Encyclopaedia Britannica* Jonathan had perused for hours in his bedroom on rainy days in Tel Aviv before his family moved to the United States. His father's IQ was 128, not as high as Jonathan had imagined. Avi's motor reflexes and peripheral vision, by contrast, were off the scale. He had easily passed every physical and psychological test. There was nothing to indicate any medical problem. Month after month, Avi's blood work was perfect, his blood alcohol level never above negligible. He had apparently been nothing more than an accomplished social drinker. And his EKGs were all normal. Of course, Jonathan's were always normal too. There was no mention of any affiliation with Israeli intelligence or any matters related to the Germans working at NASA.

"Would you like to break for lunch now?" Frutiger asked. "It's almost one o'clock. We've got a pretty good cafeteria upstairs."

Jonathan assessed the linear feet of paper he'd covered and the amount left to review. "Something quick."

They returned to the main level. The cafeteria was standard General Services Administration, generic and sterile—the walls painted pale blue, the floor tiled in a checkerboard pattern, the tables white Formica with chrome legs. No artwork on the walls, only posters about the government's retirement plan and an upcoming session about healthcare coverage. A canary-yellow AED emergency kit hung behind the cash register at the end of the food service line.

"Beef stew's the special today," Frutiger said. "It's not bad."

Jonathan picked up a prepackaged tuna salad sandwich and a diet soda.

"Your launch is in November, I think. You'll forgive the occupational reflex. I did a little extra research."

"That's our target."

"You're a pilot, I presume. Must be hard not to have your dad here to see all this."

With head down and his sandwich in his mouth, Jonathan looked at Frutiger through the tips of his eyebrows.

"I didn't mean to offend," Frutiger said, his soup spoon frozen in midair, a few inches from his mouth.

Jonathan finished chewing, letting the man sit in discomfort. "It's all right."

By his late twenties, Jonathan had already taken his first steps toward the Moon—flying lessons. Whether the result of rollicking weekend flights with his dad, like the time they took a loaner biplane on low-flying sorties over the Everglades and attacked enemy alligator "tanks" with water balloons, or the weightier ambition to preserve a legacy, Jonathan felt the pull of the cockpit. When he flew, and particularly when he flew solo, his father was not so far away.

"Sport, recreational, private, commercial?" Frutiger asked.

"Commercial. Do you fly?"

"Heavens no, but I've filed away more FAA and NTSB reports than you can fit on a C-130 transport. I have to admit I sometimes like to read about the accidents." He used a paper napkin to wipe tomato residue from the corners of his mouth. "It can get a little tedious, spending most of your life downstairs. You know what the most common ones were?"

"Small aircraft, bad weather."

"That's right. Like what happened to JFK Junior. Usually it's pilots who had just been certified IFR. You've got to trust your instruments. That's what they say."

"It was Dale Lunden's mantra." He had packed Jonathan's head with tragic anecdotes of pilots who couldn't resist the temptation to look out into a sea of clouds and suffered the ultimate consequence. "Dale must have told me 'instruments, not instincts' at least a hundred times."

"The missus and I get a glossy color retirement brochure with his big pearly whites at least twice a month. Can't figure out all those annuities. We just stick to treasuries."

"Me neither. Glad it's not my dad's face stuffing your mailbox. I mean, who wants to watch a huckster at work?"

Frutiger started to laugh. "But Lunden's cash cow sure jumped over the Moon."

Jonathan shrugged and segregated his plastic for recycling. "You ever meet him—Dale?"

"Just on TV. Wife says he looks like Van Johnson. Quite smitten at one time she was. Of course, you're too young to even know that name."

Jonathan flung his scraps to the trash. He had never noticed the resemblance before. "*A Guy Named Joe,* 1943," Jonathan said. "My dad's favorite war movie. Van Johnson played the young pilot, Ted Randall."

Frutiger slapped his knee. "That's where she got it. We used to love that picture. Spencer Tracy was great."

Jonathan hated the film, but when he couldn't sleep, he sometimes watched it, alone, in his media room. Tracy's character, Pete Sandidge, was shot down by a German fighter but came back from Heaven for one last mission—to serve as Randall's guardian angel. Randall survived the war and got Sandidge's girl. And Sandidge's ghost shambled back to the clouds. Jonathan always cringed at his resignation, like he was almost happy about how things had turned out. "Yeah, he's a good actor, I suppose," Jonathan said. "Would you, by any chance, have any documents about the decision to put Dale Lunden back in command of Apollo 18?"

Frutiger polished an apple on his sleeve. "Might take me a bit to locate, if we have anything. I'm pretty backlogged, but I suppose I can scrounge around, tomorrow or the next. I'll give you a holler if anything turns up." Frutiger's eyebrows pressed together. "We know where to find you," he said, in a menacing baritone. Frutiger struggled to sustain the feigned gravitas, but his lips betrayed him, cracking an impish grin. "Maybe I'll find a dashing Lunden headshot for the missus while I'm at it."

The final box contained the autopsy and an audit of the procedures followed to monitor Avi's health. Jonathan had delayed his review of the medical examiner's report, dithering as he had before reading Cassandra's account of his father's death, as if the letters on each page floated above the paper, swirling in a vortex of gobbledygook, settling into words and coherent text only when he looked at the first page.

He made a fist under the table, pressing it into his thigh as he read. His father had been found at 10:22 a.m. ($10 + 2 - 2 = 10$), on the floor of his room, naked, face up, halfway between his bed and the door. Toxicology was negative. Blood alcohol content 0.01. The report called the BAC result "a potential false positive" and in any event *de minimis*. It offered no explanation for the presence of alcohol in a quarantined location. When Jonathan reached the report's final conclusion, he slowed down to mouth every syllable.

"'Given the absence of atherosclerosis, severe coronary artery spasm presents as the most likely precipitating cause of acute myocardial infarction.'" Most likely.

He wrote down the unsurprising cause of death, leaned back in his chair and lifted his head. The rectangular fluorescent lights whited out his vision before he closed his eyes. The pinkish outlines of the overhead bulbs lingered on his optic nerve until all went dark.

"You drink, Mr. Frutiger?"

"Other than wine at communion and a rare eggnog at Christmas, no."

"Maybe you should try the hard stuff sometime."

Frutiger remained silent.

"Only a joke, man. You know us Jews, always keep 'em laughing. You know why we do that, don't you?"

Frutiger shook his head.

"They can't shoot straight when they're laughing." Jonathan coughed up a forced chuckle and returned to the few files that remained. He found a list of every NASA employee with access to the Apollo 18 astronauts during prelaunch quarantine. Each of the ten names was followed by a job description and a summary of the man's NASA employment history. No Germans. According to military police summaries, Avi's crew members hadn't heard or seen anything unusual. He couldn't have followed up with them anyway. Both had been dead for years. All appeared in order, just as Frutiger and Lunden had promised. After spending over four hours plowing through reams of brittle logs and fading mimeographed reports, Jonathan looked forward to returning to his computer. The files corroborated what he had always been told, but the official, dispassionate confirmation failed to provide the expected consolation. The cold records left him feeling empty and unsatisfied. The sterile accounts felt like form-letter rejections, his apparent victory over Cassandra like a draw. Natural causes. He would have to learn to live with the twinge, to survive with it.

He had filled a sheet of paper with random notes including the medical examiner's name, the time of death, and a handful of facts about his father's medical history: Avi had the measles at six years old, an above average sperm count (Why did they test for that? Why couldn't he have inherited that trait instead? Why was he an only child?), and the same blood type as Jonathan. "My dad was A plus, like me."

"You mean A positive, I think," Frutiger said.

Jonathan reached under the table and picked up the first box he had reviewed to run through some of the details on his father's training regimen one last time. His hand slid along the short side of the box, and he felt a sticky spot. He ran his hand back across the same area again and felt the familiar feeling of a place where a piece of tape, or a dot, had fallen off—or been removed. Frutiger, apparently unaware, read a trade magazine for librarians. Jonathan turned the short side of the box toward him. The stickiness was covered by the black horizontal leg of a capital "L," the last letter of an eight-digit code written in thick permanent marker. The horizontal stroke seemed too long, but the handwriting in general looked irregular. Cassandra's cries of cover-up rushed to mind.

"Anybody else been in here lately to look at these files?"

"I'm afraid I can't help you there." Frutiger didn't look up from his magazine. "The classified files visitor list is—I suppose not surprisingly—classified, above even your clearance."

Jonathan knew that basic top-secret clearance wasn't that rare. Thousands of people who worked in the defense industry had it. Even Susana got it when she consulted with DARPA (the Defense Advanced Research Projects Agency) on nanobot technology. But he was ahead of himself. If there were no dot, it couldn't have been peeled off by anyone.

He had to check the av room. He pretended to read a file while his head churned with options. Could he trust Frutiger? The thought sent him into a spiraling frenzy of paranoia. Maybe Frutiger hadn't researched Jonathan out of occupational curiosity. Maybe he'd been briefed. Jonathan imagined that if he were to share his suspicions with Frutiger, the courtly librarian would slip a finger over a button under the table, summoning a pair of men in dark suits and sunglasses, and he would disappear. It did seem strange that the files were still classified after so many years, and that it took nearly a month for him to gain access.

A janitor-sized key chain hung from Frutiger's belt. Jonathan couldn't possibly steal the keys, or even figure out the right one to use. He took out his phone. Before asking to look for tapes or film, he would let Frutiger eavesdrop on a few calls in which he would casually note his location, the time, and the name of his apparently very accommodating host. Cassandra's warning felt prophetic: "Assistance is the most powerful form of control." The phone's display screen showed no bars, too deep underground. He asked Frutiger for permission to go upstairs where he might get some reception to update "a few colleagues" on his progress. Frutiger agreed, but reminded him that he could not wander around on his own.

In the lobby, Jonathan called Susana and his assistant. He spoke in the urgent, hushed voice of a fugitive in a telephone booth. He gave them the precise location of the room where he reviewed documents, the code number of the dotless box, and a description of Frutiger. Both promised to await his all-clear—his assistant, unquestioning and dutiful; Susana, incredulous and amused. After he hung up, he wasn't sure he could go through with it. He thought about bolting out the front door, aborting the mission. He could always say he had been called away because of an accident at one of his facilities. As he started for the exit, he saw a group of kids entering through the main doors. They must have been in sixth or seventh grade—no acne yet and the boys much shorter than the pubescent girls. Each student held a spiral notebook and sauntered in a loose single file. A young, petite woman in a bright pink silk blouse and knee-length navy skirt energetically welcomed the field trippers. Jonathan leaned against an informational kiosk and watched them snake through rows of computer terminals and bookshelves.

Thirteen-year-old Jonathan was called out of English class on the day it happened. He thought they had wanted to go over the details. That weekend he had filled a journal with comprehensive notes on the launch sequence, mission objectives, and astronaut trivia. His whole grade was going to be there to see it. The school nurse was sitting in the principal's office. Outside, a gym class played dodgeball against the back of the bus garage. Red rubber balls ricocheted with loud reports off the cinder block wall. Thirty years later, he could still hear them, pounding. The principal lit a cigarette and took a strong drag. "There is no easy way to do this," he said. "There's been a terrible incident. It's your father. It looks like he's had a heart attack." Then they lied to him, said his father was still alive. So did Lunden, when he picked up Jonathan to rush him to the hospital, shifting gears like a Formula One racer. His mother had wanted to be the one to tell him the truth.

Jonathan turned away from the students to go back underground. "What if NASA had lied to her too?" he asked himself.

Back at the table, opposite Frutiger, Jonathan took up a file and leafed through it. After waiting what felt like an appropriate amount of time, he lunged toward the box like a pouncing cat. He pretended to rifle through a series of files in search of something specific, something he knew he had seen. He felt the box again. His feverish movements drew Frutiger out of the magazine. "Anything I can help you with?"

"I saw in these records, somewhere, a reference to the medical examiner's dictation. That would be done on audiotape, I think. I assumed it wasn't kept, but I just felt the side of this box, and it seems there may have been a dot stuck on this side, covering this 'L,' that maybe has fallen off. Here, feel it."

Frutiger seemed interested in Jonathan's theory and felt the box. "It's sticky. Do you want to check audiovisual? Those dots have been known to peel off now and again."

Jonathan's body went limp. He felt the same cool relief he experienced after waking up from a forgot-to-study-for-the-final-exam dream. He couldn't believe that a few seconds earlier he had contemplated his grisly end at the hands of secret government assassins. Frutiger was all too happy to help.

The dot probably fell off. Natural causes.

Frutiger asked Jonathan to open the heavy metal door and let him conduct the search. Without much effort, he found a sealed manila envelope with a few handwritten notes ("Apollo 18" and "classified-top secret") and a NARA label bearing the corresponding box code. The flap was covered with strips of Scotch tape browned with age around the edges. It looked undisturbed, no apparent tears. Jonathan felt a round object inside. He held the envelope up for Frutiger and in a ripping pantomime asked if he could open it. Frutiger reached into his sweater and pulled out a letter opener. Inside they found a tape reel. Jonathan asked if they had a machine that could play it. Frutiger said there was one that worked two floors above and went to retrieve it.

Jonathan waited in the research room, holding the reel with two hands. Despite his invention of the medical examiner's dictation as a way to camouflage his suspicions, the tape was likely nothing more than a clinical recitation of the autopsy. Reading the report had been bad enough. He didn't know if he could handle it—listening to the detached, workmanlike description of the weight of his father's internal organs. He checked the wastebasket under the table.

Frutiger returned with a dusty reel-to-reel player on a pushcart. He threaded the tape and started the machine. After a few moments of the hiss and crackle of old, monaural recordings, a male voice could be heard.

"This is Blaine Naughton for Armed Forces Radio."

The broadcaster had an old-time radio voice, a stylized way of speaking, no discernible geographic roots, the kind of voice incapable of irony or expletive.

"We are lucky to have with us today Captain Abraham Stein, a member of the Israeli Air Force and, more significantly for our purposes, a part of the Apollo 18 crew that leaves for the Moon in about t-minus five days. Thanks for taking the time to speak with us today, Captain."

"You are welcome."

That voice, which had been fading away for so many years in

Jonathan's mind, receding relentlessly toward a vanishing point, roared to life with startling fidelity. He felt hot all over, the heat radiating from deep inside as if he were being bombarded with microwaves instead of sound waves. He leaped out of his chair to stab the STOP button.

"You all right, son?"

Jonathan stepped back from the machine, arms folded at his chest. "It's not every day you hear your dad's voice after so many years. That kind of time warp, it packs a hell of a wallop."

"I can see it right there on your face, plain as day."

Jonathan patted his cheeks as if taking his temperature. "I'll be fine, really, but maybe this might be a little easier with some privacy? Would that be all right?"

Frutiger looked back and forth from Jonathan to the tape player. "I'm pretty sure nobody knows the regs around here like I do. Shoot, wrote most of them myself. But I suppose I don't see any reason to intrude on family matters for the sake of bureaucratic technicalities."

"That would help, a lot. Did you know about this tape?"

"No, of course not." Frutiger picked up his magazine. "I'll drag a chair into the hallway. Just let me know when you're finished."

As soon as Frutiger left, Jonathan stood his briefcase on the table to shield his digital mini-recorder from view.

One . . . Two . . . Three . . . Four.

He pressed RECORD and restarted the tape player.

"Captain Stein, could you please tell us what this upcoming mission to the Moon means to you and your people?"

"It is, of course, a great honor to be the Israeli first in space. The Jews for sure have escaped annihilation throughout history. When I plant our flag on the Moon, it will be a symbol of our resilience . . . even if it must fly beneath your Stars and Stripes."

The interviewer cleared his throat. "So . . . so . . . ah, describe the training you, ah, have done here in the States to prepare for the mission."

"Extensive endurance preparations, but nothing too difficult. The Israeli Air Force and my combat experience have prepared me."

"That's good to hear, Captain Stein, but I have to believe the space-age technology NASA is famous for must be entirely new to you. Am I right?"

"Not really. The technology for the Apollo program is not so new. Nineteen-fifties engineering, solid and simple. I have not either had to spend too much time with the Nazi engineers. I have, however, been very interested to learn about the guidance computers for the shuttle program—integrated circuits I mean. We do not have any technology in Israel like that, not yet anyway."

"I'm sorry, I think you meant to say NASA engineers." Naughton sounded frazzled.

"No, you heard me quite correctly, young man. Can it be a secret that US military brought over Wernher von Braun and his compatriots to win the space race? He is big celebrity here. I don't think so."

Jonathan stopped the tape player and the mini-recorder. A cold stream of sweat ran down his spine. He checked to make sure the digital device was capturing his father's interview. Satisfied with the sound quality, he started the tape again and began to pace, hands on his hips.

"You mean," Naughton said, "the German professors who were forced to work for Hitler's war machine?"

After a moment of dead air, Avi responded. "If you want to put it that way. So many unfortunate innocents forced to work for Hitler—Jews, Gypsies, Dr. von Braun, Secretary General Waldheim, the list goes on. What a shame for all of them."

"Right, so this mission is really another outstanding example of America's staunch support of the Jewish nation, isn't it, Captain Stein?

"You could say that I am pleased the American government has made at least a small effort to make an amend."

"So Captain Stein, what have you been do—I'm sorry, did you say make amends?"

"Of course, I don't just mean America's decision to support the Munich Olympics. Do you think that American military intelligence did not know what was happening in Europe? Patton? Don't get started. Putting an end to our suffering was not vital to strategic, national interests . . . but this mission is at least a small step in a right direction. So, yes, to answer your question directly, yes, we appreciate the small step."

There was a brief pause in the recording. Jonathan imagined the young, white-bread reporter floored by his father's blunt remarks. He wasn't surprised that Avi might have held such beliefs, but he was shocked that, with only days until launch, his dad would be so cavalier with a journalist from a military news outlet.

"I know, Captain Stein, that bad weather has pushed back your launch date by a few days at the last minute. What have you been doing with the extra time? Any chance to relax?"

"Not really much extra time. We go through a whole prelaunch procedure from the beginning: equipment checks, malfunction logs, science experiment protocols, et cetera. But I have had a little time at night to read. In fact, I've just read a very interesting book, and it's helped me put things in perspective, let me tell you. It's called . . . well . . . how would you say it in English? I'm not sure of a translation, but it has to do with tolerance. What individuals can put up with. This, of course, is a subject so close to the Jewish heart. The intolerance has been the most powerful force at work on our people for centuries, scattering us, even over an ocean. In fact—"

"Well, Captain Stein—"

"I'm not finished yet. This book I read puts the tolerance of human beings in a new perspective. I don't think it's been widely read, I'm sure, but I recommend it very highly. Everyone should read it. It has helped me to better understand my friends here in the United States and also my enemies."

"Well, looks like that's all the time we have, Captain Stein. Thanks so much for talking with me, and . . . Godspeed."

Jonathan sat on the table, hunched over, his feet planted on the seat of a chair, holding his face like it might fall off. The tape reels, still turning, wheezed a white-noise *ostinato* while competing questions clanged inside his head, a cacophony of unease and perplexity. Why had his father acted like that? An altercation with the Germans? Who were his "enemies"? Why hadn't his mother ever mentioned the interview? Why hadn't Dale? Were they protecting him? Guarding a secret? Had they even known about it? Had his father been drinking? Why was the tape classified? Could Avi have been a spy? Was he speaking in code? What was that book? What happened to the dot on the box? How did Cassandra get his information? Jonathan slipped the recorder into his briefcase, rubbed his hands through his hair, untied and retied his shoes, put on his suit coat, and invited his chaperone back into the room.

"Was it helpful?" Frutiger shut off the machine.

"It didn't answer any questions. That's for sure."

"You look a little peaked. You all right?"

"I guess hearing my father after so long, it made me feel like . . . like I was a kid again, thirteen years old, like he was never gone. But he felt farther away than ever too. It made me feel funny to be dressed up in this suit." He rubbed his sleeves. "Like I've been pretending to be a grown-up."

"Don't tell my grandkids," Frutiger said, "but that's what we all do."

"What happens with the tape?" Jonathan asked.

"I'll reseal the envelope and make sure to get a bright new sticky dot for the box." Frutiger rewound the recording. "And don't worry. I know I said I get bored down here, but I won't listen. You can count on it. I'm not supposed to review classified material unless I have a legitimate archival purpose. FAA reports are different, they're public. I have to record that the envelope was opened today and by whom, but that's it. I'm a very good grown-up." He smiled as if they were old friends keeping a secret pact.

"You really can't tell me if anybody has been through these files lately?"

Frutiger looked up at the ceiling and moved closer to Jonathan. "Mr. Stein, I'm not unsympathetic to your quest. But to put it in simple terms, I'm too close to full pension, son."

"Anything?" Jonathan pleaded.

"Nobody ever found that tape before."

"But that means—"

Frutiger seized Jonathan's elbow and thrust a rigid finger against his lips. "I'm just a librarian, that's it," he whispered. Frutiger stepped back. His voice returned to normal volume. "You flying back tonight?"

"I've got a dinner, so tomorrow."

"Enjoy that sunny weather. You go on ahead. I'll straighten up."

In the elevator, Jonathan put two fingers to his neck and probed his carotid artery, his throbbing pulse masked the faint valvular burp that he believed would kill him. Though it terrified him, he wanted to feel its ominous vibrations. He took comfort in its presence, as if that inborn cardiac tic were a homing beacon setting the course and tempo of his predetermined march along Avi's path. He just needed more time. But Frutiger and that tape recording had amplified Cassandra's message. His next steps were unclear, no footprints to guide him, no guardian angel.

He called a car service and waited by the curb. He tossed pebbles against a flagpole while competing conspiracy theories swarmed him. Was Cassandra on the inside? Did he have a well-placed mole? Had Jonathan's archives request triggered an interagency alert? Who was worried about what he might find? The louder his conjectures buzzed the more he wanted to drown them out. He had left his mind too wide open, and now he couldn't dismiss the possibility of murder. He called his assistant and Susana—to let them know he made it out alive—and cancelled a dinner with defense industry lobbyists. He put away his phone, threw a few more stones, and pulled it out again. He made sure the caller ID block was on.

"Hi, Cassie. It's Jon, the Jon from the airplane."

"Still got your tattoo? Would've sworn you washed it off by now."

"No, I did, but I'm too good with numbers. I couldn't forget it if I tried. Are you free tonight?"

"Massage?"

"Maybe."

"Hell, I was supposed to come back tomorrow anyhow so I'm wide open."

"Great. I'll call you at seven. Let's meet for a drink first."

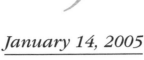

9

January 14, 2005

8:42AM

The Jaguar crawled in a rush-hour caravan along I-95 on the way to his mother's house. Jonathan listened to his father's last interview (copied onto a CD), and then listened to it three more times, searching for a clue hidden behind the accent, a hint buried inside Avi's irregular inflections, long pauses, curious wording. His mind ran in unbridled spurts with the possibility that Avi had sensed trouble. Was there a secret message? Each time Jonathan let loose his imagination, he slammed on his mental brakes, reminding himself that his father's belligerence during the interview, bizarre and inexplicable as it was, didn't constitute proof that Avi was the target of a brazen murder plot.

Idling in bumper-to-bumper traffic, he checked in with his administrative assistant. She reminded him about a one o'clock conference call with an MIT robotics group working on a mobile laboratory to be left on the Moon. He asked her to track down the military reporter, Naughton, gave her the little information he possessed, and told her to be discreet, no direct contact. He would make the call.

Jonathan parked on his old block. Recently retired from teaching, Eva Stein continued to reject her son's offer of a new condo on the beach. She had lived in the same house in Hollywood for nearly thirty years, a modest two-bedroom ranch with an off-white stucco exterior and faded coral pink shutters. The foundation was skirted by a wide ribbon of sunbaked stones, dotted with a few acacia trees and laced with bougainvillea. A dowdy Subaru station wagon sat in the driveway, its bumper plastered with causes from Darfur to deforestation.

Jonathan found his mother in the backyard vegetable garden despite the unusually hot January weather. When she saw her son standing on the screened-in back porch, she pulled off her gardening gloves and stood up, wearing a look of mild discomfort. The top of her head no longer reached his eyes, unless she wore heels, which was almost never. Her white hair, once strawberry blond, was woven into a braid that reached the middle of her back. Her cheeks sank in deeply beneath her high cheekbones, and sharp creases of crow's feet drew attention to her pale green eyes. When Jonathan smiled, people noticed the family resemblance in their toothy grins and prominent jaws. She usually wore too much perfume, her sense of smell dulled from decades working with paint.

He met her in the yard with a firm embrace. Beads of sweat collected in a row outlining her upper lip. He gestured with open hands and shrugged shoulders. "You know I can hire someone."

"Don't be silly. You can take the girl out of the kibbutz, but you can't take the kibbutz out of the girl." She peered up from under the brim of her flower-covered straw sun hat. "I spoke to Susana this morning. She sounded fatigued. I was the same way with you." Eva patted her stomach.

"She's been working too hard, as usual," Jonathan said. "A little temperamental, no more nausea, thank God. Shower plans coming along?"

"Invitations went out yesterday," Eva said. "Anything for my grandson." She winked. "For you too. Such a shame Silvia's not with us anymore. That's got to be hard for Susana, especially now."

"She's been preoccupied with Europa. Not getting much data. Nothing good anyway."

Jonathan followed his mother to the porch, where she sat on a white wicker couch with sunflower yellow cushions covered in a wavy lattice of jungle green vegetation. He leaned against the doorjamb, next to a metal shelf stacked with empty flower pots, organic pesticides, and a "World's Best Teacher" coffee mug half-filled with frayed paint brushes. He snatched a fly swatter from a hook on the wall and waved it like an orchestra conductor. "What happened to

Tevye?" A pot-bellied, weather-abused garden gnome lay face up on a work bench, a serene expression still plastered on his badly pock-marked face. The black paint on his long beard (added by Eva to make him less Santa, more *hamish*) had faded away, and his pointed hat had a jagged crack like Frankenstein's scar.

"Reb Tevye's had it," she said. "I thought I might fix him up one more time, but he's too far gone."

"All those times I knocked him over with the lawn mower," Jonathan said. "It's amazing he lasted this long."

"Susana said you just got back from Washington. Anything interesting?"

"I need to talk to you about Dad." He let himself drop into the couch, wedging into the corner where the armrest met the back cushion. "What do you remember about his heart?"

"You mean the day it happened?" She took off her hat and wiped her brow with the back of her wrist.

"No, before that. Any warning signs?"

"Nothing." She leaned closer, squinting as if she were struggling to hear him. "Are you OK?"

"I'm fine. No, I'm just getting ready for all those interviews I'll be doing. What did they tell you after? About what caused it?"

"Sudden artery blockage. No way to see it coming."

"Did you ever think that his death might have been something more?" Jonathan twisted against the armrest to study her reaction.

"Why would I think that?" The question lingered in her blank expression.

"Did Dad ever say anything unusual before he died?"

"What's on your mind?" She rubbed his shoulder. "It's not interviews, is it?"

"Mom, can you think for a minute?" He stood up. "Was there anything, anything at all?"

"We couldn't talk to him that much then, right before launch. He was in quarantine. The couple of times we spoke he sounded normal, excited."

"He never said anything strange to me either." Jonathan gently rapped the fly swatter like a riding crop against his thigh. "He did say 'take care of your mother,' but I thought he meant to take care of you until he got back. I still do." He picked up Reb Tevye and placed the squat statue just outside the screen door. "I'll put him to the curb when I leave."

"What's this all about, Jon?"

He returned to the sofa and explained what he'd found on eclipsedtruth.com. She listened without interrupting him, frowning, rolling her eyes, shaking her head.

"That's the craziest thing I've ever heard," she said. "How can you put any faith in that Internet *schmutz*? See why I won't get a computer." She took both of his hands and spoke in the reassuring tones she had once used to convince him there were no monsters under his bed. "You know better. Of course it's nonsense. Remember how you used to yell at the TV screen whenever one of those hillbillies told a reporter he'd been kidnapped by aliens?" She smushed his cheeks with one hand. "What happened to my little *skeptnick*? Come, let's go inside. I've got something to show you." She opened the sliding glass door leading to the kitchen. "Some winter, huh? Could you wind up that hose for me before you come in?" He tossed the fly swatter to the shelf and went back to the yard.

The bronze spigot coming out of the house was still open. He reached for the hose and began to spool. The hose slid backward through the thick blades of grass and around the base of a dwarf orange tree, like a dead garter snake corkscrewed in the early stages of rigor mortis. At the end of the hose was the scratched, dull metal spray gun his mother had used since he was a boy. The trigger felt cold and wet. He made sure his mother was inside and closed his eyes, recalling a game he used to play with a chubby kid named Barton who lived across the street. He twisted the flow control dial ("jet," "shower," "mist," "full," "off") clockwise four times, put the nozzle to his right temple, and extended his neck out like a turtle. Reverse Russian Roulette. Only "off" was safe. He squeezed.

Nothing.

"I did it," he whispered. Still wearing a self-congratulatory grin, he noticed the nozzle was set on "jet." His eyes leaped to the spooled hose. He'd been saved from a second morning shower by a kink in the middle.

Eva's cramped kitchen was outdated with no hope of achieving retro status. She pulled a red-and-blue Superman onesie from a shopping bag to show her son. "Remember, Jon? Of course you don't. You were only a baby, but you had one exactly like it. Your dad used to hold you over his head and run back and forth in our apartment, like a wild man, making airplane noises. Then he'd hold you close to his face and say, 'Do you know what the S stands for? Do you? Do you? It stands for Stein, and in German that means 'stone' 'cause we're—'"

"'Unbreakable,'" Jonathan said. "That part I remember. Susana will love it." He reached to take the outfit, but Eva yanked it back.

"Not yet," she said. "It's for the shower. You want something to eat?"

He went straight to the refrigerator and pulled out a bottle of ice tea and leftover coffee cake. He ate with his hands.

"Take the rest of that cake with you, please," she said, giving him a fork. "It's too rich. Got to watch my cholesterol."

"Is it high?"

"Borderline, a little above 200. Have you had yours checked?"

"My numbers are good so far. Don't worry."

She asked him to grab a water pitcher from a high cabinet shelf. He found a handle by feel and pulled one down.

"Still using this thing?" He remembered the stack of proofs of purchase they'd mailed in to get the cherry red Kool-Aid Man pitcher.

"You used to love those commercials, when the pitcher came crashing through the walls to save the day." She sighed. "Nice memories." She filled the smiling pitcher with tap water and sat down on a stool next to a narrow strip of open counter space. "Before you sit down, would you mind going to the basement to bring up my easel? I might paint outside tomorrow. It's supposed to be cooler."

"More sea cows?"

"The preservation coalition wants me to do a shock-and-awe design for their new campaign. I'm thinking about a manatee floating behind a motor boat, its back lacerated like a slave's, a water skier passing by—young, beautiful, completely unaware. You remember the line, 'Their cries rising in waves still as the skillful yachts pass over.'"

"Stevens?"

"William Carlos Williams."

"Right, sorry. Couldn't you paint a bowl of fruit like the other retirees at the JCC?" He grinned, and she shrugged. His mother was the only person he knew who could recite poetry from memory. She had recited some of Plath's "You're" to Susana's abdomen after they told her about the twenty-week ultrasound. *Right, like a well-done sum. A clean slate with your own face on.*

"Sorry hon," she said. "I'm just a hippie at heart, more interested in life still than still life."

In their neighborhood, many residents had a pool, but only the lucky few had a basement. His old haunt was little changed—the unmatched furniture, the outdated television and bulky stereo equipment, the shelves filled with art supplies, model rockets, trophies and ribbons from math and science competitions, his Smith-Corona Super G manual typewriter in its aquamarine carrying case, and a jumble of toys and games that had escaped charitable donation, flea markets, and yard sales. He rummaged through a cardboard vacuum cleaner box held together by masking tape and packed with a mish-mash of military figures. It contained various shades of plastic troops, less than a division of tanks, and a few pieces of artillery. Below a platoon of forest-green rangers, he found folded sheets of paper on which he'd written out meticulous battle plans complete with crude topographical maps.

Young Jonathan had recreated some of the greatest battles of the twentieth century—El Alamein, Iwo Jima, the Battle of the Bulge, and more. One of his favorites was Operation Moked, the devastating pre-emptive airstrike launched by the Israelis at the outset of the Six-Day War. Avi's plane always flew in first and fastest. Among the tactical sketches, he found a heavily creased carbon copy, the first letter to Armstrong he'd written on his new typewriter. He'd typed it on the floor of his bedroom, near midnight, after using a world atlas to trace the route his father might have flown in Operation Thunderbolt.

> *4 July 1976*
>
> *Dear Lt. Armstrong,*
>
> *We just got home from the fireworks. Mom and I watched them from Miami Beach, down by the water, with a youth group from our synagogue. There's no way I'll be able to fall asleep.*
>
> *It was like Independence Day squared. Our rabbi played the guitar while we sang and danced a hora on the beach, kicking up sand like crabs as we flew around in a circle. A group of senior citizens gathered to clap and sing along. Whenever the white lights of a starburst pattern lit up the sky, I could see that some of them had numbers on their forearms.*
>
> *Can you believe what the Israeli commandos did in Entebbe last night? It was unbelievable! 102 hostages freed. I can't wait to hear all the details of the mission. Even the Pentagon has to be impressed. Mom says Dad would have known all the pilots who flew in the raid. I know he would have volunteered to go too if he could have. He wasn't afraid of anything.*
>
> *Only one Israeli soldier was killed. He was named Yonatan, just like me.*
>
> *I hope you had a happy holiday, and that you hate Idi Amin as much as I do.*
>
>

Sincerely,
Jon Stein
>

He dug deeper into the box and found a faded, chipped figurine sitting in the passenger seat of a jeep with no wheels. It was the Hamburglar, one of the original McDonaldland gang, a puckish burger thief from the fast-food chain's early advertising campaign. Always dressed in black-and-white-striped prison garb, the Hamburglar had no illusions about his future. Jonathan had saved his allowance to

buy five of the petty patty snatchers (along with an obligatory chocolate shake). He needed them for his reenactment of the Treblinka
concentration camp uprising of 1943. They served as the leaders of
the revolt. Their inmate stripes were horizontal, not vertical, but they
were the best that he could muster.

He searched the other shelves but couldn't find any more. He had
to be holding Jankiel Wiernik, the only organizer to survive the brazen escape attempt. When Wiernik passed in 1972, Avi taught his son
about the heroic carpenter, who had been forced to build gas chambers for his own people, and the bravery of the Treblinka prisoners.
A reenactment of the incident became a regular part of Jonathan's
repertoire. He examined his sketch of the prison yard, complete with
labeled buildings and fleeing Jews cutting through barbed wire fences.
"The first kind of flight," he whispered. The handwriting seemed like
the script of a different person. He no longer wrote like that. It was
familiar but inaccessible.

Jonathan picked a few unlucky soldiers, their mouths still open
in full battle cry, their weapons at the ready, and placed them on a
miniature ping-pong table, along with his favorite mechanized piece,
a missile launcher. He calculated the trajectory by sight and fired on
the veterans, knocking down two of them. Satisfied with the effort,
he returned his plastic troops and their materiel to the shelves. But he
couldn't leave Wiernik to the same fate. He smuggled the lone refu-
gee to safety in his pocket.

Across from the toy shelves sat a boxy old Magnavox. Its tubes
had been blown out for years. The set weighed a ton, and his mother
never bothered to have it removed. Above the television hung a photograph of his father, white pants and shirt, red sash around his waist
and matching scarf, running down a narrow street, a cloud of dust
billowing behind him. Avi and a few other astronauts had jumped a
cargo flight to an air force base in Zaragoza and run with the bulls in
Pamplona. Eva didn't speak to him for a week, but she later confessed
her love for the "vibrant kinetics" of the picture. "Who else would
strap bombs to their backs?" she had told her son.

Jonathan sat on a salmon-colored loveseat opposite the television, recalling a moment, at that very spot, when Mary, his high school chemistry lab partner, awkward but effective, had made him ejaculate. Polished technique wasn't required in those days. He'd been so afraid of getting caught. Their tentative, exploratory pawing now seemed laughably innocent. The massage therapist from Baltimore had Mary's red hair, but much more competent hands. He leaned forward, elbows on knees, hands behind his head in the airline crash position. The two encounters took on such different characters with the passage of time, one inspiring sweet nostalgia, the other burgeoning regret.

"It's Jon, from the plane. Sorry I never called."

Cassie replied immediately to his text. "Never expected it. U didn't pocket the platinum til after we landed. How's tricks?"

He turned his hand over, examining his ring.

"Fine. Busy. Stuck in Miami for now. Crazy heat wave this winter."

"I could use some natural rays. Doc says I got to stop going to cancer in a box. Maybe I'll come down for a visit?"

His fingers couldn't type fast enough.

"I really just reached out to apologize. I can't see you again. You understand."

"No tears here, big boy, but I've got your number now, just in case :-)"

He dropped the phone as if it were a pinless hand grenade, picked it back up and deleted the conversation. Sweat flooded his armpits. "So stupid," he said. He paged through screens until he figured out how to block her. But that wouldn't be enough. He'd have to change numbers. He could blame the switch on a string of mysterious calls, dead air then hang-ups. Maybe it was Cassandra, he'd say. He would take advantage of a fortuitous nemesis and a hard-won reputation for overkill to convince Susana. "Still covering tracks," he whispered.

Eva called from upstairs.

"Yeah Mom, I'll be right there." He picked up the easel and grabbed a scrapbook of family pictures and newspaper clippings about his father.

In the kitchen, his mother had put a deli-sized slice of cake on a clean plate. He sat at the counter and took a few bites. "I talked to Dale about the website."

Eva poured herself more water from Mr. Kool-Aid. "What did he say?"

"Called it 'nonsense,' of course, just like you. How did he act back then, right after? He kept a stiff upper lip for me, but with adults, with you—"

"Devastated, completely," she said. Eva sat next to her son and drew parallel trails through the condensation on her glass. "You know how those two were." She looked at her watch. "Time for my bone boost." She grabbed a clear plastic case with seven daily pill compartments.

"But Dale got his old spot back," Jonathan said. "A few times, I remember, when Dale came for dinner, he would needle Dad about his 'special treatment,' getting to cut the line for Eighteen. Said he didn't believe in 'affirmative action.' One time, he was sitting right at this counter." Jonathan mimed a glass and bottle in his hands. "Pouring a scotch and soda right here. Dale teased Dad with a smile, but the way he said it, his tone, always put me on edge. The truth is if Dad had lived, Dale would have never made it to the Moon." He pushed the cake plate away. "Eighteen . . . some lucky number, huh?"

Eva wagged a slow finger at her son. "Dale was pissed at the politicians, but he never blamed your father. He felt sick about taking Avi's place, even came over to ask my permission when they offered him the command. Brought me an amaryllis." A thin smile spread across her face. "I don't know what I would have done without his help in those first few weeks, sorting everything out."

"But you two aren't that close any more." Jonathan flipped through the scrapbook.

She paused for a moment, and Jonathan imagined seeing her eyes mist. "Think of how many parents divorce after the loss of a child," she said. "Of course our relationship was nothing like that, but the pain became more intense, whenever we were together." She rubbed his back and closed the scrapbook. "How's the nursery coming? Pick out any wallpaper yet?

The warmth of her touch made him decide to tell her more. "I went to the National Archives to review the NASA files about Dad."

"Because of a silly website? Oh, Jonathan, don't you have enough to keep yourself occupied without wild goose chases?"

"Not exactly wild." He left the kitchen for the living room, planting himself on a pale-yellow couch across from a mirrored china cabinet containing what Eva used to call "Mom's Tower of Tchotchkes"—a Chagall-like fiddler-on-the-roof music box, matching black-and-gold Damascene plates with Stars of David in the center, a silver Nambé bowl, and three Lladró figurines. A dark brown Kahlua bottle made to look like a tiki god perched on the top shelf, a housewarming gift from Lunden, the first one his parents had received in Florida.

Eva followed and sat in a wing chair covered in tangerine-colored felt. Jonathan picked up a chipped ceramic knight from a green-and-white chess set sitting on an acrylic coffee table and rolled it between his fingers. "The official documents were no surprise. But I did find something else, a recording of an interview Dad had done with Armed Forces Radio a few days before he died. He must have been in quarantine already."

She squinted and rubbed the left side of her face like she had a mild toothache. "I don't remember that one. Did he?" She grimaced, her eyes cast down, and leaned forward to pick a grape Jolly Rancher from a beveled dish. "What's so strange about an interview though? Your dad did lots of them."

"This one never went on the air, I'm sure. It was supposed to be a soft-news story, but Dad sounded really strange. He was flippant, even hostile, and his answers were totally nonresponsive, like Dad and the reporter were in different conversations. He spoke about off-the-wall stuff—the government's failure to help the Jews during the war, the German scientists at NASA, and a book he read, in Hebrew, on how people need to tolerate each other. Does it ring a bell? Anything?"

Eva creased the candy wrapper, folding it into increasingly smaller squares. "I don't remember it." She furrowed her brow, looking paler. "Did you ask Dale?"

"Not yet. He didn't mention it when we talked about the website. That wouldn't be the kind of thing he'd forget if he knew about it. I asked him if there was anything strange."

"That doesn't sound like your father. He could be volatile, like most Israeli men, but he always controlled himself in public."

"Could Dad have been drinking?"

"You mean when he did the interview?"

"Dale told me once that he could really put it away."

"But he was in quarantine."

"Dale said those guys could sneak out if they wanted to. It wasn't exactly Fort Knox."

She unwrapped another Jolly Rancher and rolled it around in her fingers as if she were cycling through prayer beads. "Never. He liked a good party, but with his work he was as serious as he could be." She stuck the candy in her mouth.

Jonathan checked for text messages. "Dad wasn't one of those playboy astronauts, was he?" He looked up at the Kahlua god.

"Skirt-chasing? Your father? That wasn't his thing. One of the reasons the IDF picked him. Most of his flyboy pals would've caught the clap after a weekend in the States. Your dad told me about a few of the other astronauts." She palmed her cheek. "Felt bad for their wives."

"Did Dad ever say those kinds of things to you? Like calling Patton an anti-Semite?" Jonathan plucked the Kahlua bottle from the cabinet. A whiff of its dregs planed his face and burned his nose. "He was clearly unhappy with the Germans, and the Americans, in that interview."

"Your father wasn't alone in thinking America was more interested in winning the war than in stopping the Shoah." Hard candy rattled against Eva's teeth. "We knew von Braun had brought over a rocket crew, but your dad didn't have to deal with any of them as far as I know. Of course he didn't love the idea of Third Reich engineers at NASA—didn't love a lot of the Americans to tell you the truth—but he never lost sight of what the mission meant for Israel. That always came first. He used to say '*We're* going to the Moon.'"

Jonathan thought about the incident at the gymnasium during space camp but said nothing. He had never told her. There might have been things that Avi never told anyone. "Was Dad a spy?"

"Your father, please." She waved a hand in front of her face like she was shooing flies. "He couldn't keep a poker face." She extended an arm and tapped the inside of her wrist. "Wore his heart on his sleeve. I had to make him swear he'd stop playing cards with the boys after two months in Florida. Put him on a strict weekly allowance. He was no Wild Bill Hickok. Couldn't bluff worth a damn."

"What about that book, the one on tolerance? Sounded like code when he mentioned it. Did you ever see it? Talk about it?"

"He wasn't a big reader, your father. I was the bookworm. Of course, he believed that people—usually he meant Arabs and Jews— had to find a path toward coexistence, but I never heard him talk about any kind of book like that. None of this makes him Mossad."

Jonathan placed the empty idol on the coffee table and sat on the couch. "What about Armstrong?"

Eva's eyebrows rose and the corners of her mouth pinched together. "What about him? The last I heard he still lives like a leper."

"Cassandra, the website guy, actually e-mailed me about him."

"How'd this Cassandra even find you?"

"It wouldn't be that hard. He says Armstrong stays out of the public eye because he knows the truth about NASA's secrets, including what happened to Dad, says I should try to make contact."

"Cassandra?!" Eva rolled her eyes, tossing her head.

"I know, I know." He closed his eyes and waved a hand at her incredulity. "It's all categorically ridiculous, but maybe I should talk to him, finally, after all these years. I'm doing other research too, but what if Armstrong never wrote back because he knows something, something he can't, or won't, get into it? There has to be a reason for his silence. What if this is it?"

"I'm sure that's not why he never wrote back. He's a hermit, son." She spat a candy shard into the wrapper. "I don't get it. It's like you and this . . . this Cassandra are playing 'Simon Says.' Cassandra says 'Go visit Armstrong,' and you do it, just like that." Eva returned to the kitchen. "How can I forget all the times you ran to the mailbox hoping you'd get a response? If he didn't bother to write back to the young son of a dead astronaut, what makes you think he's going to talk to you now, after so long?" She sighed and poured more water. "Why couldn't you have written to Aldrin instead?"

Back at the counter, Jonathan flashed a palm when Eva held up the pitcher to offer a drink. "I've always respected Armstrong's privacy—too much I guess. Confronting him, finally, might do me some good. I don't want to go to NASA yet, and there's something Dale's not saying. Armstrong's been an unchecked box in my life for too long. It's time to try something besides letters."

"Forget about him. He was just a man in a space suit who got out first. The most famous man without a face."

"So, Mom." His voice wound up like a lawyer firing his last question on cross-examination. "You don't think there's *any* possibility there could have been foul play?"

"No, and Neil Armstrong is certainly not going to be any help . . . unless maybe he can lend you a spade." She faced him holding her hands fist over fist in front of her stomach, pretending to shovel. "Remember? How you wouldn't do it? You're about to become a father. It's time to bury your dad. Your child deserves it. You *know* how he died, but you don't want to believe it. You're seeing foul play in whatever you find—the website, this interview, even Armstrong's silence. You'll take anything if it lets you deny the randomness." It was then that her voice broke and tears misted her eyes. "Why are you making me do this?"

Jonathan felt bad that he'd made her grief resurface. He flipped the scrapbook open to a photograph taken when he was eight. The family had hiked up the Snake Path to the top of Masada. He stood between Avi and Eva, surrounded by enormous sun-bleached boulders. He wore khaki shorts, a gray T-shirt with a New York Knicks logo, and an oversize white fisherman's bucket hat. He remembered little from the excursion, except that his hat kept sliding down over his eyes, and that his father had carried him part of the way. "Look, Ma, remember this trip?" He showed her the picture as a peace offering.

"That hat." A laugh escaped. "It was your dad's, but you insisted on wearing it." She dried her eyes with a dish towel. "Are you looking for a reason to cancel the mission?"

"Of course not. What's that supposed to mean?"

"Maybe you're a little afraid." She put her arm around his waist. "Worried for your son, or reluctant to overtake your father. No boy ever feels too great about beating his dad in a foot race."

Jonathan could feel his pulse. He wouldn't tell her about his heart condition, fearful that even speaking the words would set his fateful future in stone. "I thought digging up those old records would actually help me bury him, but it hasn't. Can I at least play you the interview?"

"I don't think that's necessary."

"I've got it right in the car."

"It's not going to change anything, Jonathan. You have to let it go, let *him* go. He died of a heart attack in 1974. That's it. Take a look at my bookshelf. You'll see what I mean. Rabbi Kushner is right there. Bad things happen to good people all the time—and more so, it seems, to good Jews."

"Doesn't what I told you about the website and the interview matter?" Jonathan paced in a tight circle, clutching the scrapbook. "The website talks about the NASA Nazis and then so does Dad. That's a pretty big coincidence. Doesn't it stir anything?"

She stepped in front of him and put her hand on his chest. "Pain, Jonathan. That's all it can stir. What I know is that my husband has been dead for thirty years. I soldiered on as a single working mother. As wonderful as you were, are, it wasn't easy. Of course I miss him. My heart aches for him, all the things he missed—we missed together— but some online fiction is not about to disturb the peace I've worked so hard to make. In the end, nothing will ever bring him back."

"I know he's not coming back. That's not it." Jonathan put down the album, picked up his car keys, and pecked her on the cheek. "I get why you don't want to look back, but I have to. I've got no choice. There's a reason murder has no statute of limitations."

10

January 21, 2005
7:31PM

Jonathan had left work early to set up a new, professional-grade telescope in the backyard. Susana joined him to help with the calibrations. It looked like a sawed-off cannon. Mature coconut palms, lit by a low waxing gibbous moon, cast long shadows over the manicured lawn. After a friendly squabble over azimuth calculation and some meticulous fine-tuning, they took turns surveying the lunar landing zone. NASA had just approved Jonathan's site—a smooth volcanic plain dotted with a few scattered narrow craters, like sand traps on Scottish links.

Once he had tested the Celestron's automated features, Jonathan changed into swim trunks and mixed a dark and stormy under an enormous pergola wrapped in strands of white light. He sat at a patio table stacked with papers next to an amoeba-shaped pool while Susana did water aerobics to salsa tracks from Mark Anthony. "This stuff from the underwriters is totally incomprehensible," Jonathan said. He was finally reviewing the estate planning documents their lawyer had sent weeks earlier. Susana didn't respond. The music was too loud for her to hear. He had requested a quote from a London insurer for a special purpose policy—life insurance coverage if he didn't make it back. Jonathan raised his voice. "They want $250,000.00 for two million. I should remind them nobody's ever died on the Moon." She nodded without losing the beat as she marched in place. The term sheet contained an exclusion for preexisting conditions. A chill rippled through his body at the thought of his own autopsy. He shoved the stack aside and grabbed his phone to make a call.

First, he checked for any unwanted texts. He could hear Zubin scolding him for imagining Cassie like Glenn Close in *Fatal Attraction.* Jonathan knew Susana was no "forgive and forget" Anne Archer wife. She would definitely shoot him first. While the phone rang, he stepped inside a changing cabana that looked like a sultan's tent.

"Frutiger speaking."

Jonathan apologized for calling so late. He had intended to leave another voicemail. Frutiger said he had stayed after hours to finish an overdue year-end report.

"Any luck on those files?"

"Took longer than I expected. Just one memo. Think that might be it. I was going to call you. I'll drop a copy in the mail first thing, if that's all right. Nothing classified."

Jonathan asked him to fax it. Ten minutes later, he was standing in his study with the document in his hands. The memo concerned a requested deviation from personnel protocol. It began by outlining the normal procedure for prime crew replacements, including citations to the NASA policy manual provisions outlining the purposes of a backup crew on every mission. The request for an exception came from Dale Lunden, then set to command Apollo 19. He had asked for a meeting with NASA officials a week after Avi Stein's death and presented his case: a proposal to switch places with Avi's backup commander. He argued for the exception based on the unique circumstances of Apollo 18. Putting him in command, Lunden contended, would simply be a return to the *status quo ante* before the Israeli pilot had taken his spot. Making sure to emphasize the limited nature of its decision, NASA ultimately decided, "in this unique and unfortunate situation," to grant Lunden's request.

Jonathan raced back to the pool and shut off the outdoor speakers. Susana froze, her arms thrust high above her head. "*Carajo!* What is it? I love that song."

"From the archives." He waved the paper above his head. "Dale volunteered to take my dad's spot, even lobbied for it. He lied to me." Jonathan dropped in a chaise lounge to reread the memo.

She held her pose for moment before letting her arms splash in the water. "Of course he did."

"What do you mean 'of course he did?'" Jonathan imitated her faint Puerto Rican accent when he repeated her words.

"It was Dale's mission *first*. By then, everybody had heard rumors about budget cuts. He knew Apollo 18 would be the last moonshot. Your dad would have done the same thing. That doesn't make him a criminal." Susana swam a lazy backstroke to the far side of the pool. "So he's an opportunist. Join the club."

Jonathan pursued her on foot. "But why did Dale lie to me?" He could smell the damp stones of the Old Cemetery in Tel Aviv. "When I was a kid, Dale told me that Mom had to convince him to go. Shit, that doesn't match up either. Mom said he came to *her*, to ask permission. He must've lied to her too. Can't even keep his story straight."

Susana climbed out of the water and wrapped herself in an oversize beach towel. "Semantics, Jon." She wrung the water out of her hair. "Convince, permission; he said, she said; whatever, it's been thirty years. What was Dale supposed to do? Throw himself in an open grave? It's not India." She took a V8 from the outdoor kitchen's mini-fridge and sat on a teak chest. "Dale saw men die in Vietnam, a lot of them. What happens? Next man up. I'm sure he didn't feel any need to explain himself, or feel guilty about it."

"Why lie then?" His mind replayed a scene from *A Guy Named Joe,* when Sandidge's friend shoved the dead pilot's picture into a drawer.

"What was he going to say to a fatherless child?" Susana asked. "'Listen kid, them's the breaks. Dad's bad luck was the best thing that ever happened to me.' *No hay mal que por bien no venga.* Haven't we all, in some way, depended upon the misfortune of others?"

"But what if Dale wanted him dead?" Jonathan went back for his drink.

"We all commit thought crimes, Jon. You want to go to jail for every South Beach model you ogle?"

Jonathan shook his head. "No . . . I mean, what if Dale actually *did* something?" He stabbed the air with a finger. "He knows about that interview. I'm telling you he's hiding it." Susana, like his mother, had dismissed any connection between the interview and Avi's untimely death.

"Now you sound like that *mamabicho* who started all this, that Lunatic tow truck driver, Wyatt. Just go talk to Dale. Ask him about the damn interview. Play it for him. I'm sure—" She hunched over and put her hand on her stomach. "Wait. I think the baby just moved. A smile burst across her face. "It was like he was knocking on a door, tap, tap, tap. Come, feel it."

Jonathan approached with an outstretched hand. She took it and guided him to a spot just above her hip. "I can't feel anything."

"Wait a minute. There, did you feel that?"

He pressed firmly against her flesh. "No, nothing."

"It's stopped. I felt him earlier today at work, more like a kick. What I wouldn't do for a knock like that from Europa."

"Still quiet up there?"

"Not a peep."

They sat side-by-side on the bench in silence. Water gurgled from a brass spout pouring into the pool. A mixed chorus of katydids and crickets sang in the shadows. "Maybe Dale didn't have to do anything," Jonathan whispered. "Seize the moment, keep your mouth shut. Don't ask questions. No looking back."

"*Por díos*, Jon." She stood up and tightened the towel around her shoulders. "It's like you actually want you father to have been killed by somebody."

Jonathan shot to his feet. "That's ridiculous." He stepped toward the house before executing an abrupt about-face. "Why, why would I want that? Armstrong, Cassandra, that interview, this memo—something happened. My dad deserves the truth, doesn't he?"

"Just because you want to find something doesn't mean it's there. Believe me." She pointed to the twinkling night sky. "I'm reminded of that every day."

"But you're still looking, aren't you?" Without waiting for her reply, Jonathan ripped off his shirt and dove into the pool—lap swimming to cool down. The official account was losing its authority. Lunden's angry protests at the diner had been too loud, his professed reluctance to replace Avi a self-serving sham. What had he done? Jonathan emerged from the water after ten minutes, chest heaving.

He scrub-dried his hair with splayed fingers and returned to the telescope for one last look. "Everything we see is in the past," he told himself. The moonlight firing his retinas was already 1.3 seconds old. "We're always looking back."

11

January 27, 2005

7:41AM

Jonathan flashed his ID badge at the guard hut and parked behind
the Kennedy Space Center's training facility. Twice a month, since
October, he had risen before dawn and piloted the Cessna due north
to have his world turned upside down. He started each visit with a
session in the MAT (Multi-Axis Trainer) room, pitching, rolling, and
yawing in a gyroscope to simulate the disorienting effects of a tum-
bling spacecraft. Head back, eyes open, breaths even, mind clear. He
had long understood the MAT's value.

His father had talked endlessly about the lessons of the Gemini 8
mission, the 1966 orbital docking exercise gone horribly wrong. The
spacecraft's death spiral, caused by a thruster malfunction, reached
one revolution per second, enough to cause blurred vision, uncon-
sciousness, catastrophe. Avi Stein had marveled at the poise of the
young command pilot on his first mission: Neil Armstrong. On the
brink of disaster, Armstrong methodically activated the reentry control system to steady the ship and brought her safely back down to
Earth, averting the first fatalities in space. Armstrong had a three-
year-old son at the time. Once, when Eva passed through the kitchen
and heard her husband preaching to Jonathan for the millionth time
about the brilliance of the Gemini 8 reentry, she put a finger to
his lips and added a line from Kipling. "'*If you can keep your head
when all about you are losing theirs. . . .*'" "Exactly," Avi said. "That's
it. That's what got him the right to be first one on the Moon. Grace
under pressure."

After hundreds of hours in a variety of cockpits, Jonathan never
had a problem with the MAT. He even had the machine's operator

flash lights and blast punk rock, the Clash or the Sex Pistols, to inten-sify the sensory overload. He would be ready for anything.

"Got a good one today, Mr. Stein," the operator said as he strapped Jonathan to the chair for a five-minute ride.

"Don't tell me, Hank. That damn song's been on the radio non-stop. U2, right? 'Vertigo.' Clever, but I can't stand Bono. Thinks he's the messiah or something."

"No sir, nothing that commercial." Hank stepped behind a com-puter console to initiate the spin. Music exploded from its speakers: The Ramones, "Too Tough to Die." Head back, eyes open, breaths even, mind clear. Jonathan knew the lyrics. *I tell no tales I do not lie.* Ceiling, wall, floor, wall, floor, ceiling. "Doing all right, Mr. Stein?"

"Yep. Fine."

"Looking good, sir. I'll crank her up to eleven."

Jonathan twisted and turned with increasing velocity. Floor, wall, floor, wall, ceiling, floor. At the highest setting, he imagined himself like the blades of fan, a blur in all positions. He pictured the scene from outside his body. Shards of Avi's interview interrupted the MAT's high-pitched whir. "Endurance . . . combat . . . intolerance . . . ene-mies." *Halo round my head too tough to die.* Head back, eyes open, breaths even, but mind, not so clear. He saw flashes of Cecil Frutiger, the cheerful archivist, donning a crimson armband; Cassie, the mas-sage therapist, at his front door with a suitcase and a baby bump; his teary mother holding a garden hose; and his father, wrinkled and bald, the old man he never was. *In real good shape I have no fear.* Jonathan would look just like that in thirty years.

"Thirty more seconds to go, Mr. Stein."

His stomach sloshed and burned. It didn't have to be a heart attack. Assassination, sabotage, a malfunctioning spaceship somer-saulting silently through space. Susana in all black. His infant son too small to salute, like JFK Jr. Not even a casket to salute. Acid crawled up his throat. He forced air through puffed cheeks and kept his eyes shut while Hank counted down from ten. *Halo round my head too tough to die.*

Once the MAT stopped, Hank released Jonathan from the harness.

"A little green under the gills this morning. Throw back a few last night, did you?"

"Wife mixes a stiff drink," Jonathan said. He hadn't had a drop since before he visited his mother.

"From the look on your face, I'd say too stiff, sir. Your pulse really spiked up there at the end. Ease off the sauce would be my advice."

Jonathan excused himself and quickstepped to the men's room, where he spent the next three minutes dry heaving, his hands pressed against the sides of the stall. He spit up yellowish strands of saliva that hung from his lips until he wiped them away with scratchy toilet paper. His throbbing heartbeat was slow to return to normal. He would schedule another battery of tests.

"Forget it," Dale and Eva had said. "We were there. Natural causes." Were they like the nonchalant policemen telling bystanders to "move along" at a crime scene? "Nothing to see here." Wrapping yellow tape around his past? Protecting him from a sight too graphic to view? From something about Avi, or about themselves?

Jonathan cupped water to rinse his mouth out and slapped his face to return color to his cheeks. *If you can trust yourself when all men doubt you . . .* He smudged an X on the mirror over the wash basin. "I will not 'move along.'" There had to be an answer. He could solve it, just like any other equation or crossword puzzle. He owed that much to his father.

After the MAT session, Jonathan and his crew logged time in NASA's virtual reality capsule, going through launch sequences, module separation, reentry, emergency procedures, and abort scenarios. He managed to stay composed throughout the run-through, focusing on the clipped commands and status reports ricocheting like pinballs between crew members and mission control. The final exercise was lunar touchdown. Jonathan seized the joystick and calculated his angle and rate of descent.

"You're coming in too hot," his copilot said.

"I've got it."

"You've got to fire the thrusters now," a flight controller demanded.

"Not yet."

The charcoal gray basalt of the simulated lava bed raced forward, filling the wall-to-wall screen. Jonathan hit the thrusters and pulled on the joystick, but the lander slammed hard against the surface. Billowing clouds of smoke covered the moonscape, quickly overwritten by flashing red letters in blasé Courier font: "Lander fail. Excessive angular acuity and descent velocity."

"That's why we practice, Jonathan," said a calm voice over the intercom. "You'll get it."

He'd seen pictures of his father going through the same motions. His mother used one of them to paint a portrait of Avi that now hung in Jonathan's office. She had mimicked LeRoy Neiman's bold splotches of reds and yellows, blurred borders, and energetic strokes. Avi, wearing the familiar communications Snoopy cap, smiled over his shoulder, his disintegrating fingers stretched over an array of countless dials and knobs that all seemed to swirl at once. Jonathan felt dizzy again, just thinking about it. His rehearsals wouldn't be in vain, like his father's had been. He would solve the past and the future. He looked around at the crew. "Don't worry, guys. I'll be ready when it counts. Never failed a test in my life."

Following the training exercises, he chaired a teleconference of NASA scientists and his own R&D team on the progress of solar panel and biodome component experiments to be conducted on the Moon. The new materials were essential to the future construction of a facility for the processing of helium-3, precious metals, and other rare elements to be mined from the Moon—the commercial justification for the mission.

During the meeting, Jonathan said little, putting more effort into doodles on a legal pad than the action items on the agenda. The financial incentive for his investors was a necessary means to an end. His blue-pen sketch was a bullfight scene, a matador with a cape in one hand and a sword brandished high in the other. At the opposite end of the yellow sheet stood an angry bull, like the ones chasing his father in Pamplona, head lowered, eyes wide, ready to charge.

"Jonathan . . . Jonathan," said a voice over the phone.

"Yes, what?" He dropped his pen.

"Anything else for today?"

"No. Just keep, um, keep the payload maximums in mind. Can't be overweight. Food, water, and oxygen come first, always."

One of the NASA scientists stood to shake Jonathan's hand before leaving. "Jon, that's not how it works."

"Of course not. You think experiments are more important than life support. You sound like my wife."

"No, your drawing, the *corrida*. I studied in Seville, undergrad. The matador keeps the sword hidden until the very last second. Bull never sees it coming."

Jonathan ripped the sheet from his pad and tossed it to the trash. "I've only seen them in cartoons."

"It's like Sun-Tzu," the woman said. "All warfare is based on deception, and all defeats, at least in part, on self-deception. I added that last bit. The loser has to bear some responsibility, right?"

"So it's the bull's fault too, I suppose?"

"Yeah, maybe. Maybe he knows exactly what's coming. Maybe his brethren told him in the pen. But he thinks it's gonna be different this time, for him. *He's* gonna win. Overconfidence is just another form of self-deception. That's why NASA loves mission checklists. Failure is not an option, eliminating human error and all that jazz."

"You really should meet my wife. She thinks all manned space flight is, per se, human error."

"But you think differently."

"I have to."

Had Avi's enemies hidden their swords? To get up close? Who then? Wouldn't his father have seen the Germans coming a mile away? Had Avi been blinded by overconfidence? Had Lunden been an accomplice, betraying his friend like Brutus? Who were the "enemies"? Who were they now? Pictures of former NASA administrators, smiling white men with receding hairlines, lined the far wall of the conference room. Was Jonathan in their midst already?

Before flying back to Miami, he drove out to the Beach House. It was time to return. As he passed Launchpad 41, the cottage's beige roof rose above the dunes. It looked freshly painted, pale yellow clapboard on the second floor, exposed gray concrete on the first. He climbed the stairs to the back deck, where Eva and Jonathan had said goodbye to his father thirty years earlier. Jonathan stood in the precise spot where Avi had handed him a Medal of Valor, Israel's highest military decoration, awarded for bravery during the Six-Day War. "Hold this for me until I get back," his father had said.

Jonathan faced the ocean just as they had on that day for the *Tefilat Ha'derekh*, the Traveler's Prayer. His father had brought an IDF compass—motivated more by a love of navigation than strict adherence to Talmudic imperative—to make sure they had the required holy orientation, facing directly toward Jerusalem. The ocean was calm, like it had been for their farewell, the fenced-off beach deserted but for a few seagulls stripping the last bits of meat from a mutilated fish carcass. Jonathan reached into his pocket and pulled out a faded and frayed yellow ribbon with a silver Star of David displaying a sword and an olive branch. He turned the medal through his fingers and tried to remember that prayer. With no compass to guide him, Jonathan used the sun's position to align himself as best he could. He was certain he got the direction right but the words wrong. He could manage only the first few lines. "Lot of good it did him," Jonathan muttered. He stared at the horizon, dreaming of what it would be like to see the roundness of the Earth—a sight his father never saw.

He tested the sliding door and found it open. Three young employees, probably engineers or meteorologists, ate bagged lunches around a glass-topped table with a wicker base and matching chairs. The interior still looked like a low-budget beachside rental. A portrait of Director Debus hung over a black leather coach. When he died, a German newspaper broke the story that, like von Braun, Debus had been in the SS. "Still got his brown shirt, I see," Jonathan said. After listening to Avi's interview, he knew *Herr Direktor* had never made any effort to make his father feel welcome. Jonathan imagined tense, awkward exchanges, veiled hostilities, lips bitten raw.

The three NASA employees stopped talking and looked at Jonathan as if he might be lost. "As you were, guys. Just here to check out the collection." He pointed to a pair of floor-to-ceiling liquor cabinets, glass doors and cherrywood frames. Bottles crowded every shelf, some slapped with mission decals, others scrawled with autographs. "My dad's on one of these."

"Awesome," said an Asian woman, a waifish twenty-something in a Ludacris T-shirt.

An overweight man with a full beard, wearing Birkenstocks and black-rimmed glasses, swallowed a mouthful of hero in one gulp. "I got it. You're totally familiar-looking. It's Young, he looks just like him, John Young." The man pointed a chubby finger at Jonathan. "Apollo 16, April 1972, eighth man to walk on the Moon."

"Idiot, Julian," said the third member of the group, a pencil-thin, pasty man-child in a short-sleeve plaid shirt. He threw a balled-up Fritos bag across the table. Julian held up his hand to block it. "Young was the ninth. Irwin was eighth. Right, Scarlett?"

Both men looked to their female colleague. "Pay up, Julian," she said. "Garth's right." Julian slammed a five-dollar bill in the center of the table.

They were engineers.

"You're Jonathan Stein, aren't you?" Scarlett asked.

"Wow, Jon Stein," Julian said. He jumped out of his chair. "I knew I recognized you. Great to meet you. What you're doing, it's great, really great. We should've gone back years ago, totally." The others nodded in agreement. "Six American flags on the Moon, every one of them now bleached snow white by the Sun. That mean we surrender?"

Garth edged Julian out of the way. "I really admire what you've done with Apollo, turning the company around. I'd love to, I don't know, have lunch some time, talk about some ideas I have for satellite delivery systems. Totally innovative stuff."

"Guys, he's not here for a job interview," Scarlett said, herding them away from Jonathan. "Give the man some space."

"Good one, Scarlett," Garth said, laughing. "'Space.'" Julian and Garth high-fived.

"You want us to leave?" she asked.

"No, it's fine. I just want to look."

"There are two Armstrongs in there," Julian said. "I wrote a memo. Those cabinets aren't even alarmed. The glass isn't shatterproof. There are no motion sensors, not one, in this entire house. It's ridiculous."

Jonathan opened one of the cabinets. He searched through spent champagnes, gins, vodkas, and burgundies, saw Cernan, Schirra, Aldrin, Lunden, Slayton, Worden, and on a bottle of Stolichnaya, Armstrong and Scott, the Gemini 8 crew. He turned the bottle in his hands, took a whiff, no scent left, and put it back on the shelf. After a few minutes in the other cabinet, Jonathan found his father, a 1965 Mouton Rothschild. "A full bottle of this would be worth about $4,000 today," he said. He held it up for the engineers to see. Avi's autograph was on the front label. Below it there was a small inscription in Hebrew. It was so tiny, the letters so squished together, that Jonathan had trouble reading it. "Got a magnifying glass around here by any chance?"

Julian ran to the kitchen. Garth pulled a mega-deluxe Swiss Army knife from his pocket and flipped a glass open.

Jonathan took the bottle and knife out on the deck to read by sunlight. The engineers followed. It was a biblical citation, Proverbs 31:8, and the words "forgive me." He spun around to face the curious trio. "Proverbs 31:8. You know it?"

"Sorry," Julian said. "My parents raised me Baha'i."

Jonathan looked at Scarlett. "Buddhist."

He turned to Garth. "Twelve years of vacation bible school. Finally good for something."

"So what is it?" Jonathan asked.

"'Speak up for those who cannot speak for themselves.'"

"About what?" Jonathan said. "Speak up about what?" The engineers shook their heads, bewildered. Was it something from the tape? Why did Avi have to ask for forgiveness? Jonathan was certain no one had ever seen the inscription. Cassandra, Lunden, Armstrong, his mother—none of them knew about it. He asked Garth to hold the bottle while he retrieved a camera from his briefcase. He took pictures of the label, and then, at their request, a few with the engineers. He collected business cards and promised to e-mail the photos.

The clues were mounting but the puzzle grid was still blank. He'd had no luck finding Cassandra or cracking the mystery book on tolerance. With Susana's permission, he had recruited her postdoctoral assistant, Helmut Schneider—an astrobiologist, Jonathan's occasional tennis partner, and a famously indefatigable researcher—to help track them down. Two weeks into an exhaustive online sweep, they had found nothing, not even a promising lead.

Jonathan's administrative assistant had fared better in her search for the military reporter, but even a meeting with Naughton would have to wait. He had retired two years earlier from his last post, a radio station at Ramstein Air Base, and resided in a retirement community south of Ocala. When Jonathan had called Naughton's home, his wife said that he was in the hospital, recovering from double hip replacement surgery. Jonathan explained, in vague terms, his desire to speak with her husband. Mrs. Naughton provisionally agreed to let Jonathan visit in a few weeks.

After finding the bottle, Jonathan would have called Cassandra on the spot if he could've. Flying back to Miami, he studied the wine label in the camera's view screen. "What did my father do wrong? Who couldn't speak?" His suspicions about Lunden continued to grow. He needed to find out if Armstrong held the solution key, or at least another clue. There would be no more letters, not even a search for an unlisted number. Jonathan knew that their first encounter would have to be face-to-face.

12

January 30, 2005
8:56PM

"Warp drive would be amazing," Susana said, "but it's not going to happen. I seriously doubt if there's even enough energy in the universe to get me out of this bed. Could you get the Sunday paper for me? I can't move."

Jonathan had propped her up with three overstuffed pillows in the middle of their memory-foam mattress. Her hair, pulled back and up in a white scrunchie, formed a cockeyed, Seussian ponytail. She wore an extra-large sweatshirt with an image of the Puerto Rican flag in gaudy colors, like something a tourist might buy off the gangway in Old San Juan. She had been reading an article Jonathan had given her on negative energy requirements needed to fuel an Alcubierre warp engine for faster-than-light travel. The author claimed it could never be built. Jonathan had hoped Susana might disagree.

"But it's so late," he said. Jonathan sat in a reclining chair, studying the next month's training schedule while spinning a pencil at the base of his thumb. "And I've still got to make myself dinner since you obviously forgot to order the Chinese food I'd asked for. I went in and out of the driveway three times today. No paper. The delivery guy's still mad I didn't give him a Christmas tip. And I'm already dressed for bed." He wore tartan plaid pajama bottoms and a white T-shirt with cartoonish red toadstools captioned "I'm a fun-guy."

An hour earlier, they'd been arguing about Avi's interview. Susana couldn't understand why her husband was waiting to talk to Lunden, or confront NASA. "You do want to get answers, don't you?" she'd said. "What are you waiting for?"

He wanted answers but disagreed on how best to get them. He remained determined to work covertly, gathering more evidence before taking on Lunden or NASA. He didn't trust the bureaucrats and knew that Lunden would sugarcoat the truth as long as he could, acting like Obi-Wan Kenobi, protecting Jonathan, or himself, from any painful or shameful revelation. He wanted to build as much of the case as he could before the cross-examination he was planning.

Susana tossed the warp drive article to the floor and turned on the television. A *M*A*S*H* rerun neared conclusion. Captain Pierce tried to go to sleep on a cot under a spotlight outside his tent. Surrounded by a tight, barbed-wire enclosure of his own creation, Hawkeye was determined not to fall victim to a practical joke. But the joke was on him. The mere promise of a prank was enough to get him to build his own prison.

"I saw the paper around lunchtime," Susana said. "I know I did. It was behind the mailbox post. *Pleeeze*. I really want to do the crossword before bed."

"The *Herald*'s?" He recalled helping Cassie on the flight to DC. He stood up, having decided to give in and look for the paper. "That puzzle's only for idiots. You're a lot better than that. It's not worth your time. Or mine."

"Nothing too taxing. Need to relax the synapses before sleep. Would you rather me read trashy chick-lit, or maybe watch some *telenovelas*?"

"I'm going."

Jonathan put on his sneakers and walked down the long drive, lit by dim in-ground lights, like a runway. The air was cool and dry. As he approached the mailbox, the hairs on his forearms tingled as a legion of goose pimples popped up like at-ease soldiers scampering to attention for a surprise inspection. He found the paper, sheathed in a thin blue plastic bag, where Susana said it would be. He knelt to pick it up and saw a black Ford Expedition pull to a stop across the street. Government plates. Two men in dark suits got out and approached him. A black Chevy Impala, similar plates, parked behind the SUV, and another man, similarly dressed, got out of the driver's side but remained next to his car.

"Jonathan Stein?" one of the men called.

"Yes." Jonathan clutched the paper under his armpit and rubbed his forearms.

"I'm Agent Rose." He opened his jacket to reveal the badge at his hip. "This is my partner, Agent Cranston. Department of Defense, Special Operations Division. You're under arrest."

Jonathan felt a sudden urge to pee. He contracted every muscle in his lower abdomen, straining to hold it in. The enemies had arrived. He glanced at the third man now standing on the passenger side of the sedan. He tried to make his worried face seem quizzical.

"That's Agent Fuentes," Rose said, following Jonathan's gaze.

Was this a real roadblock? Had mild-mannered Frutiger been an FBI plant? Maybe too good at being a grown-up? Was it the White House? Who had been to the archives before him? Would they search the house? His surreptitious recording of Avi Stein's classified interview sat clearly labeled on top of his desk. Theft of classified information meant jail time. No Moon. A prison infirmary. Would they even bother with the courts? Would he be found naked and beaten to death on the beach? Found at all? Were these guys CIA, or even farther off the grid? Would his son grow up without a father? "Can I see your identification?" Jonathan asked. He clasped his hands behind his back to keep them from trembling.

Rose and Cranston showed their credentials. They didn't flash them like motion picture con men, opening and closing their wallets in one slick motion. He got a decent look. He had seen IDs like them before, at the Pentagon. They looked genuine. "What's this all about?"

"You'll know soon enough, sir," Rose said. "Until then, I advise you not to say a word."

"Who sent you out to my house to arrest me on a Sunday night?"

"Orders came straight from General Fielding, sir," Cranston said. "You can take it up with him."

"You can bet I will." Jonathan had once met General Fielding at a fund raiser for disabled veterans in Miami. Fielding had won his post as head of the US Southern Command by compiling an enviable military record, spotless but for a few well-timed and fortunately placed battle scars. He told himself Fielding wouldn't be involved in any sort of covert ops "extraordinary rendition" of a prominent US citizen. That supposition, however, left him with another possibility, only slightly less disturbing. He was genuinely being arrested and charged with a crime.

What could he have done? His tax returns were immaculate, his investments subject to law firm due diligence, and his housekeeper and gardener on the books. The regional subdeputy in Beijing? He refused to believe it. That was pennies compared to what other multinationals were coughing up to do business. It wouldn't even add up to a misdemeanor. And why would the Defense Department be involved? "This has got to be some sort of mix-up," he said. He felt embarrassed as soon as he said it, sounding like a character actor in a prime-time crime drama. "Can I please have a minute to change and tell my wife? Call my lawyer? She's pregnant."

"Your lawyer?" Rose asked.

"No, not my lawyer, my wife. Can't I come down to your office in the morning? You must know who I am."

"No sir, we were ordered to bring you in immediately," Rose said.

Cranston moved in a semicircle around Jonathan, imposing himself as a barrier to retreat up the driveway. "We know who you are. It's no mistake."

"Excuse me?"

"Sir, this is a national security matter," Rose explained.

"Can't you give me a minute? My wife's gonna think I was kidnapped. You want her to lose the baby?" Jonathan searched for any facial tic when he suggested that abduction might be their true purpose. National security matter? Maybe Fielding was merely executing a bogus arrest on someone else's order, unaware of the extralegal animus behind it. That's how the play would work. Misdirection at all levels. Why were they trying to stop him? Who were "they"? He was obviously getting too close, but to what? What's so top secret? The agents remained stone-faced, their cheeks and jaws carved with right angles like the soldiers in a G.I. Joe comic book.

"We need you to come now, sir," Rose said. "Agent Fuentes will speak to your wife and explain the situation."

Jonathan burned to call Rose an asshole. "I really need to go to the bathroom first. Please. At least let me do that."

"Hold it or piss in the plumeria," Rose ordered. He gestured toward the bushes. "We've got to go now, and you are not having an accident in my backseat." Cranston, the more physically intimidating of the pair, took a step closer to frisk. Shadowed by the agent, Jonathan stepped behind a row of shrubs to relieve himself, after which he was handcuffed. He walked to the SUV with the agents on either side. Rose opened the rear passenger door, and Cranston put his hand on Jonathan's head as he bent down to get in.

"What the hell?" Jonathan shrieked. He recoiled from the meaty fingertips on his scalp.

"Standard procedure," Cranston said. "We wouldn't want you to get a nasty boo-boo now, would we?" Cranston punctuated his snide remark with a carnivore's grin and patted Jonathan on the forehead.

"Count yourself lucky," Rose said. "We could've given you the super-deluxe Seal team treatment." He grabbed a phone from the cupholder and chirped the push-to-talk feature. "Sully, you up?"

"Copy. Over."

"We've got Stein. Let the general know. Over."

"Copy that."

"Where are you taking me?"

"You really should keep your mouth shut," Rose said. "It's for your own good."

Jonathan sat alone in the back, thinking about the absurdity of what was happening, shocked at how willingly, almost unconsciously, he had suspended his disbelief. This had to be a bad dream, like the time he dreamed he'd gone to Hebrew school wearing nothing but his Flash Gordon pajama top. Maybe his defective heart really wasn't beating out of his chest. Had he fallen asleep while Susana worked a crossword? Maybe the puzzle had stirred up guilt about Cassie. There was one sure way to tell. Without the use of his hands, he managed to slip a sneaker off and raise a bare foot to his lap. He bent down low to take a deep whiff. The dank musk, like the sweaty funk of a middle school locker room, made him hack. The accelerating heartbeats were real.

"You all right, sir?" Rose asked.

"I'm fine. It's nothing."

After Agent Cranston read the Miranda warnings from a card, movie-style, he explained that Jonathan was being charged with multiple violations of Title 18, United States Code, Section 1001.

"What's that?"

"Lying to a federal officer or agent," Rose answered.

"I don't even remember the last time I spoke to a federal agent."

"You're familiar with the Buy American Act, aren't you?" Cranston asked.

"Of course." As CEO of a major vendor to the Defense Department, Jonathan had to certify that parts used to fill orders from the armed services were obtained from domestic sources.

"You signed those forms for the government procurement officers, didn't you?"

"I think I'll wait for my lawyer before I answer that one." He had signed dozens of them, all with fine print about certification under penalty of perjury and a string of statutory citations. Maybe the charges weren't a ruse. It would almost be a relief.

"We found a bunch of Chinese parts in that communications satellite you just delivered to the navy," Rose said. "Traced them back to your supplier in Shenzhen."

The knots in Jonathan's stomach began to loosen. The arrest at least had nothing to do with the Chinese official, and the parts from his Shenzhen supplier were scrupulously segregated from government projects. He even had a stack of memoranda from the senior quality control manager, one for each Defense Department order, including the navy satellite in question, assuring him that only domestically sourced parts had been used for military contracts. There could have been a mix-up in assembly, but he hadn't lied to anyone. "You two are going to feel like shit when you see what a stupid mistake you've made . . . and you better pray that my wife is all right."

"You sound like you're on *Law & Order*, sir," Rose said.

Jonathan didn't care about how he sounded anymore, didn't even care about his still thumping chest. He was furious and certain he would be swiftly vindicated. This was no clever government ruse. It was a routine government fuckup. One of Jonathan's lawyers had served as the deputy attorney general in the prior administration. After his one phone call, he'd be back at home in a few hours where he would immediately begin the execution of a plan to get Fielding transferred to Fallujah and the agents to Kandahar.

Rose drove without lights or sirens toward downtown Miami. About fifteen minutes into the trip, he parked on the shoulder of the highway and chirped his phone.

"Sully, you copy?"

"Go ahead."

"Are you ready for us?"

"All set, Rose. You may proceed."

Cranston joined Jonathan in the backseat. "Mr. Stein, we're taking you to a secure facility for preliminary processing. This is all standard procedure. No need to be alarmed."

"I think we passed alarmed about three miles back. So what now? Chloroform?"

Cranston pulled a black blindfold from his pocket and cinched it over Jonathan's eyes. "We'll take this off as soon as we get there."

"Standard procedure," Jonathan said, his hackles on fire. "You can't be serious. Nothing about this is standard. I demand to know what the hell is going on." He felt a pair of hands grabbing his ankle. "What do you think you're doing?" Jonathan writhed against the seatback, his head gyrating in a vain attempt to loosen the blindfold's knot.

"I'm trying to put your shoe back on, sir."

"Agent Rose, I deserve a goddamned explanation. Christ, you'd think I was in al Qaeda."

"All you're gonna get, sir, is radio silence from now until we're inside. SOP. Just be patient."

How could he possibly be "patient"? He had been snatched from his lawn on a Sunday night by a couple of DoD goons on some obviously trumped up paperwork technicality. The whole escapade reeked of black ops subterfuge. It had to be a sit-down with some shadowy spymaster. They would take him to a man who would stand just outside the circle of a lone spotlight in a deserted warehouse. The mature, self-assured voice would tell him to back off, to stop digging. He couldn't possibly understand the potential consequences, the man would say. And, of course, no explanation would be offered, only vague references to fragile international alliances and long-term strategic partnerships.

Jonathan even entertained a more outlandish possibility—that he was going to be shown the X Files, informed of alien encounters, or of ancient extraterrestrial artifacts found on the Apollo moonwalks. He would be told to keep quiet about what he saw up there. The voice from the shadows would deliver a stern lecture about the peril of potentially destabilizing revelations, and just before being deposited back onto his front yard, the agents would obliquely warn him that rocket launches can sometimes go wrong for no apparent reason.

Jonathan forced out his lower lip to blow up at the blindfold and strained to rub his face against his shoulder. He tried to get the previously responsive agents to start talking again, promising lawsuits, congressional committee hearings, and internal affairs referrals. After what seemed like an eternity, Rose parked the SUV. Jonathan could hear the sounds of a busy street as the agents led him by the elbows.

"I'm being kidnapped," Jonathan yelled. "My name is Jonathan—"

A thick hand clamped over his face. "Don't you remember, Mr. Stein," Cranston whispered. "We *are* the police. Protect and serve. You're in safe hands."

They hustled him through a door and into a silent room. Jonathan surmised it was a large, airy space with a tiled floor, given the pitch and volume of the echoes made by the agents' hard-soled shoes. They walked him in a straight line for what seemed a great distance. He couldn't help imagining his demise at the end of a pirate's plank or before a firing squad.

"Here we are," Rose said.

Cranston removed the handcuffs and the blindfold. It was a huge corridor, dark but for the diffuse white spray of low-beam security lights and the fuzzy red glow of exit signs over doors to the right and left. "Where am I?"

"You don't recognize it, sir?" Cranston asked. Jonathan twisted around as his eyes adjusted. Behind him stretched the main atrium of the Miami Museum of Science. The three men stood before the entrance to its planetarium.

"What the hell are we doing here?"

With the perfect unison of well-drilled cadets, Rose and Cranston opened the double doors. The dimly lit celestial theater-in-the-round was vacant, its concentric circles of burgundy cinema seats unoccupied. A cool, androgynous voice, sounding like Kubrick's HAL, poured out from speakers surrounding the room.

"Come in, Jon."

"What the fuck?" Jonathan glared at Rose and Cranston. His breaths quickened, a breakneck pulse pounded against his temples.

"Happy birthday, sir." The agents smiled wide, apparently satisfied with an Oscar-worthy performance.

Jonathan half-collapsed, bracing his hands on his thighs, struggling to catch his breath. "Holy shit." He wiped a glaze of sweat from his forehead, pressed his other hand against his chest. "Where is she? Where the hell is she?"

"Go on in," Cranston said. He invited Jonathan to enter the planetarium with the sweeping hand of a ringmaster.

Susana made her entrance through a side door, dressed in a shimmering black evening gown. Her emerald necklace glittered underneath the soft lights. Jonathan, his ribcage still heaving, shuffled into the theater, his jaw unhinged, the way a dead atheist might enter the pearly gates. The doors closed behind him.

"Got ya." She hugged him with one arm and cradled a remote control in the other. "Geez, your back is soaked. I guess I got you more than good. Surprise! Happy birthday, Jonathan."

"But it's not . . . not for three more weeks."

"You think I could pull this little stunt off on the actual date? You'd be on red alert. We're not going to have a night out like this for a long time once the baby's born. You're not too freaked out I hope? I almost called the whole thing off, after the way you were acting at the National Archives, but Zubin, my partner in crime, convinced me we had to go through with it."

"I'm fine, really," he lied. "I thought we'd lost millions on a botched-up satellite job, that's all. Fielding? Seriously? How—"

"I know," she said, giggling. "I had to hold my nose and call the RNC. They got someone from the White House to help me enlist the general for my little *travesura*."

"And the museum?"

"They accept donations, especially large ones."

"How'd you get here so fast?"

"Agent Fuentes has a very heavy foot."

"Of course he does. Those agents were right out of central casting."

"They were so gung-ho for this. They wanted to gag you and toss you in the trunk and then take you to the brink of a rubber-gloved cavity search. Be thankful I reined them in."

"Gee, thanks."

"You ready?"

"I doubt it. Ready for what?"

"This." She pressed a button on the remote control.

Two young men, in black pants and white dress shirts, entered the planetarium from the central double doors, pushing an oversize cart carrying a round bistro table topped with a white linen table-cloth and formal place settings for two. They put the table in an open space in the middle of the room. As they left, a young woman entered from the opposite side of the room with an ice bucket and a bottle of champagne.

"Hope there's no dress code." He plucked at his T-shirt. "They wouldn't let me change."

"Don't worry about it, 'fun-guy.'" She traced one of the toadstools on his chest. "I needed to keep you out of the house while I got ready. It's *your* birthday anyway. You can wear your birthday suit for all I care." She sat across from him and pressed another button. The entire room went dark except for two electric candles on the table, both flickering with red light.

"What the—"

"Just wait. Look up."

A night sky filled with stars appeared on the concave screen covering the domed ceiling.

"Okay, contestants," she said, "when is it and where are we?"

Jonathan's eyes bounced from side to side, examining the constellations. In preparation for his mission, he'd spent hours honing his star-spotting skills—still the reliable last resort for mapless explorers.

"You give up?"

"No, no, give me a minute . . . looking at the lineup . . . Aries, Pisces, Aquarius, almost directly above us, and Ursa Minor on the northern horizon . . . I'd say we're in the summer months and in the Northern Hemisphere, but I . . . I'm not sure where, or what month."

"See if this helps."

Among the twinkling stars, tiny sparks flickered and danced, sputtering across the sky like newly hatched water bugs.

"The Perseid shower. And no moon. I should've known. August 13, 1982, the night we met in Arecibo. It was so dark on the beach once I got away from the party. Remember how I tripped over you? I thought I'd stumbled onto some couple *in flagrante*, not some geeky meteor hound. I should've known. You know I don't like surprises, but this is different . . . amazing." He took her hand. "You're amazing."

"Let's try another," she said.

"Wait a minute. I want to look at this one some more." He studied the stars, trying to retrieve from his memory a clear picture of the night sky from when they'd first met. After the pause, Susana clicked the remote again. The ceiling went dark before hundreds of stars rose at once. Jonathan craned his neck, stretching to look at the sky behind him.

"Well?" she asked.

"I've got this one. Look at the upward sweep from Neptune to Uranus to Mars, kind of like pearls on an ecliptic necklace, and Virgo directly above. We're in the Northern Hemisphere again, and not that far from the vernal equinox. The full moon, that's the clincher. Mom always said it was a bright, full moon the night I was born."

"Not bad. Here's the last one."

The virtual sky went black before gleaming with another cosmic array.

"This sky looks nearly identical to the last one, maybe a month or two later. Late April or early May?"

"And?" she asked.

"It's not our anniversary. Not my launch date. No birthdays or holidays I can think of."

"It is a birthday."

"Whose?"

"It's my due date."

He shook his head. "I wasn't even thinking about the future. Been stuck in the past."

Susana shut off the sky. The planetarium's recessed lights, encircling the theater right below the dome, painted the walls with an intimate penumbra. "The past has its place," she whispered. "It's more of who we are each day, but our future is coming . . . and fast." She patted her bump. "You need to catch up."

"I'm trying. I promise. I am trying. Are *you* ready . . . Mommy?"

"Ever since you told me about your dad's bottle inscription, I've had this strange urge to read the Bible again. First time in decades. Can you believe it? Some women crave pickles and ice cream. But me? *Ni modo.* Truth is it doesn't really age that well."

"Now who's stuck in the past?"

"There's this verse from Ecclesiastes. You might know it, chapter nine, verse eleven."

He tilted his head sideways and shifted his eyes. He didn't recall it by citation. The numbers, however, captured his imagination as usual, his mind rearranging them, looking for patterns $((9 + 1) \times 1 = 10)$ and connections. The first link was obvious: the attacks of September 11. The next hit closer to home. The citation had the same numerals, rearranged, as the quote from Psalms on his father's tombstone.

The last association was a dead-center bull's-eye. 9-1-1: the numbers to be dialed frantically when the timer inside his chest reached zero. "Nope, I don't know it."

"'The race is not to the swift or the battle to the strong, nor does food come to the wise or wealth to the brilliant or favor to the learned; but time and chance happen to them all.'"

"In other words, shit happens," he said.

"Exactly. That interview was strange, and cover-ups were easier in those days, but you can't abandon Occam's razor. There's not nearly enough real evidence to overcome its presumption. You have to be willing to accept that Dale and your mom were only telling you like it is, like it was. You can't fight bad luck, you can't change what happened, and you'll never be able to make perfect sense of the past. There's always incompleteness. It's time to move on, think ahead, think of us."

Jonathan leaned back, his legs and arms crossed. "Is this a birthday party or an intervention?"

Susana made a crooked face and grasped her side.

Jonathan's own stomach churned in alarm. "What is it?"

"Oof! It felt like something dug into my kidney." She pressed her palm against the table to brace herself, knocking the remote to the floor. It hit the concrete like a firecracker, and the dome blazed with a panoply of stars. "Blue Moon" crooned from speakers overhead.

"You OK?"

"I'm fine. Another Braxton-Hicks contraction. It's better now."

"You sure?" He picked up the remote and began clicking randomly, turning the stars off, then on, then off again.

"Yeah, it's gone." She snatched the controller from him to shut off the music.

"If it happens again . . ."

She nodded and took a few sips of water. "I'll stop. I'm only trying to give you some perspective. Just don't expect to be able to fill in all of the blanks. Please, don't be mad."

"I'm not. You deserve some slack after pulling this off. I'm just not ready to give up yet."

She raised a flute. "A toast to your birthday and to 2005, our best year yet."

He gulped. She sipped.

"You hungry?" she asked.

"Starved. Chinese food, finally?"

"No, no takeout cartons tonight. Your special-occasion, artery-clogging favorites: lobster bisque, stone crab claws, hash browns, and butterscotch bread pudding for desert."

"It's . . . it's just perfect. I don't know how you found the time."

"It's easy to do for someone you love."

"I love you too." He leaned across the table and took her hands. He squeezed them as if his grip could speak the words of apology she deserved but would never hear. They kissed. "Can I ask a favor?" he said.

"Of course."

"Since the stars brought us together, could we go back just one more time?"

With a click, she relit their shimmering first night. He stared up in silence, his mouth open wide.

"I've been thinking about baby names," she said. "Do you want to name him Avraham, after your dad?"

"We can't."

"Why not? I thought he just couldn't be alive."

He lowered his gaze, snapping out of the past, to answer her. "That's not the only Ashkenazi prohibition. If he died as a result of foul play, we can't do it. Only when we know for sure he died of natural causes. Otherwise, it would be—"

"Bad *mazel*," she said.

"Correct. We might not be able to fight bad luck, but we don't have to summon it."

13

February 19, 2005

10:45AM

Susana stopped in the middle of the stroller aisle at Babies "R" Us. "My phone's vibrating." Jonathan was examining an endless variety of European infant transporters with space-age polymers, developmental gadgets, and hidden storage compartments that would put the latest planetary rovers to shame. The ingenious engineering of the infant industry proved an unexpected but welcome diversion.

"I can't, I can't hear you that well," she said. "Speak up and slow down."

"Is that Helmut?" Jonathan asked.

Susana nodded and closed her eyes, her face taut like she was ready for impact. During the last year, Helmut had regularly worked twelve-hour days, seven days a week, on the Europa project, usually sleeping on a grungy, eggplant-colored futon in his tiny office. Talented and excitable, he never hesitated to call Susana at home—sometimes to go over routine mission data from Europa that could wait until morning, and other times because he'd lost a quarter in the building's vending machine.

"Helmut. I can't understand you. The reception's spotty. You're talking too fast. What? Organic? What? Helmut?" She threw her purse on the floor in frustration and sat on a conveniently placed glider rocker. She shook her head intermittently, twirling her hair with a free hand. "Haven't the sensor readings been anomalous lately? Yes, I know . . . I know . . . you have to calm down. Have you checked the calibration? How long was the transmission? What's it doing now? Helmut . . . Helmut . . . I lost you again. Helmut?"

Susana tried to get him back. "My phone sucks. Let me use yours."

Jonathan handed over a spotless new Blackberry. She shoved her phone into her purse and struggled to get her third-trimester body out of the plush, thickly cushioned chair. She tried her husband's phone twice without any luck.

"What's up with spastic man?" Jonathan asked.

"He would drive anybody to Paxil. Helmut thinks the probe picked up a promising signature for organic matter, but the data hasn't been reliable lately. The sensors have been generating strange results, probably related to transmission interference from solar flares. I'm not getting my hopes up. It's way too early to tell if there's a pulsating amoeba swimming around down there."

"If it's there, you'll pick it up again," he said. "It's not like the Wow! signal. That's exciting though, more interesting than his usual interruptions." Jonathan put his hands on the upturned handlebars of a dark blue Peg Perego stroller and popped a wheelie. "Anything on the book?" Jonathan already knew the answer.

"You know he's done a zillion searches. He's even started cold-calling university libraries in Israel. It must have been really obscure even back then, out of print for years. If Helmut had found it, he'd show up on our doorstep in his *Star Trek* pajamas with a faxed copy of the whole thing at three o'clock in the morning."

Jonathan squatted to admire the efficient modular design of the latest Pack 'n Play, with its removable bassinet, collapsible changing station, and side panel of clicking dials, brightly colored squeezable knobs, and mirrors—all approved by an ad hoc board of developmental psychologists. "Let's get this one." He loaded the awkward rectangular cardboard box into their cart at an angle, a quarter of it extending over the handlebar. He had to extend his arms and lean left to push. "You should really try to cherry-pick some of these design engineers for your next probe. Their work is categorically inspired. Maybe I'll poach a few for myself."

Susana inspected an $1,100 Austrian carriage, complete with a built-in iPod port and speakers to pipe downloaded lullabies into little passengers' ears. "Are you sure the book is that important? It was a weird comment, but probably not a coded communication."

"I need to find out if that reference meant something more. I'm not ready to say it didn't." But after dozens of replays, he was almost ready. Maybe his father had simply had enough—enough of the silent treatment, the insults veiled as humor, the condescension disguised as sympathy. At camp, Jonathan had wanted to vandalize the Germans' sedan after a brief and, in retrospect, trivial encounter. Maybe his father needed his own brand of symbolic retaliation. He was a proud, driven man, the polar opposite of the stereotypical cowering shtetl Jew. They would have had to kill him to get him on a one-way train. It had to have been excruciating for him to swallow his pride, like eating fire, to never strike back. Is that why he needed forgiveness? There must have been plenty at NASA who wanted to see him wash out—the Germans, the homegrown bigots, even Lunden—men who might have tried to goad him into a disqualifying misstep, like the white ballplayers who taunted Jackie Robinson. That kind of stress would have been enough, more than enough, to cause him to lash out. Maybe he was just blowing off steam, not encrypting a message.

Jonathan picked up an electric baby wipe warmer from an end-aisle display complete with a looping demonstration video. The images were predictable—a cold wipe provoking eardrum-scraping screeches for an exhausted mom trying to calm her inconsolable infant and a warm wipe evoking heart-melting gurgles and coos, a serene image of Madonna and child. "Our kid will grow up pampered enough." He returned the warmer to its shelf. "A cold *tuchus* is a relatively mild introduction to the harsh realities of life."

They meandered down an aisle lined with plastic bottles, nipples, breast pumps, sterilizers, and a vast assortment of novelty bibs. Susana picked one up and flashed it in Jonathan's face. It had an empty baby bottle laid on its side and read: "I drink until I pass out. Just like Dad."

"That's stupid," he said.

"Lighten up Jon, *por díos*. It's a bib joke for God's sake."

"Sorry," he mumbled. He scanned the racks for a fitting riposte, trying to be a good sport. "How about this one?" With his back to

Susana, he snatched a powder blue bib with white block letters from a high clip and just managed to tie it around his neck. He faced her with a guilty smile, the kind a baby might wear after loading his diaper. Susana's cheeks ripened as she read, "Whose boob do I have to suck to get a drink around here?"

She tried to yank it off him, but he jumped back and nearly fell into a young couple. The man covered his mouth to silence his laughter as he pointed at Jonathan's chest and nudged his ready-to-burst wife. The woman frowned and pushed their overloaded cart past him. Holding her small chin upright and stiff, like a minister's wife on Sunday, she whispered to her spouse in Spanish.

"What did she say?" Jonathan asked.

"She told Claudio that if he ever bought a bib like that she'd put arsenic in his mofongo."

Jonathan put it back, and Susana pushed the cart toward cribs and mobiles. "What's next, after talking to that reporter, Naughton?"

"It's Armstrong, despite what my mom says." He paused next to an Italian crib. A mobile with stuffed snowy owls hung from a hooked arm fastened to its railing. He cranked a dial at the base of the bracket and heard a soft, chimey version of "Rockabye Baby." He waved at the mobile, like a model on a game show, with an enticing open palm.

Susana frowned. "I don't like it."

"You think it's crazy, chasing Armstrong?" He slid his fist through the slats of the crib, measuring the gaps. "Because of Cassandra."

"No, I think you *should* go."

"Really?"

"But not because of Cassandra." She worked her way down the aisle, testing the drop-down side rails on a row of cribs. "You think Armstrong owes you an explanation for his silence. That's why you should go."

"That's what I told Mom. It's time for something besides letters." They moved on, past the cribs, to a nearby selection of bouncy seats. "Listen, the guys at work told me, categorically, that we have to buy this. These little vibrating chairs are supposed to work like magic when the kid's screaming his lungs out. It apparently shuts them right up and puts them to sleep. Maybe we could get an adult-size bouncy chair for someone I know."

"Very funny Jonny, but I already have something that vibrates. It's not a chair, and it definitely doesn't shut me up."

Jonathan's concessionary laughter trailed off when he, almost involuntarily, began to fantasize about Susana using a bouncy seat to masturbate. He felt certain someone had tried it already.

"Did you just get horny thinking about me and my vibrator?"

"Let's get out of here," he said.

"Wait," she said, standing next to a wall of diapers.

"What is it? Contraction?"

"My phone again."

He assumed she was about to hear another breathless report from Helmut. She looked at the screen. "It's blank. Wait, there goes my purse. It must be your phone. I forgot to give it back. Here."

"It's just an e-mail," he said.

"It vibrates for e-mails?"

"I was playing with the settings this morning. I hate the marimba. Shit." He leaned against stacks of extra-absorbent Pampers wrapped in violet plastic shrink-wrap.

"What is it?"

"Cassandra."

"Read it."

"I'm not reading it out loud. I don't even know if I can open it."

She put her chin on his shoulder. "Let me see."

The subject line read "Cassandra's last warning." The sending address had once again been blocked, but this time he was able to access the text.

> Have you given up already? Written me off as a false prophet with delusional disorder? The world might brush me aside, but you cannot. I know you can't. You must expose the truth. The world will listen to Jonathan Stein.
>   Remember you've got no friends at NASA. Institutional memories are the most selective, and all

institutions want to persist in their being. NASA wants to remain NASA, like a rock wants to stay a rock. Armstrong is the closest thing you've got to an ally. He knows what happened. They've never been able to fool him about anything.

Isn't anybody outraged? Aren't you, Mr. Stein? Our government did everything it could to coddle its amoral Nazis. Is it any wonder they left your father's case unsolved? Has it been too long? Have you all gone soft? Is that why so many German cars fill synagogue parking lots? Nobody has ever seen *Triumph of the Will?* Victorious Hitler parading down a Nuremberg *strasse* in a Mercedes convertible. Who cares that Ferdinand Porsche gave his beloved *Führer* a Volkswagen for his 50ᵗʰ birthday? Let bygones be bygones. Luxury is the only legacy that matters. Is that it? Game over?

"We should've gotten the Volvo anyway," Jonathan said.

Haven't you ever seen that 1950s photo of Walt Disney with his hand on a model rocket, standing next to Wernher von Braun? They appear so pleased, so unconcerned, so congratulatory. Walt even wanted to use the old SS officer as a technical consultant. If you can't save the Fatherland by sending slave-built V-2 rockets to kill women and children in London, why not put on a pair of mouse ears and help build Tomorrowland? "Who's the leader of the club that's always *Juden* free? A-D-O, L-F-H, I-T-L-E-R . . . Forever let us hold our banners *heil, heil, heil, heil.*" Same sleek rocket designs, target audiences instead of targets.

"You're not the only who doesn't like Walt Disney," Susana said.

"Shh, let me finish."

"Stop tilting the screen down. I can't see. He sounds pissed. Thank God you changed your number."

"Thank God," he said.

It's no surprise the extent of von Braun's decorated service to the Reich wasn't exactly spelled out in the official NASA biography of its vaunted Director of the Marshall

Space Flight Center. And what about his good friend Kurt Debus at Cape Canaveral? Both were loyal German soldiers—not in the Wehrmacht—in the stone-cold, Führer-worshipping, bloodthirsty SS. At least Herr Waldheim was only regular army.

By the way, who exactly was the "reformed" von Braun visiting when he took a break from his important work at NASA to travel to Brazil and Argentina in October 1963? You think he went to South America just to learn the samba or the tango? When you dance with the devil, the devil always leads. And if you dance a jaunty allemande with *Doctor Faustus*, you're as bad as he is. You, Mr. Stein, of all people, shouldn't have to be reminded of the unassailability of the transitive property.

The truth will out, but never from NASA. Even today you can visit the Dr. Kurt H. Debus Conference Facility at the Kennedy Center Visitors Complex. It's probably available for kids' birthday parties—maybe even *bar mitzvahs*.

You could be our only hope. Camp outside Armstrong's house if you have to. You've seen *The Odessa File*. Be like Jon Voight. Don't give up. Neil knows what happened. The clock is ticking. You must act now.

Cassandra

P.S. They couldn't even let your father rest in peace. Check out von Braun's grave marker. Ivy Hill Cemetery, Alexandria, Virginia, Section T, Plot 29, Site 5.

Jonathan stood up straighter. Two packages of Pampers clung to his T-shirt, damp with sweat. They fell to the floor when he stepped away.

"Jon, this guy's really starting to scare me. He's like a stalker."

"He's not threatening anyone. He's got some unorthodox motivational techniques, but I'm not too worried he wants to hurt me." Jonathan bent over to pick up the fallen diapers. "Let's get out of here. I need to get to a computer."

"We can go to my office," she said. "I need to see what's going on with Helmut. Should we call the FBI? What about those weird hangups? What if he thinks you're not listening to him? People like him don't like to be ignored."

"You're really worried about a virtual gremlin who paraphrases Spinoza? You did catch the—"

"Of course I did. So what? What the hell does *that* matter? The Unabomber was a Harvard grad with a PhD in mathematics."

They found Helmut sitting in his darkened office. The flashing images on his computer screen provided the only light. He was watching Japanese anime.

"Jon . . . Susana." He flailed to click shut the open window on his desktop as he leaped out of his chair. Susana switched on the overhead lights. Crumbs from Combos littered his black T-shirt. Some of the larger chunks on his chest tumbled off a glossy image of actor Carrie Anne Moss, frozen as Trinity from *The Matrix,* in a midair, kung fu pose. Helmut blinked rapidly when he shook Jonathan's hand. He had a face only Brueghel could love, round like a loaf of peasant bread. He looked like he'd been stuffed into his tight European flea market jeans, the kind with too much back-pocket stitching. His bowl-cut, sandy blonde hair made him look like a grown-up-sized little boy. "I tried to call you at least five times, Susana, but I couldn't get through. Thank God, you're here. I really want to show the data. It could be organic."

Jonathan excused himself to use the computer in Susana's office. The virtual wallpaper, added in December, was a still shot from her ultrasound. He clicked on a search engine and ran a query for the unfamiliar movie. His leg twitched as he read a summary of *The Odessa File,* released the same year his father died, 1974. The suicide of a Holocaust survivor led German journalist Peter Miller (Jon Voight) to discover an underground organization devoted to protecting former SS officers from capture or prosecution. Despite attempts on his life meant to thwart his search, Miller tracked down the SS butcher of Riga, who had also killed Miller's father, a German soldier. According to the Internet encyclopedia, much of the film had been inspired by real persons and events. Jonathan found a copy online and ordered it for rush delivery.

A search for von Braun's grave produced exactly what Cassandra had promised—a simple, rectangular marker, black background with raised bronze letters, the rocket engineer's name, his years of birth and death, and a biblical citation, Psalms 19:1, the same passage quoted on Avi's headstone three years earlier.

"Goddamn it!"

"You OK?" Susana called.

"Yeah, but you need to see this."

She and Helmut rushed to the office and stood behind him at the desk.

"It's the same," he said. "Von Braun's grave has a citation to the same verse from Psalms that's quoted on my father's. 'The heavens declare the glory of God, and the sky above proclaims his handiwork.'" He closed the search engine to make the tombstone disappear, leaned back in Susana's chair, and gripped the ends of the armrests, his evenly spread fingers clutching like talons. He spoke without moving his jaw. "If these people hated us so much, why did they have to steal our religion too? Weren't Loki and Thor good enough for the master race? I guess if you take our homes, our art, our fillings, our hair, our lives, you take everything. Kill all the Jews, but keep praying to their dead prophets and worshipping their God. That makes perfect sense."

After a moment of silence, Helmut spoke in a halting whisper. "My grandparents, on my father's side, Catholics from Westphalia, fled with their families to Switzerland in 1937. Their parents had been active in trade unions. It wasn't everyone."

Jonathan spun around. "I know that. Of course I know that. I wish you could find that damned book."

"I'm trying everything I can think of."

"Not to fuel the fire," Susana said, "but how does Cassandra know what's engraved on your father's stone?"

Jonathan whirled back to the keyboard and entered a new search, holding his breath until he saw dozens of pictures of the inscription. Cassandra, like everyone else with a computer and an Internet connection, had easy access to his father's grave.

"Perhaps it's pure coincidence," Helmut offered. "Von Braun was quite religious, and this passage has obvious meaning to anyone associated with space exploration."

"I don't think so," Jonathan said. "My father's funeral was really big international news. My mom's scrapbook has dozens of obituaries, all of them quoting that verse. Von Braun wasn't at the funeral, of course, but being at NASA and so close to the press, he had to know about it. He had to."

"So it can never be used again, like Clemente's twenty-one?" Susana asked.

"No, of course it can be used again, but *he* shouldn't have used it. I'll tell you another thing. Cassandra's no redneck bunker builder with a talent for web design. He knows something. I don't know what exactly, but he's not taking a shot in the dark. Maybe he used to be on the inside. Maybe he still is."

"So you're going to Ohio," she said.

"I have to."

14

February 21, 2005
12:47PM

Two days later, Jonathan stood on Ocean Drive in South Beach outside a bistro where he'd arranged a luncheon for a congressional candidate. In a belt of green between the street and the beach, barefoot Brazilians played foot volley over a net tied between palm trees. On the sidewalk, a pair of high-heeled moms jabbered in Spanish while they drove their toddlers forward on push-handle tricycles. Jonathan, already sweating through his undershirt, stayed in the shade of an awning. The guest of honor was late, and Jonathan couldn't reach her campaign manager. After leaving a barrage of exasperated voicemails, he called Zubin.

"Jon, thank God you called."

"What? Why?"

"I came up with an amazing idea for a start-up. Auto repair shops run by Mormon missionaries. Think about it. Those kids in thin ties and short-sleeved dress shirts would be the ultimate honest mechanics. People would line up around the block. Can I put you on speaker? I'm in a conference room with the guys from Greenwich. They're pretty excited."

"I don't want to talk about that now."

"Hold on, Jon. Just one. Don't you think—"

"Stop it. I need you to listen to me. Just stop it, OK?"

"No worries, man. I'll step out in the hall. What's up?"

"I got another e-mail from Cassandra."

"Let me guess. The lost tribes of Israel were found living on Mars."

"I want to visit Neil Armstrong."

"Seriously?"

"Absolutely. I sent a private detective to watch his house yesterday. He's home. Will you come?"

"Hell, yeah. Can be at LaGuardia in an hour. Cincinnati, right? I'll bring maps, a GPS, binoculars, night vision goggles. What else? Oh, a Taser. I will most definitely bring a Taser . . . just in case."

"You sound like you're ready to kidnap him."

"You know what Brother Malcolm says—'by any means necessary.' There's no way I'm missing this. I have been watching you—for freakin' years—this sad sack waiting to hear from Armstrong. I told you the same thing a hundred times. 'Why don't you call somebody at NASA? Why don't you drive to his fucking house?' And every time I had to hear the same pious bullshit about respecting his privacy, his personal space, about how he signed up to be an astronaut, not a celebrity. Shit, dude volunteers to be the first man on the Moon and then gets his nose out of joint about being famous. You don't know how close I got to kidnapping *you,* back in college, just to drag your ass to Ohio. I was gonna get you drunk and say we were going to count cards in A.C. I'll see you tonight."

"Wait a minute," Jonathan said. "I can't go just like that. I've got to call people, make arrangements, maybe tomorrow afternoon."

"Dude, it's been 'ands' and 'buts' for years with you. Let's go, now. Tonight. Send a few e-mails and jump on a goddamn plane. Don't give yourself the chance to back out."

"Why would I have called you if I didn't want—"

"I tried to tell you 'why' twenty years ago. It's Psych 101. You spent way too much time with Albert and not enough with Sigi. It's transference, bro. Maybe you wanted Neil to stay silent so he could be two men at once. Psychological superposition."

Jonathan had wandered into a playground on the small beachside park. He sat on a white rocking horse. He felt disoriented, unable to focus. He rocked with his feet on the tiny footrests, knees nearly in his chest, his stretched blazer squeezing his shoulders. "But you know how he is. I didn't make him that way."

"Sure his weird behavior made it easy for you, but look at all you've accomplished. If you really wanted to communicate, you could've made it happen, years ago. Quit finding excuses. Forget that NASA conspiracy crap. Let's just go. Today."

Jonathan stopped rocking. Beyond a row of palm trees skirting the beach, a speeding jet ski pulled a bright yellow banana boat parallel to the shore. A huddled train of orange-life-jacketed, impossibly blonde kids let out a burst of thrill-ride screams with each hard bounce over the waves. "I'll meet you at the hotel inside the terminal. We'll go to his house first thing tomorrow morning."

"No way," Zubin said. "We should go to his house tonight, right when we get in. Otherwise, I'll wake up to a Post-It note on the nightstand politely informing me you took the first flight home."

"I won't back out, I promise. Take my wallet and phone and lock them up in the room safe."

"What if I handcuff you to the bed?"

"Enough with the handcuffs. Zudu, this isn't my bachelor party. Trust me. I won't run away."

The next morning, Jonathan set the heat in their rental car as high as it would go, but Cincinnati's sharp morning chill seeped in from all sides. The temperature was a seasonal 38 degrees, but he was underdressed in a lightweight fleece jacket. A smooth sheet of low dishwater clouds pressed down from above.

"What are you gonna say when we get there?" Zubin took a bite of an apple he'd picked up from the breakfast bar at the airport hotel.

"I haven't really prepared anything." Jonathan's eyes bounced between the road and the unfamiliar GPS unit in their Chevy Malibu. He fought an urge to go back to his plane, to break through the grimy slab—soaring from dingy gray to brilliant blue, like Dorothy when she walked out of her house after the tornado. He lied about not preparing. He had been running simulations all morning, preparing a variety of responses, each with a tone finely calibrated to match Armstrong's potential attitudes. Shy reluctance would be met with patient reassurance. Dismissive irritation with righteous indignation. Open hostility with unbridled fury. Heartfelt apology with forgiveness and acceptance.

"You've got to practice, Jon. You know you're much better when you're prepared. Let's do it. I'll be Armstrong."

"This is stupid. I'll be fine."

"It's not stupid. Let's go." Zubin sat up with a stern expression. In an impatient, deeper voice, he said, "Listen Stein, I left public life years ago. I have made it crystal clear I want people to respect my privacy. I signed up to be an astronaut not a celebrity. I did my job in 1969, and now I want to live out the rest of my life in peace and quiet and solitude. I'm not interested in talking to you or anybody else."

Jonathan remained silent, his eyes fixed on the road, his hands gripping the steering wheel, his wrists rolled forward toward the windshield.

"See what I mean?" Zubin said. "You're gonna freeze up. Just tell him how you feel. You were the little boy of a dead astronaut, and you were looking for words of encouragement from a hero. 'Neil, how could you have ignored me?' That's what you should say."

"I'm not gonna say it that way. Maybe he has a perfectly legitimate reason. According to you, our failure to communicate has mostly been my fault. Juvenile self-sabotage, remember? I'll be fine."

Zubin asked to listen to the interview. Jonathan had it preloaded in the CD player. "'Nazi engineers,'" Zubin said, repeating Avi's words. "No way they let that on the air."

"No way," Jonathan said. "But why the hell did they make it top secret? Other people must have known about it."

"Jesus, your dad had a massive pair. Going after Patton with a military reporter?"

"Here's comes the part about the book on tolerance. Listen."

Jonathan cranked up the volume. "Hear that? Why is he, all of the sudden, talking about a book on tolerance, making reference to the diaspora, talking about his enemies?"

"That was definitely bizarre," Zubin said, after the replay had finished. "That line about Waldheim . . . now I know where your sarcastic streak comes from. Did they put your dad on any meds before the launch, you know, for the stress, or the weightlessness? Could that have affected his mood?"

Jonathan turned down Armstrong's street. "Watch for the address. It should be coming up on your side, soon." The boxy, well-spaced homes, vintage early eighties, sat a notch below mansion class, with long driveways, landscaped yards, and at least two chimneys each. Some had tarpaulin-covered pools and netless tennis courts. "I've run through a thousand possibilities. Prelaunch jitters, worries about Mom and me. I thought he might have had a run-in, maybe more than one, with the Germans, like I did. I know for sure he felt torn up about being in America during the Yom Kippur War, guilty about not being there for his squadron. He lost some good friends. He even volunteered to leave the space program to go home and fight, but the IDF ordered him to complete the mission. He was probably under a lot of different pressures, but I'm not sure any of it, even when you put it all together, explains why he acted like that during the interview."

"And that book about tolerance," Zubin said. "It was almost like he knew that somebody would know what he was talking about. Look, there it is. That's his mailbox."

Jonathan imagined his letters stacked up inside. He parked past a fire hydrant on Armstrong's side of the street. "Dad wasn't talking off the cuff. And then he died three days later. Cassandra knows something. Neil's silence has to mean something."

The house was a two-story colonial—white Doric columns, gray clapboard siding, black shutters, a ruby-red front door, and an attached three-car garage. Mature red maples and black and white oaks, denuded of leaves, brittle and exposed, surrounded the grounds. Tiny specks of snow sailed on the currents of a swirling wind, mixing with the hopeful smell of fireplace smoke. A high wrought-iron fence protected the property, and an imposing gate hung between two ten-foot stone columns on either side of the driveway, each one capped with a security camera. Zubin pushed the intercom buzzer. After a short delay, a female voice crackled through static. "Yes, who's there?"

Jonathan gestured for Zubin to respond. His friend, however, held hands up in a "don't shoot" pose and stepped back. Jonathan stood immobile until the voice returned. "Hello, is anybody out there?"

He stepped to the intercom and pushed TALK. "Yes, we're here. I mean, my name is Jonathan Stein. My friend and I would like to speak to Mr. Armstrong." There was a long silence. He glanced at each camera and whispered that there was no way they were getting in. "He's not the most social fellow, you know."

A prolonged buzz accompanied the clank of a bolt retracting from the gate's lock. Zubin, without uttering a word, walked straight through the unlocked gate and up the lengthy driveway. Jonathan followed close behind.

Zubin, in $800 sunglasses, ripped Levi's, a brown hooded sweatshirt, and a pair of ratty Chuck Taylors, looked like he just rolled out of bed. That was the intent, of course. With a deliberate hitch in his step, he unzipped and removed his hoodie, revealing a lemon-yellow T-shirt with an oversize iron-on decal of a green bottle of Tang.

"Dude, a Tang shirt? Really? You're forty-two years old, and it's freezing. You look ridiculous. No wonder you're still single."

"What are you talking about? It's like your wedding day. How can you *not* show up in a tuxedo? I knew we'd meet Neil eventually, so when I saw this vintage baby on eBay last year, I snatched her up. I've been saving it ever since. You gotta sport the *Tang* tee when you meet an astronaut. It's de rigueur, motherfucker."

"Who do you think you are? Some slick character from a Tarantino flick? That's so, so . . ."

"I think the phrase you're looking for is fin de siècle."

"You're such an ass."

On the front porch, Zubin snapped his head toward the door clapper.

"You do it," Jonathan said.

"No, no way. I got you to the door, Neo. It's your red pill, not mine."

Jonathan reached for the brass handle and smacked it against the plate. After what seemed like an unusually long delay, a heavy-set, apron-wearing woman in her sixties answered. She had white hair pulled back in a bun, clear blue eyes, and a flat face like the back of a shovel.

"Can I help you?"

Jonathan's eyes bulged, and he swallowed hard. Zubin's slow nod made clear he shared the same thought. "Ah, I mean, yes, I, I hope so," Jonathan said. "We're here to see Neil Armstrong."

"I'm his housekeeper and personal secretary, Maria."

"It's kind of important. I'm sorry, I have to ask you. I noticed an accent when you spoke. Are you—"

"I was born in Germany, Dortmund, but I've lived here for more than thirty-five years. Why do you ask?"

"No, no reason. My father was an astronaut in the Apollo space program, like Mr. Armstrong, and I need to ask him a few questions. This is my friend, Zubin Dukkash."

"And I suppose you can't ask your father these questions."

"How do you know that?"

"Aren't you Avi Stein's boy?"

Jonathan stuttered again as he confirmed that he was. Zubin nudged a subtle elbow into his ribs as if to say the day promised to get much more interesting.

"You're wondering how I know this I suppose. You think Mr. Neil does not read newspapers or watch television? We both know about your mission. It has been very well-publicized. He is very interested."

"Interested, really?" Jonathan asked.

"He's read several articles and watched all the news programs about it."

"May we speak with him?"

"He's not here. Gone away. Out of town."

"When did he leave?"

"That's not really your business, I'm afraid. Not really."

"Is his wife home?" Zubin asked.

"No, she spends a lot of time traveling. She is second wife, you know. Divorced after thirty-eight years. Can you believe it? After thirty-eight years."

"How long have you worked for, ah, Mr. Neil?" Jonathan asked.

"About eighteen years. Excellent boss. Eighteen years."

"So, when will he be back?"

"It's hard to say. He went ice fishing. He doesn't have a telephone at the cabin. No phones up there. Sometimes he's gone a few days, sometimes a few weeks. Could be days or weeks."

Jonathan felt like he had written another letter that would go unanswered. Zubin pressed forward. "My friend wrote several letters to Mr. Armstrong and never got a response. Do you have any idea why?"

"Mr. Neil gets so much mail, not as much now, but even ten years ago, you cannot imagine how much. So much mail. Everybody wants something from him: money, time, favors, even parts of his body. He is a very private person. He doesn't write back."

"Did he ever read any of them?" Jonathan asked.

"He used to read them in the early days, but it became too depressing."

"Why?"

"Sick kids and poor kids asking the first man on the Moon to help. He is a very sensitive man. He was an astronaut not a miracle worker, not even a social worker. Even you are not here to see the real Neil Armstrong, the flesh-and-blood real Neil Armstrong. No one even ever thinks of his real face. Not his real face. They think of him up there. His face was a visor. You know what it looked like, don't you, Mr. Stein?"

"A convex mirror," he said.

"Yes, it was a mirror. You see your own reflections. Everybody does."

"What does he do with all the mail?" Zubin asked.

"He has a post office box to receive his important correspondence. The letters and packages he gets at home I sort through when I can. When I can. If it looks important and I can't decide, I send it to his attorneys first. That's the way he wants it. Send it to his attorneys."

"What happened to my letters?"

"Maybe NASA has them? Were they old? Mr. Neil told NASA to stop forwarding correspondence years ago."

"I've had his home addresses since I was in college."

"Honestly, I don't remember them, but I probably tossed them out. Before 1986, I can't really say. Just can't say."

Jonathan felt limp, as if the blood in his veins had plummeted to his feet. Maria couldn't have known that her explanation, blunt and heartless, had punched him in the gut. He couldn't believe that he had suffered a lifetime of unanswered letters because of Armstrong's rigid fan mail protocol and his own self-defeating approach.

"Could I use your bathroom?" Zubin asked.

"No, we really should be going." Jonathan felt an overwhelming need to leave.

"But I really have to go."

"I suppose," Maria replied, looking at Jonathan. "I feel like I know you, from the news. Would you like a piece of cake before you go? I made it this morning, pineapple upside-down. Just this morning."

"Thanks, but—"

"That would be terrific," Zubin said. "Mind if we look around a little? It's such a beautiful home . . . and spotless too."

"Zubin," Jonathan said, his jaw clenched.

"It's OK, it's OK, as long as you don't touch anything. You can't touch, *ja*? I'll go to the kitchen and get the cake for you. Give me a minute or two to heat it up. The bathroom is down the center hall behind the staircase. There, underneath the staircase."

Once she left the vestibule, Jonathan grabbed his friend by the forearm. "What the hell are you doing?"

"We're here, aren't we? Let's look around, maybe find his computer. I'll kiss up to the *hausfrau* and see what I can learn." Zubin freed himself from Jonathan's grip and headed toward the bathroom.

Before Jonathan had a chance to voice his objections, his intrepid companion had bolted down the hall and out of sight. He leaned against the front door, wondering how he had ended up in Neil Armstrong's house. He could feel his body swaying, like a palm tree stirred by the outer bands of a hurricane. He shouldn't have skipped breakfast. His breaths were shallow. How did he end up on a covert ops mission, doing "recon" on a national hero? He felt blanketed by a thick, impenetrable haze—unable to see where he'd been or even two feet in front of him. Was this what the moment before fainting was like? Before a heart attack? Was this it?

He'd spent his life striving to be the astronaut's son, so thoroughly dedicated to realizing the unfinished journey that he even found solace in a shared affliction. He felt more fully his father's offspring and more certain, more resolute in his commitment to realize Avi's dream. Was he about to pay the price for that connection? His rib cage tightened like a vice around his lungs. Would he die in Neil Armstrong's house? He squeezed the doorknob and hunched his shoulders, bracing for a shooting pain in his left arm.

What would Cassandra write? Neil had him killed? The CIA had assassinated him because he was about to get Armstrong to talk, to expose the truth? There would be more cover-up chatter. The Internet would buzz with reinvigorated rants about fake moon landings and Nazis. There would be no lunar mission, and his father's legacy would be left even more clouded by rampant speculation. Cassandra would be canonized, the latest and greatest prophet of conspiracy theory. His pregnant wife. The son he would never know. He heard a high-pitched ringing. His face twisted in anticipation. He reached out, staggering to reach the staircase. Was this it? 9-1-1?

He dropped to the bottom step. He closed his eyes, concentrated on his breath, trying to slow it down. The ominous ache in his left arm never came. The ringing subsided. A panic attack. He shook his head as if to expel any lingering effects. He knew what Zubin would say. Another self-imposed barrier to Armstrong, like his feckless correspondence.

"I can't stop now. I can't go back to letters."

The house was quiet, except for the faint sound of the exhaust fan rattling and humming in the bathroom. Jonathan explored the first floor, inspecting the main hallway, the formal dining room, the parlor, and the living room. He found no indication of Armstrong's lunar landing—not one plaque, photograph, or certificate honoring the many accomplishments in his long career of service to the United States.

The furniture was a predictable, conservative mix of Ethan Allen and Thomasville. What stood out, instead, was the art. It was an eclectic collection. Jonathan recognized most of it from years spent paging through his mother's books. Hanging in the main hallway were prints of Warhol's *Marilyn Diptych*, Rubens's *Prometheus Bound*, the mythological fire thief chained to the rocks while an eagle gorged itself on his liver, and Doré's *Wandering Jew*, the old man cursed to walk aimlessly beneath the shadow of the crucifix.

In the living room, above the fireplace, he found an unfamiliar work—an original but unsigned Chuck Close-style painting of the last frame of Truffaut's *400 Blows*. The young runaway, Antoine, glared back at the camera after finally reaching the sea. On the opposite wall hung a lithograph of Lichtenstein's *Drowning Girl*. It was as if the young French boy was cursed to watch the woman sink, powerless to step out of the frame and rescue her. Jonathan never imagined Armstrong as an art lover, but the astronaut's curious curation made sense to him, though he couldn't articulate his reasons. He thought about what Maria had said, that Armstrong was a sensitive man. The artwork seemed to confirm it, making him an even more complex equation to solve.

Jonathan wandered about the house, mulling over Maria's assessment. Was she right? Was Zubin? Had he created his own personal Neil Armstrong, distorted by his own preoccupations and expectations and galvanized by Cassandra? Near the kitchen, he could hear Zubin peppering Maria with questions about baking recipes—buttering her up and stalling. She sounded thrilled to have the attention. Resolved to follow through, to break from a history of a half-hearted efforts, Jonathan took advantage of the extra time to explore the basement. He had always liked to poke around attics, garages, and basements—places where the only masks were from Halloweens past. He wondered if Armstrong might be hiding there.

The basement didn't fill the whole footprint of the house. At least half was empty crawl space. The rest was unfinished—a utility area for two furnaces and a hot water heater, a few metal shelves stacked with old paint cans, rusted tools, weather-beaten camping gear, and a pile of duck decoys, a motley flock of canvasbacks, pintails, and mallards, all badly faded and chipped. The only light came from a pair of hopper windows, adorned with cobweb valances, and a few bare-bulb, ceramic fixtures, each one operated by its own beaded metal chain. A white, no-frills refrigerator sat in a corner next to a rectangular multipurpose table with a white plastic top and crude oil-black legs. Jonathan cracked the refrigerator and found rows of clear packages filled with blood. Each was labeled "For Use of Neil Armstrong Only" with the name and address of a law firm typed below.

"Stockpiling. Figures."

More surprising was what he found sitting on the table, an out-dated IBM Thinkpad. Its peculiar location and connection to the Internet—via a telephone line hanging from an exposed beam—made Jonathan's hands shake and breaths quicken. Stooped like a cat burglar, he inspected the rest of the basement over his shoulder. He dragged a folding chair to the table and turned on the laptop, looking back and forth from screen to staircase. A sudden rumble and snap bounced him out of his seat. After a quick sweep behind a fired-up furnace, he easily defeated the password protection of the outdated operating system.

One . . . Two . . . Three . . . Four.

What he uncovered was a disappointment—no evidence to suggest that Armstrong was Cassandra's puppeteer nor any sign of the sophistication needed to design and operate the website. Nothing of significance—no draft of any memoirs, no notes on the Apollo program, and no mention of Nazis, Dale Lunden, or Avi Stein. The computer's memory contained only letters to Armstrong's attorneys. In them, he declined all business opportunities—offers to put his name on restaurant chains, amusement park rides, and camping equipment. He refused to speak at trade conventions or serve as the grand marshal in any parades. The webpage history in his browser recorded visits to sites on First Amendment law, ice fishing, and bowhunting.

Jonathan left the computer as he found it, shot up the basement stairs, two at a time, and ducked into the bathroom. He flushed and left the exhaust fan on. In the kitchen, he blamed the delay on the lousy Indian food his friend had made him eat the night before. After a few nibbles of the pineapple upside-down cake and the obligatory compliments about the immaculate house and the mouth-watering dessert, Jonathan asked to see Armstrong's study, said he would love to see his book collection. Maria seemed reluctant. To convince her, he described a prospective renovation of his own home office, said he might get some design ideas. Zubin's enthusiastic confirmation of the project persuaded her to consent. She led Jonathan to the stairs and pointed to Armstrong's study. She climbed the stairs to shut bedroom doors and told him to stay out. After she reiterated the "don't touch" rule, Zubin coaxed her back to the kitchen with a request for more cake.

The study had forest-green walls with intricate cherrywood wainscoting, matching crown moldings, and prints of Victorian fox hunts. A motion sensor mounted high on the wall opposite the doorway flashed a red dot as he entered. No security cameras in sight. The still air smelled like pine-scented furniture polish. The mostly empty bookshelves contained a set of World Book encyclopedias and a couple of textbooks on constitutional law. There were no family photos and no books on aeronautics, the military, or space. There were a few coffee table books—photographs by Diane Arbus and paintings by Rothko and Van Gogh—and two shelves filled with binders containing copies of the last twenty years of Armstrong's state and federal income tax returns. Like the rest of the house, there was no indication that he had ever been an astronaut.

Armstrong's desk was an antique walnut rolltop placed flush against an interior wall. Jonathan was surprised to find it unlocked. He searched through its drawers, finding a well-organized system for saving receipts, warranties, and appliance manuals. Armstrong apparently kept everything from records of large purchases to grocery store tapes. Another dead end. This guy was incredibly private and wanted to stay that way. More than a full-time job for the first man on the Moon. "It's like he wants to forget everything that matters and just hold onto the stuff that doesn't," Jonathan whispered. "Putting people on a pedestal always makes them stand taller than they were."

He knew he had to get back to the kitchen, but halfway down the stairs, he did an awkward pirouette. An episode of *Antiques*

Roadshow, one of Susana's favorites, led him back to the desk. An appraiser examining a similar rolltop had shown the owner how to locate and open a secret, interior drawer.

"My letters."

He removed two narrow drawers from the center of the desk. He jammed his arm into the slot, and, with fingers spread, felt his way toward the back, picking up small splinters. His middle finger, nearly hyperextended, tripped over a small metal latch. He worried it might be a revolver inside, but kept flicking until a hidden drawer popped out, releasing the faint smell of oiled leather and bitter almonds.

He found a small black diary and flipped through its pages, looking for handwriting, any scribbling that might offer insight into the enigmatic astronaut's mind. The pages were a cascade of unadulterated white. As the empty pages shuffled off his thumb, a folded piece of paper, soft as a handkerchief, fell to the desk. He picked it up, unfolded it, and read its typewritten verse.

> *The Arboreal Tradition*
>
> *The cedars of Marathon*
> *And red maples of Manassas*
> *Drank silently the spilled blood,*
> *Incorporating into circular files*
> *The freshly hewn forensics*
> *Of youth cut down in useless shade.*
>
> *A conspiracy of teeth*
> *Grinds these pristine logs to pulp,*
> *Leaving their recollections*
> *Stained and warped.*
>
> *Only the liberty of decay confers*
> *Upon the unsuspecting conifer*
> *The ancient elements of an unknown truth.*

Could Armstrong have written it? Jonathan thought the poem a bit too clever but poignant, even lyrical, in parts. He knew what his mother would say. She would quote *Hamlet*, the graveyard scene. The ashes of Alexander the Great reborn as a barrel stopper. Jonathan dusted the top of the desk, wondering what lost history made up the reconstituted DNA in its felled wood. He ran his fingers over the poem, equally powerless to read the true history of the paper's prior incarnations. He was struck by a heavy feeling that his efforts to revisit his father's last days and to understand Armstrong would ultimately prove fruitless.

Jonathan carefully replaced the poem and the diary, put the desk back together, and rushed down the staircase on tiptoes. He went into the bathroom, flushed again, and emerged with his apologies. Zubin nodded to him as if to say "play along," and said he had explained to Maria that his friend must have been taking notes and walking off dimensions for the contemplated renovation. Jonathan knew he had taken too long and confirmed the explanation.

Maria's face grew even paler. "No photos."

Jonathan held up his Blackberry to show its back. "No camera. Just jotted some notes on wood finishes and window treatments. It's such a wonderfully maintained home."

Her taut face relaxed into a satisfied grin. Jonathan signaled it was time to go, but Zubin gave a quick head shake. "I want to show my friend the deck," he said. "Is that all right?"

"Go ahead. Make sure you look at the bird feeder on the big hickory tree to the left. I built it myself. I fill it with homemade suet for the woodpeckers. Sometimes we get the big, pileated ones. The really big ones."

On the cedar plank deck, the two men leaned against the railing and surveyed the backyard, its ground covered with the brown curly crust of a snowless February in the Midwest. A gentle downhill sloped away from the house, and a diagonal row of tall trees cut across the back edge of the property, bordering a small boundary creek. There were no woodpeckers at the feeder, only flittering chickadees.

"Man, that cake was really good," Zubin said, his hoodie back on and zipped up, the cold air condensing his breath as he spoke. He faced the house and scooted up to sit on the top board of the railing. "Did you find anything?"

"Not a thing." Jonathan stood next to him, leaned over the edge, his arms crossed. The black-capped little birds fluttered around the tree trunk, stopping occasionally to peck at sunflower seeds suspended in congealed fat. "I went through his computer, his desk, his bookshelves . . . nothing. I grabbed the directions to his fishing cabin off the hard drive, but there's no point. Armstrong's got nothing for us. I don't know why I ever convinced myself that he mattered. Maria was right. So were you. I tried to make him something he wasn't. He's an eccentric, introverted, antisocial recluse. It was a waste of time. I can't believe I let those Lunatics get in my head."

Zubin jumped off the railing and spun to lean over like Jonathan. "It might not be total loss." He lowered his voice. "I got an interesting story from *Fräulein* Maria."

"What story?"

"She couldn't help but surrender to my masculine charms. Those Germans love us handsome Indians, you know, the original Aryans."

"Don't joke around, Zudu. I'm really not in the mood. Did she say something?"

"Turns out our Maria has an interesting provenance."

"Just tell me what the hell she said."

Zubin explained she was the niece of a German scientist, Dr. Horst Schottstenger, who had worked with the air force and NASA for many years. She came to the United States in 1968 to take care of Schottstenger, already seventy years old by that time, who suffered from rheumatoid arthritis. His declining health made living alone impossible. He also needed a traveling companion to help him make frequent trips between Houston, Huntsville, and Cape Canaveral. She had always wanted to come to America, but she had limited options because of her "condition." Schottstenger was able to get her a green card and brought her over to live with him. Once she started taking care of him, she looked for extra work. She cleaned the homes of astronauts and other NASA personnel in Houston and around the Cape. That was how she met Armstrong. When the doctor died in 1986, he hired her as live-in help.

Jonathan had never heard of Schottstenger. He was far too old to have been one of the Germans at space camp. "Did she say what projects her uncle worked on?"

"She was thrilled to tell me that he was an expert in astronaut health and space medicine. Helped design the space suits for the Mercury 7 astronauts. He apparently had an air force medical library named after him and was inducted into the Space Hall of Fame."

"Did you ask her if the doctor knew my father?"

Zubin slapped his forehead with the heel of his hand. "How dumb do you think I am? Of course I did. She said he didn't know your dad. Schottstenger was really sick between '72 and '74, spent most of his time in and out of hospital in Houston. He was already semiretired, not living in Florida."

"Did she ever hear anything about my father's death?"

"She remembered hearing on the news that your dad had a heart attack, but that was it. Nothing from *Herr Doktor* Schottstenger."

Piercing shrieks scattered the chickadees. A fat blue jay, imitating a menacing hawk, swooped down from the top of a naked sugar maple at the far end of the yard and perched at the bottom of the feeder, thrusting its beak like an ice pick into the frozen bird pudding.

"Anything else?" Jonathan rubbed the bridge of his nose with his thumb and forefinger as if he had a headache.

"I asked her if the doctor had ever mentioned any book on tolerance."

"What for? You think Horst could read Hebrew?"

"We don't know what your dad meant, right? We came all the way here. Why not take a shot?"

"And?" Jonathan sat on a picnic table bench and rubbed his arms.

In mocking imitation, Zubin stood up straight, made his face blank and repeated her response, "'*Nein, nein,* I never heard *Onkel* Horst talk about any book on tolerances.'"

"Well that's a shocker. I'll do some research when I get home, just in case."

"Do you want to ask her any questions?"

"I don't think it's necessary. Let's go inside. It's too cold." At the sliding door leading to the kitchen, they heard a frantic scratching from above. A squirrel scurried diagonally across the black-shingled roof, disappearing over the top.

"What did you just say before?" Jonathan asked.

"I said, 'Do you want to ask her any questions?'"

"No, no." Jonathan raised his brows, the ridges in his forehead pinched. "What did you say right before that?"

"She said she never heard her uncle mention a book on tolerance."

"That's not what you said. Before you said 'tolerances' with an 's.' Plural. Is that how she said it?"

"I think so, yeah. You heard the way she speaks. So what? It's her accent, or her condition, Tourette's or whatever the fuck it is." Zubin moved toward the door.

Jonathan stood stock still, blocking his way. "I can't believe it," he said. "I think I might've had it wrong the whole time. I never put a question mark after it, like a crossword clue."

"What's that even mean?"

"I'm not certain, not yet. Let's go talk to her." He slid the door open and whispered, "Follow my lead."

Jonathan told Maria how excited he was to learn that she was related to the famous Dr. Schottstenger. He feigned familiarity with the doctor's work in space medicine, claiming to have read many of his published papers in preparation for the upcoming mission. Jonathan described Schottstenger's work as "groundbreaking," and Maria beamed. He asked if her uncle had any children.

"*Nein*. He was married only to his work. To his work. He said I was like his daughter."

"Any chance you might have saved any of his old research, like work papers or journals? If you have anything of his work that I might be able to study, it could be very useful to us. He was a real pioneer, a true visionary."

"He left most of it with NASA, but I do have a few journals he kept. I never read them. Never read them. They are mostly filled with mathematics, I think. But do you read German?"

Both men said they didn't.

"Could we borrow them, to photocopy?" Zubin asked. "We could have them back in an hour or two."

"I don't think so."

"We would be very careful," Jonathan said. "I've seen his papers at NASA, but I'd hate to miss out on anything else he might have worked on before he died. I promise your uncle would receive due recognition for any contribution to our mission. Particularly if that contribution saved us money, which would mean, maybe, something for you as well."

"Would he be mentioned in the news reports?"

"Definitely," Zubin said. "And you too, if you like."

Her eyes lit up. "All right then, I suppose. All right." She went upstairs and returned a few minutes later with a half-dozen journals filled with scientific equations and neatly printed paragraphs. "Please bring them right back and be careful. You must be careful."

"We will," Jonathan said. "I promise. Thank you very much for your assistance. It means a lot."

"Yeah, maybe even more than you know," Zubin added. She smiled.

Once they passed through the front gate, Zubin grabbed Jonathan. "Now tell me what the hell's going on. What the hell's going on?"

"I think I made a mistake, maybe two. I'll explain in the car."

Behind the wheel, Jonathan's face twitched, his jaw and lips contorting as if he had food stuck in his teeth. The tops of his ears felt hot. He played the CD again.

"Wait a minute," Zubin said. "You said once we were in the car—"

"Hold on. I need to hear it." They listened to the interview in silence. Jonathan backed up the recording after the part about the book.

"I thought it was in Hebrew, but maybe it wasn't. Maybe it was German."

"Did your dad even speak German?"

"It was my grandmother's first language. He was fairly fluent."

"OK, but you said 'two mistakes.' What's the second?"

"I always assumed my dad meant accepting people who are different."

"And?"

"I don't want to jump to the wrong conclusion again. Maybe this is what it was always about."

"About what? *Intolerance?* Bigotry?"

"What are the two things that would get me to hop on a plane and come to Ohio? My dad and Armstrong, right? What if Cassandra knew that? What if it was always about Schottstenger, and Cassandra sent me here *to Maria* to figure this out? What if my father knew something about the doctor?"

Zubin shook his head. "What if you're being paranoid again? What would your father know?"

"Not yet. I can't say. Let's switch, you drive. I'm too . . . can't focus." Jonathan didn't want to share his emergent theory, afraid that merely speaking his thoughts would crystallize them into an immutable, horrifying reality. He lowered the window and stuck his head outside, spitting at the ground and then turning, mouth wide open, to face straight into the wind. The stinging air made his eyes water. Jonathan slumped inside, wiping his face. He said he had a hot flash, felt like his cheeks were on fire. Zubin offered to stop, but Jonathan insisted that they keep going. "Zudu, what would you do if your life's dream was to reach the Moon?"

"You mean, like what? Sacrifices? Training, studying . . . whatever it took."

"Not just sacrifice . . . suffer humiliation or commit crimes . . . or keep secrets?"

"I don't know, Jon-o. I guess it depends."

"'Depends,' Jonathan said. "Sounds harmless enough, right? Moderate, practical. But it's always the first crack in the dam. For years you would never hear any Wagner music in Israel, not ever, anywhere. The position was always 'under no circumstances' until one day it changed to 'it depends.' Now the dam's been washed away. You can hear *Parsifal* echoing off the Western Wall." Jonathan didn't want to believe his father had learned a secret so dangerous it might have gotten him killed. He didn't want to imagine the depravity that could have inspired such drastic measures. Head back, eyes open, breaths even, mind clear. He didn't want to believe that his own heart condition was as inconsequential as his cardiologist had said. He pressed fingers to his wrist. The beat was quickened but steady. He had embraced his inheritance, determined to march in time to the legacy of a lethal, lopsided pulse. But if his father had been murdered, his own irregular beat wasn't a fatal ancestral echo—it was a false alarm.

At a local Kinko's, they divided the journals and scanned their contents onto flash drives. Jonathan felt like he was splitting in two, but he kept his unnerving suspicions and bitter disgust to himself. Before returning to the house, they stopped at the hotel. Jonathan opened his laptop and e-mailed the material to Susana with an urgent request to have Helmut begin translation. She replied within minutes, reminding her husband that Helmut had left for his sister's wedding in Munich and wouldn't return for a week. Despite his burning need, Jonathan didn't want to trust a stranger. He knew Susana would explode if he sent the work overseas. He would have to wait.

They returned the journals to Maria and drove to the airport. Jonathan accompanied Zubin to the security checkpoint before flying himself home. Zubin grabbed his friend by the shoulders. "Let me know if there's anything else I can do. You know I'm always up for it. Even if you're gonna keep me in the dark and not let me see whatever light bulb started flickering up there." He knocked his fist twice on his friend's head.

"Give me some time," Jonathan said. He took a deep breath. "And I'm sorry, so sorry you had to put up with my stupid obsession for so long."

"No apologies. You pick up the phone, I'm there. But promise me one thing."

"Of course."

"Talk to Armstrong. It'll be worth it even if what your dad meant—and what happened—had nothing to do with Mr. Neil."

Jonathan steadied his upper lip. "You got it . . . but under one condition."

"What?" Zubin smiled as if waiting for the ending of a stupid joke.

"Lend me that Tang shirt when I finally meet him."

Zubin stepped back, stripped off his sweatshirt, rolled the T-shirt off his back, and threw it into Jonathan's chest. "It'll only make my trip through security easier. You know what those TSA drones like to do with us brown people."

15

March 18, 2005

6:15AM

Jonathan struggled out of bed to answer the doorbell. Helmut leaned against the doorjamb, his worn, khaki satchel barely outweighing the dark brown bags under his bleary eyes.

"You look like you slept less than I did," Jonathan said.

"Is Susana all right?"

"She sawed more wood than Paul Bunyan."

"I'm sorry. Who?" Helmut teetered on the threshold.

"No, that's my fault. American idiom. It means she snored the whole night. Bad dreams lately. Keep waking me up."

Jonathan had been having a recurring nightmare since returning from Cincinnati. A line of helmeted astronauts digging ditches in a Martian desert. He was lost. Gusts of wind covered him with ash. He asked them for directions, coughing out his words. They opened their chrome visors at once, and his throat sealed shut. They looked like the walking cadavers in the concentration camp films—men, women, deep-set eyes, and skin like mottled panty hose. A young woman grabbed his arm and said, "It's not because of the hunger; it's because of what we've seen." They looked at Jonathan like he was alien. He couldn't speak. He sprinted along a ditch. Someone hit him in the back, knocking him in. They threw shovel loads of dirt on top of him. He couldn't climb out. At that point, he woke up, his mouth dry like sandpaper, his hair soaked.

Helmut held up his loaded bag as if to offer it. "I stayed up all night. They're done. I don't even know what time it is. You told me to come as soon as I finished."

"That's fine, good, thank you, but keep your voice down."

Jonathan pointed upstairs. Helmut had taken longer than Jonathan had wanted. After extending his stay in Munich for a few days, he returned to Miami and had worked feverishly to catch up on data from the Europa probe that hadn't been analyzed since he had left.

Jonathan led Helmut into the kitchen. "What can you tell me about him that isn't in the official biography?" Jonathan had thus far found nothing more than the familiar NASA template—innocent civilian medical researcher for the Luftwaffe and eager post-war émigré to America. He poured two mugs of coffee. "Skip the equations. Just his interests, opinions, stuff like that."

Helmut sat at the kitchen table, opened his bag, and pulled out copies of the original journals, each with a typed translation attached. "The doctor had a keen interest in the future of genetic research. He devoted several pages to cloning and particularly unsavory efforts to justify a revival of planned human reproduction. He ranted, for example, about the hypocrisy of Western society's treatment of selective breeding. 'It's praised at the Westminster Kennel Club and the Kentucky Derby,' Schottstenger wrote, 'but in humans it's supposedly an abomination.' And he lamented the lack of will in the scientific community to speak the truth about genetics. He railed against liberal Ivy League scientists, calling them hypocrites for denying the scientific validity of eugenics while at the same time engaging in 'rampant postdoctoral interbreeding.'"

Jonathan put a mug in front of Helmut and sat next to him. Helmut handed him the pages he'd quoted from. "I was afraid of something like this. No wonder he didn't give those journals to NASA." Helmut began leafing through another set of journal entries. "Did the doctor mention anything about his work during the war?"

"I'm afraid he didn't. At least not with any specificity."

"Anything about human physiological limits?"

"For aviation? Is that what you're really looking for?"

"Not just that. What else you got?"

Helmut sipped his coffee and kept his voice low. "In his last journals, he displayed an obsession with the growing movement against animal testing. He despised PETA and compiled a list of several important medical advances that would not have been possible without sacrificing lab rats, pigs, and monkeys. He saw the animal rights activists as 'degenerate anthropomorphizing scum.'" Helmut blushed. He looked like a child whose father had just slapped him in public. "That was his term."

"I understand."

"Schottstenger couldn't believe human beings were sacrificing scientific advancement to save 'expendable vermin.' Probably the most interesting and troubling references to his work before NASA came in a diatribe against the Humane Society. It was a bit of a non sequitur, but if you allow for certain assumptions, it's fairly disturbing." Helmut pushed his mug to the center of the table, reached for a journal, and turned to a paper-clipped page. "Here it is. My best translation is: 'Look what I did for these Americans, what I gave them to keep their men safe, and now we have to save a three-legged mutt at the expense of a cure for cancer. They were once all too happy to have the benefits of my research, despite the collateral consequences. Now, it is only a matter of time before the iron-willed, purebred Chinese overrun them.'" Helmut sat up against the chair back and sighed. "I'm sorry, Jon, that's what it says."

Jonathan nodded to dismiss Helmut's embarrassment. "Your results confirm my worst fears."

Susana's voice poured down from the master bedroom. "Jon, can you make me my fruit smoothie? I'll be down in a minute."

When her husband didn't immediately reply, she called his name even louder, in two syllables with an ending uptone. "Jah-ahn?"

"I'm making it," he answered through a locked jaw. He got up from the table and took out a twelve-inch chef's knife from a drawer in the middle of the massive granite island. He lined up peeled bananas, mango cheeks, and pineapple slices on a butcher block next to the blender.

"What were their *tolerances*? That's what I missed." He massacred the fruit as he spoke. "The design of NASA space suits was a product of Nazi atrocities. That's what my father was trying to tell me, trying to tell somebody. Nazi and NASA scientists, like Schottstenger, used knowledge from wartime experiments on concentration camp prisoners to develop the protective clothing worn by the first American astronauts." Jonathan stabbed the point of the knife into the butcher block. "I bet those fuckers stood there, supremely serene in their lily-white lab coats, dutifully marking time, temperature, and pressure while old Mr. Bernstein shivered into an indelible blue and little Miss Perlmutter chattered her baby teeth to pieces."

Helmut moved his lips as if he had forgotten how to speak.

"And they winced," Jonathan continued, "only for just an instant, when gasping Mrs. Shapiro collapsed on the floor of a hyperbaric chamber with her hands at her throat. And when they were finished, they strolled outside and stood in a circle of smokes and jokes with reams of notes and not a drop of remorse. Too cold for that."

Helmut sat motionless, elbows on the table, eyes wide. His hands cupped his face like they'd been painted by Munch. "I don't know what to say, Jon. 'I'm sorry' seems so inadequate to such enormity. It sounds almost offensive. I don't—"

Jonathan tossed the knife, draped in stringy pulp, into the sink where it clanked against the stainless steel basin. He scooped up the flesh in his sticky hands and dumped it into the blender. "Schottstenger gave them their research, his book of human tolerances, and NASA gladly used its statistics and his expertise, stained with the blood of the *untermenschen,* to keep Alan Shepard and John Glenn safe and warm. That's it, isn't it?" Jonathan hesitated before washing his hands, conscious of the symbolism of the act. "My father was trying to speak for them." He thought of the poem hidden in Armstrong's drawer. "I don't even want to go anymore. Jesus, we knew about Mengele hiding out in Brazil. But this? Apparently, the Angel of Death didn't have to go that far, or even hunker down in the rainforest. NASA would have given him good pay, a fat pension, and an engraved plaque for his fine contributions. It makes me sick. How the hell can I go?"

"Your father must have made the decision to go, unless—"

"Unless what?"

"Suppose he didn't know so much," Helmut said. "Maybe he heard only rumors, had suspicions; perhaps he never heard of Schottstenger.

The doctor obviously kept a profile much lower than von Braun."

Jonathan ran the blender, wiped down the butcher's block, and returned to the table. "What am I supposed to do now? Confront NASA? Go to the press?"

"I think," Helmut said, leaning back in his chair, "that we need help, getting more evidence first." He had a blue-eyed stare, empty and penetrating, like Jon Voight.

"Have you seen *The Odessa File?*" Jonathan asked. Helmut shook his head. Jonathan had watched it three times in the past week. The film made him even more convinced that Cassandra had wanted him to find out about Schottstenger. "When a reporter needed help tracking down an old SS commander, he met with Simon Wiesenthal, the famous Nazi hunter. That's what we should do, in real life. I think he's still alive, but like ninety-four."

"There's the Holocaust Remembrance and Research Center in Berlin," Helmut said. "Maybe they could help us."

"Anything would be better than NASA," Jonathan said. "I'm not so sure Uncle Sam would be quick to give us what we're looking for."

Susana tottered into the kitchen wearing loose-fitting gray sweatpants and an oversize maternity T-shirt, stretched tight nonetheless, with the words "*res gestate*" on the front—a gift from a college roommate who had become a law professor. "Hey, Helmut, what brings you here? Oh," she said, seeing Schottstenger's journals spread on the table. She poured the fruit smoothie into a tall glass. "Come up with anything?"

"No smoking guns," Jonathan said, quick to speak before Helmut could open his mouth, "but the journals are damning. There's stuff about the virtues of animal testing and eugenics. I'm certain the doctor was involved in sadistic camp research. My hunch about the space suits and what my dad said has to be right."

"You know what I think," she said. "Not everything is as certain as a crossword answer."

"Helmut thinks we should reach out to the holocaust center in Berlin for help."

She clicked her tongue and took a first sip. "You should talk to Dale already. Real life isn't the movies, Jon. Stop ducking him in the hallways and just ask."

"If he knows about that interview, about what Dad was talking about, I'll need all the leverage I can get to pry the truth out of him."

"It's not like you've only got one chance, counselor."

"Not yet." He slapped his hand against the table like a gavel.

"Suit yourself, but to get any answers fast, you're gonna have to donate more to that center than I gave to the science museum."

"You're probably looking at the newest board member," he said. "Once we've got a researcher assigned, I'll put him in touch with you, Helmut. I know you're ridiculously busy, but is that all right?" Jonathan glanced at Susana, who nodded her approval.

"I would have volunteered if you hadn't asked," Helmut said. The two men shook hands, and Jonathan patted him on the back. Helmut gave Susana an awkward perpendicular hug, left the journals and his translations behind, picked up his empty satchel, and shuffled out the front door.

Susana took his place at the table. She split a double chocolate muffin in half to eat with her smoothie. Jonathan joined her with a bowl of yogurt and granola. He stirred his breakfast, dropped his spoon in the bowl, and took his wife's hand.

"I have a heart condition."

Susana's face inflated like a balloon. "How long have you known? What is it?"

"A few months. Mitral valve prolapse. It's totally asymptomatic, apparently one of the mildest conditions you can have."

"*Coño,* why didn't you tell me?" She yanked her hand away. "Is that what your dad had?"

"No way to tell. His tests were clean. The cardiologist said probably not, but he couldn't rule it out categorically. He said it's nothing to worry about."

"Why didn't you tell me? *Hostias.*"

"I didn't want to worry you. The doctor was adamant that it wasn't serious. But I had convinced myself it was a fatal family curse, passed down from my dad, one I had to fight on my own, one our son might have to fight. I'm sorry." He took a spoonful of granola, his eyes fixed on the bowl. "Even though I knew it could kill me—and this is weird—it brought me closer to him. It was this special bond, our only living link left, like at least part of my dad had been reincarnated, even if the bad part. I wanted to defeat the curse for both of us." He peered up at her, ready to be scolded.

"But Jon, if it wasn't a heart attack—"

He put up his hand and wouldn't let her finish, wouldn't let her say what he already knew to be true—that proof of Avi's murder could lift the curse, that the unspeakable alternative might have inspired his fascination with Cassandra, his relentless drive to uncover a secret conspiracy. He felt like he had even willed it into being. He took her hand again. "I'm sorry, for everything. You had a right to know."

"And I have every right to be furious," she said. "You have responsibilities." She pointed to her stomach. "The land of make-believe is for *him*, not his father. Seriously." She shoved her plate away, crumbs scattering like shrapnel.

"I said I'm sorry. I promise, no more secrets." He stood up and wiped the table with a napkin. He wished he could confess everything, but the unfiltered truth was impossible. There would be a few tawdry secrets he would have to keep locked up and hidden away, like a secret diary he could never share. He felt like a craven hypocrite, searching for the truth about his father while fabricating a chaste image of himself for his wife. "I should have been open and honest with you, and with myself, from the start. I was horribly selfish, but I don't, I can't, regret the chase. Look what I've found." He waved his hand over the papers strewn across the table. "It's bigger than me, even than my dad. I have to keep going."

She stood up to grab him by the shoulders. "But you've got to put us first, the three of us, from now on. We're in this together, as a family. You can't keep yourself locked up inside this fortress of solitude anymore," she slid her hands to the sides of his head, "indulging in fantasies that make you feel better. You live on a peninsula, not an island. Connected. Understand?" She took his hand and placed it flat on her stomach. He could feel a small protrusion, a rounded knob, like a knee or a heel. "The last person on Earth you want to be is—"

"I know. Neil Armstrong."

16

April 3, 2005
11:17AM

The gambit had worked. Helmut summoned Susana to work on a late Sunday morning with a frantic call about a loss of contact with the probe. Jonathan pretended to be irritated when she asked him to drive. With only a month to go, Susana didn't like the steering wheel so close to the baby. When they entered her lab, she flipped on the lights and met a shower of confetti and shouts of "surprise" and "*sorpresa*." Susana's older sister had flown in from Ponce, cousins from San Juan, and college and grad school friends from across the country. The remaining guests—a mix of faculty, lab assistants, and neighbors—stood around a circle of metal folding chairs.

"Congratulations," Susana said. She hugged and kissed her family members and her husband. "You got me good, Jonny. Now we're even."

"Least I could do. Didn't even need handcuffs." He palmed her stomach. "I just planted the seed. You're the constant gardener. You deserve it."

Garlands of multicolored crepe paper and bunches of Mylar balloons decorated the room. Jonathan had special ordered a spherical cake made to look like a globe-sized Europa, but given the disappointing results thus far—no signs of life—he switched it at the last minute for a standard sheet. In the center of the room, three identical adult-sized blow-up dolls—bug-eyed, hairless, gray-skinned aliens—hovered over a brand-new bassinet. Eva presented them to Susana "as three really wise men who came from across the galaxy, following a distant star, just to see my grandbaby."

"Fascinating," Helmut said. "When I was a small boy, I always carried the big star on the Sixth of January with our village *Sternsinger.* We call it *Dreikönigstag.* Here it's Feast of Epiphany. Maybe that's how I became interested in astronomy."

"It was an eye-opener for me," Susana said. "Got my first telescope from *los Reyes Magos* when I was eleven, converted me into an atheist by fourteen. Probably not the epiphany my parents were hoping for."

"Susana, the shower," Jonathan said, shifting his eyes and tilting his head to the line of guests waiting to greet her. He turned and raised his voice. "Well, ladies, looks like it's time for Helmut and me to shove off. Enjoy."

"Where to?" Susana asked.

"Ocala, to meet with that reporter, Naughton. He's finally well enough to see me. Mom'll drive you home."

"Don't forget to make a couple of barrel rolls," she said, winking at her assistant, who blanched. Jonathan had taken Helmut swordfishing in October. The young man not only failed to catch any fish in the rough seas but spent most of the day heaving over the side of the boat.

"Don't worry," Jonathan said. "I don't plan on mopping any spit-up for at least another month."

It was a good day for flying, twenty miles of visibility and light winds. Jonathan leveled off his Skylane at 7,000 feet, 130 knots. The plane neared Kissimmee.

"Why is Berlin taking so long to get back to us on Schottstenger?" Jonathan asked. "Wasn't my check big enough?"

"It's only been two weeks," Helmut said. "Jürgen's still digging through stacks of Nuremberg files."

"Grab the binoculars and look to the right," Jonathan said, banking slightly.

"Yes, I can see it. Disney World."

"What do you think?"

"Impressive. I've never been. My stomach doesn't tolerate thrill rides very well. I don't even enjoy the autobahn. This flight is the most I can handle."

"I can't stand the place," Jonathan said. "My motto is *Free marketeer 'til death, but death before Mouseketeer.* I'm not against amusement parks *per se*, but I never liked Walt Disney. Did you know when he was a kid, Walt pulled an owl from a low branch and stomped it to death? True story. Who does that? Serial killers, right? And, by the way, he was no big fan of the Hebrews either."

"Isn't a Jew the chief executive of the Disney company?"

"Michael Eisner. I guess that makes it a little more bearable."

"What's that big silver orb?"

"Spaceship Earth. It's awful. Epcot's the worst of them all. Stillborn kitsch."

"Your child will want to go in a few years."

"Don't remind me."

"You're looking forward to becoming a father, aren't you?" Helmut removed the binoculars to glance at Jonathan.

"It's a big change for a forty-something. I'm not sure I'll have the patience."

"Excuse me for saying, but that's nonsense. You'll be a wonderful father. You've been like an older brother ever since I arrived in Florida, helping me find a place to live, bargaining with that awful used car salesman, teaching me the rules of American football. You have no reason to doubt yourself."

Jonathan searched his backpack for chewing gum and offered a stick to Helmut. He declined and instead pulled a half-eaten bag of Combos from his jacket. "Want a few?"

"Not with gum in my mouth. I'll pass. Maybe you should too, at least until we land." Unlike Wyatt, the tow truck driver, Jonathan had no stash of airsick bags.

"Whenever I'd made a mess in my bedroom," Helmut said, "spilling glue or paint, usually from building model sailboats, my mother used to say she couldn't stay mad at me because I had my *opa's* eyes. Seeing a relative's face alive again, maybe even seeing your own face in your children, must change everything." He picked up the binoculars again. "It's the only kind of immortality we've achieved thus far." He leaned closer to the windshield and adjusted the focus. "What's the name of the big castle out in front?"

"Cinderella's Castle," Jonathan answered, ever prepared for a pop quiz. "Based on Neuschwanstein, the Bavarian castle of Mad King Ludwig. Told you Walt Disney had a German fetish. Only problem with that kind of immortality is we're not there to enjoy it. The clock strikes twelve, and we turn back into dust."

"You didn't sound like that last November, at the announcement. You talked about a giant leap forward into outer space for the benefit of posterity. That speech, it was about a legacy to the future, to future generations. It's always been about legacy, hasn't it? Every mission to space must be. One lifespan simply isn't enough. Isn't that why you've kept your father's dream alive these many years?"

Jonathan opened a thermos of ice water and took a slow drink. "I think I was looking back more than forward when I said that, but I've been trying to see things your way." He remembered how Eva had compared his father to Moses at the unveiling.

"Time is running out for the real Spaceship Earth," Helmut said. "Flood, fire, and ice are inevitable. What you're doing is the start of a global evacuation. What's that American saying? We can't keep a chicken's eggs only in one basket? They have to be spread out across the galaxy. That's why Armstrong's 'giant leap' was for mankind, not man. It will, of course, take millennia, but someday, on a distant planet, you may be revered as a great pioneer, perhaps even as a savior." Helmut made the sign of the cross with mock solemnity.

"Wouldn't be the first time that happened to a Jew, but I'm no second coming." Jonathan had never before thought of his lunar expedition as the beginning of an exodus. It was like combining the two kinds of flight his father had described: adventure and escape. Exploration on the run. In a merciless universe, maybe that was survival, an endless hunt for greener pastures by small steps and giant leaps. "Moses or Noah?" Jonathan asked.

"You mean who's my favorite biblical hero?"

"No, baby names."

"Despite my unfortunate lack of sea legs, I like all things nautical, so I would have to choose Noah."

"Me too."

The two men picked up a rental car in Ocala and drove south on Highway 75. Helmut read from the directions Jonathan's assistant had printed. They passed innumerable billboards advertising either the distance to the Ron Jon Surf Shop or the number of days (eighteen apparently) after conception when the fetal heartbeat begins. Jonathan averted his eyes each time an anti-abortion advertisement— euphemistically emblazoned with a "pregnancy counseling" hotline number—came into focus. They had always made him feel uneasy, having joined the Grand Old Party for fiscal and foreign policy concerns, not to regulate the uterus.

After thirty minutes, they arrived at a sprawling active-living retirement development fifty thousand strong and growing called "The Community," block after block of one-story, sandstone-colored houses, each one only the slightest variation on its closely built neighbor. There were no bikes or toys in the yards and no basketball hoops in the driveways. Ersatz was everywhere, from the themed neighborhood squares, ready-made reproductions of quaint fishing villages, and gold rush boomtowns, to the lawns covered in thick, short-cut grass genetically engineered to be as close as organically possible to Astroturf. The subdivisions bore nonsensical names like Canyon Gorge and Cascade Falls and featured wide streets with low speed limits and dedicated golf cart lanes. Residents out for a stroll waved enthusiastically to one another—the men in golf shorts and striped polo shirts wearing baseball caps for their favorite sports team or service branch, the women in capri pants, cotton blouses with splashy floral prints, and sunglasses with oversize lenses. Despite the width of the roads and sidewalks and the overwhelming sense that everything was wheelchair accessible, Jonathan felt claustrophobic. "This place is like Disney World on Maalox. Are we almost there?"

"Continue straight after the traffic circle," Helmut read, "and then make the second right onto Fox Run Terrace Court Road."

"Jesus," Jonathan said.

Mrs. Naughton, a petite, middle-aged woman, welcomed them inside with offers of iced tea, lemonade, and sponge cake, all of which were politely declined. She led them past bookcases filled with dozens of rabbit figurines to her husband "out on the lanai." Naughton sat in a high-back wicker chair on the screened-in patio. The ceiling fan barely turned, as slow as if it were about to stop. A small, oval rock garden outside the patio surrounded a smiling Buddha, and a wind chime made of sea shells hung from a bracket outside the screen. In the light breeze, it sounded like ice being dropped into mixed drinks, or someone stepping on broken glass.

Naughton was in his early sixties, short and stout, with a stomach like a twenty-pound bag of flour under his black-and-gold "U.S. Army" T-shirt. His Santa Claus white hair was thick and straight, his arms compact, and fingers stubby. His cheeks drooped below his jawline, like a fringe of excess dough hanging over a pie pan.

"I'd get up to shake your hand, but it takes some effort." He no longer sounded like the young man on the recording. His voice was deeper and scratchy, like an overplayed record.

"Don't worry," Jonathan said. "How's the recovery going?"

"It's slow, like everything around here, but the doc says my hips are on target. Doing my physical therapy every day. Be glad when that's through. Gotta get back on the links. That's the only place I want a handicap, if you know what I mean."

Jonathan and Helmut pulled up matching chaise lounges to sit close and perched on the edges.

After a few pleasantries about the weather and the neighborhood, Naughton said, "So, you want to talk to me about the interview I did with your dad."

"How well do you remember it?"

"What's it been? Thirty years? I was a kid, just starting out. First time interviewing an astronaut. Only time, matter of fact. Hard to forget that, especially after what happened."

"Was that the only time you met my father?"

"Yep. First and last. Must've been hard on you. How old were you?

"Thirteen."

"Monica, my wife, said you dug up the recording. Don't know how the hell you found it. Crated up next to the Ark of the Covenant?"

"It was in the National Archives," Jonathan said. "We brought a copy with us."

"Why, after all these years?"

"I'm putting together a family history, probably going to write a book after my mission. Would you like to refresh your memory?"

"Why not? Let's hear it," Naughton said, leaning forward.

Helmut pulled a portable CD player from his backpack and played the interview. Naughton stared at the speaker during the replay, as if that focused his hearing, looking away only to watch a shiny black lizard scurry from behind a gas grill and slip through a hole in the wire mesh of the patio screen. At first, he looked puzzled, like he didn't recognize his own voice. Toward the end, he nodded as if hearing confirmation of something he'd always believed.

"I sure as hell sounded like one nervous Nellie. No disrespect to the dead, but your dad was intimidating, even though we spoke through a glass wall."

"You weren't allowed in quarantine then?" Jonathan asked.

"Of course not. It was only a couple days before launch."

"Any idea why my father spoke like that, all that unrelated stuff?"

"I was flabbergasted. I felt that way again today, listening to it. You could've knocked me over with a feather. You heard how I was trying to calm him down, steer him back on course. Not a bad effort for a greenhorn." He sat back in his chair, breathing heavily. "I have no idea why he had a swarm of bees in his bonnet, but he sure as hell did." His wife interrupted with a tray of pink lemonade and sugar cookies. "Thanks, sweetheart."

Jonathan took a glass from the tray, wrapped in a cocktail napkin. "Did the tape ever go on the air?"

"Heck, no."

"I figured as much. Do you remember how the interview with my dad was set up? What's the first thing you can recall?"

"Can't help you there. My lieutenant, Michael Watkins, called me up that morning and said to get over there, over to the Cape, and do the interview. He said we got an exclusive, only interview in quarantine. I remember that. It was supposed to be five to seven minutes, general interest story."

"Did you play the tape for Watkins when you got back to your office?"

"Never had a chance to."

"Why not?"

"The captain took it."

"What captain?" Jonathan had crept forward to the very edge of the lounge chair, which tipped the back up like a teeter-totter. He jumped and spilled lemonade on his white polo shirt and jeans. "Sorry about that. I don't think I got any on the floor." He returned his glass to the tray.

"Monica," Naughton called, "bring us a wet dish rag and some paper towels."

"That's all right. I'm fine, really. Don't go to any trouble." But she appeared as requested. "They're for me," Jonathan said. "You should probably give me a sippy cup next time I visit."

"Do you want me to wash your clothes?" she asked. "You could borrow something from Blaine."

"No, it's not that bad." Jonathan blotted the spill, which barely missed his inseam. He thanked Mrs. Naughton and apologized again as he handed her the used paper towels. Flustered, he leaned against a support column in the middle of the patio. "You were saying something about a captain confiscating the tape?"

"He was a captain at the time. He got promoted later."

"Who did?" Jonathan asked.

"Colonel Lunden, last man to walk on the Moon." Jonathan tried not to react, but his legs wobbled. He looked at the slow-turning fan and felt dizzy. He knew Helmut was watching his reaction.

"You all right, son?"

"I'm fine. Haven't eaten all day. That's all." He took a cookie from the tray. "Please continue."

"Colonel Lunden was my escort, sat right by my side through the whole thing. After your dad left, he grabbed the reel from my machine and said it was confiscated. Something about classified information. He acted real upset. He was even scarier than your dad. I think I forgot my own name for a minute there. Later on, I realized it was probably just an act, but at the time I thought I was gonna lose my lunch."

"What do you mean 'an act'?" Jonathan asked.

"I replayed that interview in my head a half dozen times that day. I wondered if I screwed something up, said something offensive, or unmilitary, or just downright stupid. But hearing that again today, it confirms what I finally figured out. The colonel was protecting your dad, didn't want him to be embarrassed for how he sounded. He even threatened to have me and Lieutenant Watkins transferred to Timbuktu if we made a stink. When I got back to the office and told Watkins what happened, he said, 'Forget it.' So I did. I don't know how in the world that tape wound up in the National Archives. Maybe there is something top secret on it after all, but damned if I know what it was."

Jonathan's eyes danced like he was rechecking a calculation in his head. He put his hands behind his back, pressing them against the column to still them. "Did you or Watkins speak to Lunden about it at any other time?"

"Nope. I got transferred to a radio station at a base in the Philippines a couple months later, where I eventually met my lovely bride. I'm sure Watkins didn't mess with it. Too close to retirement, been dead about five years now."

"Did Colonel Lunden say anything else about the interview?"

"Nope." Naughton laughed.

"What's funny?"

"No, he kept saying that it was classified, that he was actually doing me a favor by confiscating that tape. Thinking about it now, I'm sure he was pulling a fast one on me."

"Did you ever follow up on anything my father said? He mentioned a book on tolerance. Know anything about that?"

"Don't remember it. I guess I was too busy shitting a brick at the time to notice."

"Anything else at all you can remember about what my father or Dale Lunden might have said?"

He tapped the side of his head. "Not the trap she used to be. Jesus, I would've bet dollars to doughnuts the colonel tossed that tape in the first dumpster he saw."

"I knew it," Jonathan whispered.

"What?" Helmut asked.

"Later."

"You fellows want to stay for dinner?" Naughton asked. "The missus would love to hear about your mission to the Moon. She's a great cook. It's fish sticks and tater tots, but don't be fooled. All homemade, none of that frozen crap."

"It's only four o'clock," Helmut said.

"Yeah, but the wife and I are already starting to live like the real old-timers around here—all up for breakfast at 5 a.m. They call it 'Eastern Senior Time.'"

"That's interesting," Helmut said, apparently oblivious to Naughton's attempt at humor. "I once read that correctional facilities keep inmates on a very similar meal schedule. It seems they've discovered that by waking prisoners early and feeding them early, they're less aggressive, especially at night."

"I don't think aggression is the problem here," Naughton said. "First light is proof the ole grim reaper swung and missed again. The elderly folks can't wait to see it. Ain't about to go back to sleep."

Jonathan said they couldn't stay. He had to be in the pool at 6 a.m. the next day for underwater training, simulated equipment maintenance and repair. Naughton promised to call if he remembered anything else.

Jonathan and Helmut leaned against the rental car's trunk, waiting for Mrs. Naughton to go back inside. Two bald men in "Semper Fi" T-shirts rode recumbent bikes down the middle of the street. "Have a good evening," one said as he passed. Jonathan pulled up a tuft of grass to make sure it was real.

"Naughton appears credible," Helmut said. "Dale Lunden was protecting your father from bad press, or worse, by taking that tape, even if we're wrong about Schottstenger. And now, it seems, he's doing the same for you."

"But if Dale *knew* what my father was talking about—what we think he was talking about—Dale was really protecting himself. That story wouldn't have elicited much popular support for NASA, and Dale's mission was up next." Jonathan wished Lunden had thrown the reel in the dumpster. That it was sitting in the archives meant men in positions of power, like von Braun or Debus, likely knew of its existence. Had that been Lunden's true purpose in confiscating the tape? Self-promotion more than self-preservation. Maybe he couldn't wait to play it for the "right" people.

Jonathan puzzled over it, clues without a grid. None of the numbers made ten. If the interview had gone public, the Germans might have been publicly shamed, subject to ridicule, even harassment, but the government—particularly NASA and the Department of Defense—would've had much more to lose if the truth came out. The feds had handed out employment contracts and social security to war criminals instead of prison sentences, and reaped the scientific benefits of demented prisoner experiments. The government would have been just as eager—more so—to silence his father. It was still a Nixon White House, even if the worst of them had been cleared out. The crippled, patchwork administration must have been desperate for a stretch of clear air. How many more Watergate indictments would there be? Vietnam had costs billions for nothing. The economy was just beginning to recover from the devastating 1973 oil embargo imposed by Arab countries as retribution for the American airlift of military aid to Israel during the Yom Kippur War. A tabloid story about NASA's cozy relationship with its unrepentant Nazis would have been all certain liberal congressmen needed to shut down the space program for good. More money for social programs. Jonathan was certain that Cassandra would agree, doubtlessly drawing a parallel to the mysterious postwar death of Alan Turing, the celebrated cryptanalyst who had broken the Nazis' Enigma code. MI5, Britain's domestic counterintelligence agency, feared that Turing was about to spill state secrets. If Avi Stein's death wasn't the result of natural causes, the Germans might have provoked it, but they probably didn't do it. Jonathan knew precisely what that meant: friendly fire.

17

April 16, 2005

3:13AM

"Jon, did you pee in your sleep?"

"No." Jonathan checked the crotch of his pajama bottoms to make sure. He'd been asleep only twenty minutes. Ever since returning from Ocala, his insomnia had worsened. He stayed up late, woke frequently from his bad dream, and ate pints of ice cream in front of the computer screen, waiting for confirmation about Schottstenger.

"I think my water broke."

"Two weeks early?"

"Impatient little boy. No surprise there."

Well ahead of rush hour traffic, they arrived at the maternity ward in less than fifteen minutes. The obstetrician on call explained that because Susana's water broke before contractions, there was an increased risk of infection. To lessen the risk, the contractions had to be medically induced. Susana was given Pitocin to accelerate the delivery and an epidural to numb the pain. As the hours passed, the expectant couple, awaiting full dilation, watched *Lost in Translation* on the birthing suite's DVD player and worked crossword puzzles between innumerable nurse visits.

"That settles it," Susana said.

"Settles what?"

"This boy was preceded by a flood. It's got to be Noah. *Après le déluge, c'est lui.* You were right. It's perfect."

"Even Miss Havisham's clock was right twice a day."

Susana's mobile phone rattled on a nightstand next to a plastic cup filled with ice chips; it sounded like a woodpecker drilling into the trunk of an oak tree. "It's eight o'clock. Helmut probably just opened up the lab," Susana said. "I'll put him on speaker. Hello, Helmut."

"Susana, it's Helmut. I have important news."

"Me too."

"Really, what is it?"

"No, Helmut, you go first. Mine can wait. Did we get anything? Microbes?"

"What? No, I'm sorry, Susana. Still nothing there I'm afraid. In fact, given the increased battery drain, the probe will probably give out by the end of next week. I'm calling for Jonathan. He didn't answer." In the rush to get to the hospital, Jonathan had left his phone at home.

"I'm right here, Helmut. Hold on." He picked up the phone and switched off the speaker. Susana cringed at the onset of a contraction. "You OK?" he asked, his hand covering the phone.

"I'm all right," she said, her face twisting in pain. "I think we're at four minutes apart now."

"Should I get rid of him?"

"No, he said it was important. This one's not too bad. Just press the call button again."

Jonathan did as he was told, stepped away from the bed, and leaned against the doorjamb to watch for the nurse. "Hello, Helmut."

"Jonathan, it's Helmut. I heard from Jürgen. He found something buried in the Nuremberg archives, a document never admitted into evidence at any of the trials. There's a list."

"What kind of list?"

"Doctors overseeing experiments on prisoners at Dachau."

"And?"

"Schottstenger's on it."

"Does it say anything else?"

"There's only a one-line description. 'Research on physical endurance under hyperthermic and hyperbaric conditions.'"

"And the experiments were at Dachau."

"Yes."

"That's it. It's got to be. Damn it, I knew it. He was freezing Jews one minute and boiling their blood the next. Fuck."

"There are no words, Jon, to speak of such horrors."

"Helmut, don't say anything to anybody yet."

"I understand."

"You're not the only one with news. We're in the hospital. Susana's in labor."

"So soon? Is she all right?"

"She's fine. Her water broke this morning."

"Please call me after he's born. I'll be at the hospital tomorrow morning. Did she agree to Noah?"

"Just now. I'll speak with you soon. Thanks for everything you've done."

"I was happy to help. I felt I had to."

Jonathan took up Susana's clammy hands. "It's confirmed," he said. "I was right. Schottstenger was involved in involuntary human experiments, and at Dachau of all places, deep freeze and pressure chambers. My father must have known. I can't imagine—"

"This doesn't prove your father, Dale, or even Cassandra knew, or that Avi was assassinated."

"But this makes it a lot more likely. I mean, what are the odds?" Jonathan sat slumped over on the empty bed next to Susana.

"Please don't do the math, Jon. It's been thirty years. What if you're never able to prove it was murder? Guns don't smoke for that long."

"I can't stop."

"What about your mission?"

"I don't know how I can do it." He began to pace in front of the beds. "For god's sake, they shipped my grandfather, the kindly, candy-man pharmacist, to Dachau." Jonathan stopped to face Susana. "What if they turned *him* from a flesh-and-blood human being into a frozen data point? Von Braun's Teutonic rocket brigade was bad enough, but this, this is too much. You can only swallow so much before you throw up. What am I supposed to do? Say 'thanks for the lift' from the launchpad?"

"Listen to me. Ahh! *Coño!*" She clutched the bed rails like she was trying to rip them off. "Where's the fucking nurse?"

Jonathan punched the red emergency button and started for the nurse's station.

"Jon, wait, don't go." Susana strained to speak. Her cheeks were flushed, sweat glazed her forehead. "This one . . . really . . . fuck! Worthless fucking epidural!"

The nurse and doctor arrived in seconds.

"This one's the worst," Jonathan said. "They're three minutes apart, now."

The nurse checked the drip and vital signs, and the doctor checked the dilation. "Seven centimeters. You're almost there. Everything's fine. We'll be right back after I deliver across the hall. Then it'll be time to push. Hang in there. Really soon."

Susana's panting slowed.

"Contraction over?"

"Mostly. I understand, Jon, how you feel. Yes, it's horrible, unspeakable, but you still have to go to the Moon. You have to, despite what might have happened, and despite what I think about manned missions." With a limp wrist, she pointed at the rollaway table near her bed. "Give me some ice chips."

"So that's it?" he asked. "If enough time passes, who cares about the torture, the experiments, the gas chambers? Old harm, no foul? Sorry, Gramps."

"Of course not, but it's your *accomplishment* of the mission that does the most, a lot more than an angry, short-sighted boycott." She winced, slamming her head against the pillow. He jumped from the side of the bed. "It's OK," she said. "It's not a contraction. Human beings, with or without you, are going back to the Moon. You've got the chance to be the first person to do it in this century. Do you really want some thrill-seeking Russian oligarch in a gold *lamé* jumpsuit dancing around up there before you? Remember what I said on the night we met, when I got you to stop trying to calculate the odds of us meeting under a meteor shower in Puerto Rico? 'What matters most is what happens next.'"

"How's the pain now?" He put a wet wash cloth on her forehead.

"Tolerable."

"Suppose I condemn what happened. It's just lip service if I go."

"You're not condoning anything, or absolving anyone. You're *overcoming* them. It's like Barenboim bringing Wagner to Jerusalem or . . . or Eisner taking over Disney. They're not sympathizers or sell-outs. They're . . ."

"Übermenschen," he said.

"Exactly. You have to do it." She threw her head back and let out a primal scream. "I can't talk anymore. Where the hell is that *puta* doctor, *maldita sea*. Get her in here now and get this kid out of me!"

Noah Stein was born at 10:18 a.m. The twisting, slimy umbilical cord glistened in the harsh glare of the hospital lights. For perhaps the first time in his life, Jonathan suppressed the urge to make a nerdy space joke about Noah's EVA (extra-vehicular activity). He smiled at Susana, her hair soaked with perspiration, her glassy eyes fixed in a postpartum dream. After a moment of hesitation, he looked to the doctor for a nod of approval and clipped the cord.

With tiny fists held tight against his chest, Noah let out a piercing wail. The doctor looked pleased with the effort. Jonathan cradled him while a nurse put drops in his eyes. Noah had thick black hair, just like Jonathan's baby pictures. The cries came in waves, full of distress. Susana reached for her son, ready to nurse. Jonathan stroked his arm to soothe him. It felt like pure silk. He pecked a kiss on Noah's forehead and whispered in his ear. He had wanted the first words to be in Hebrew. "I promise I'll come back to you."

18

April 24, 2005
10:54AM

On the morning of the bris, Noah awoke without any notion he was about to get his first lesson in irony. A sharp cut would separate him from his foreskin and forever link him to his forefathers. Jonathan had struggled with the ritual more than his lapsed Catholic wife. During the third trimester of Susana's pregnancy, they spent several nights, just before sleep, searching for some rationale beyond the inertial pull of an ancient tribal rite and its uneasy echo of blood sacrifice. The night before the ceremony was no different.

"He should look like you, shouldn't he?"

"That's procrustean. What would I do to my son if I'd lost an arm in a childhood accident? Buy a hacksaw?"

"That's ridiculous. It reduces the risk of infections. That's good enough for me. Besides, no man really looks good in a turtleneck."

Jonathan couldn't debate the medical benefits and deferred on aesthetics, but the issue of consent—given the act's irreversibility—continued to trouble him. Noah had again refused sleep, crying relentlessly unless he was held. Jonathan carried him back and forth along the upstairs hallway like a sentry on guard duty. Susana returned him to the bassinet after a midnight feeding.

"Can we really make this decision for Noah? Is it fair?"

"Our little bundle of insomnia didn't ask for you and me to be his parents, didn't even ask to be born. How is *that* fair? He wouldn't even exist without medical intervention. Suffrage can come later."

"I'm not convinced."

"You really want to cancel?"

Jonathan rolled toward his side of the bed. "No, no . . . we'll do it."

"Why then?"

"Why else? To remember."

The caterer had arrived two hours before the ceremony. Jonathan, in need of distraction, inspected the preparations with military scrutiny. The kitchen countertops had disappeared beneath silver platters loaded with bagels, smoked fish, and spreads, and he sampled all of it. Blintz soufflés baked in the double oven. The granite-topped island of Madagascar had become the mother of all omelet stations. Bow-tied young men from the valet service waited in the circular drive. The weather was sunny, warm, and slightly humid. Two-top tables, draped in white linen, surrounded the pool. A jazz combo had arrived at 10:30 a.m. and set up under the pergola. Neat rows of mimosas and Bloody Marys lined the outdoor bar. Jonathan had one of each.

Around fifty guests milled about the living room, men in blazers and sport coats, their collars open, women in knee-length skirts, designer silk blouses, and low heels. A small group had drifted out by the pool. The ceremony would be delayed. The *mohel* had gotten lost. Jonathan patiently gave him directions over the phone—again. A judicious desire to stay on the good side of the man about to slice off a piece of his son kept any hint of irritation out of his voice.

Zubin burst through the front door, straight from the airport. Cradling two glasses and an open bottle of Veuve Clicquot, he dragged Jonathan from the kitchen into Susana's home office. "I didn't see Dale out there. Isn't he coming?" Zubin filled their glasses.

Jonathan slumped on a daybed, yawning as he spoke. "Reshooting commercials in L.A."

"Adult diapers or medical bracelets?"

"Laxatives."

"No shit?"

"Bingo."

"Have you—"

"Not yet."

"When?"

"He's back in the office tomorrow . . . so am I."

Eva knocked on the door and entered without waiting for a reply. "The *mohel* called again. He promises he's *only* ten minutes away. Susana's upstairs feeding." Eva sat next to Jonathan to kick off her heels. "I never wear these things anymore." She stood up and wiggled her toes. "Much better." She opened a window blind to let in a gush of sunlight. "Those are my favorite," she said, pointing to a mature Bismarck palm, its ghostly silver fronds waving in the breeze. "They look so out of place, like they're frozen, or unfinished." She pressed a hand flat against the pane, her eyes fixed on the tree. "'In their highest boughs the world rustles, their roots rest in infinity; but they do not lose themselves there, they struggle with all the force of their lives for one thing only: to fulfill themselves according to their own laws, to build up their own form, to represent themselves. Nothing is holier, nothing is more exemplary than a beautiful, strong tree.'"

"Joyce Kilmer?" Zubin asked.

"Hesse," Jonathan said, before his mother could answer.

"Did Jon ever tell you about that tree poem he found in Armstrong's desk? What a weirdo. Trees. Maybe he missed them up there on the Moon."

"I think I would remember if Jon had mentioned a poem," Eva said, eyes dropped to the floor.

"You would have liked it," Jonathan said. "It was about trees, not really *about* trees. It was like all poems—poetry, sex, or death. A bit overdone, but it felt like—" Jonathan left his mouth half-open as he looked back and forth between his mother and Zubin. Eva stared out the window like a statue.

"Zudu, give us a minute."

Zubin grabbed the bottle and left.

"Mom." Eva turned from the window. "You wrote that poem."

She looked frail, shrunken. "I can't believe he kept it after all these years."

Jonathan felt his cheeks turn red. He leaned back, bracing himself on the bed. One hand came down unevenly on a threadbare teddy bear he'd won for Susana at a street carnival in Boston. He swept it to the floor. His chin scraped his chest as he shook his head. Had that been it? A jilted lover? *That's* what the silence was about? "What the hell, Mom? How could you? You know what he meant to me. Jesus." He kicked one of her heels across the room. "What about Dad?"

"Let me explain, Jonathan." She tried to sit next to him, but he sprung up, pinning himself against the closed door.

"Go ahead, what is it? You're not going to tell me you two were just pen pals? I know that's not true."

She began her story. Her voice was fragile, halting. It had been a chance meeting at a charity event on the Cape, a few months before Avi's launch. He was away, training in Houston. Armstrong stood rigid like the Tin Man until he learned she was an art teacher. "If your dad had been there and I hadn't drunk those old-fashioneds, I would have never had the guts to speak to him. Seeing Neil Armstrong at a Cape Canaveral fundraiser was like . . . it was like bumping into Howard Hughes at the corner grocery . . . or a total eclipse."

Armstrong told her he loved Warhol's Campbell soup series and the Lichtenstein comic strips. She asked him if it might have had something to do with celebrity and popular culture. She mentioned an ongoing pop art exhibit at an Orlando gallery. She was so surprised he asked her to go she didn't know how to say no. "Everybody knew he never drank, smoked, or went to parties," she said, looking up at Jonathan. "Complete oddball. We all thought it made sense for him to have been the first man on the Moon—like a homecoming. Who would have guessed he was an art lover?" She snatched a tissue from Susana's desk. She blew her nose and dabbed at teary eyes, checking Jonathan with a peripheral glance.

"So that's how it began," he said. He remembered the drowning girl in Armstrong's living room.

"There was no 'it,' Jonathan. It was one foolish afternoon, temporary insanity." She looked at the ceiling. "Neil seemed so lost. I felt like I was filling a vacuum or something. I should have never agreed to meet him, but there was this powerful emptiness. I don't know what I was thinking." She locked eyes with her son. "I regretted it immediately." She took another tissue, blowing her nose as she spoke. "He wanted to see me again, but that would have been like putting my tongue on a January flagpole. When I said we shouldn't see each other, he withdrew his proposition like it was a clerical error. We never spoke again after that day, *that one day.*"

Jonathan slumped in Susana's chair. He imagined Armstrong shredding all of his unopened letters, burning them. A framed picture from his wedding day sat on the desk. Jonathan and Susana had posed on the beach in Arecibo, where they first met, barefoot and laughing in the surf. On the wall above it hung a scroll with Chinese calligraphy, a gift from a Beijing university where Susana had given a lecture on Hawking radiation. Jonathan didn't know what it said, but its bold strokes and delicate curls looked decisive, like a judgment. He wanted to scold his mother, reproach her for betraying his dad, for causing her son years of needless frustration and anguish.

"I've been unfaithful to Susana."

Time stood still when he said it. Only his mother's slow nod restarted the clock. "It's happening now?" she asked.

"No, a few times, maybe more, circumstances and alcohol. It was never an affair. Temporary insanity." He sat next to his mother. She put an arm around him. "Should I tell her? Did you ever tell Dad?"

She squeezed a spent tissue ball and tilted her head against his. "Of course not. Why would you? I never stopped loving your father. I know you love Susana. It would be selfish. We have to bear our own sins. Why should they share the load? It was a mistake, Jonathan. We all make them."

"What about the poem?"

"I mailed it to him two days after. My head was swirling with how the media manufactures images, distorts reality, how no one would ever really know what was inside Neil Armstrong's head. His rectitude, his stillness, even the quiet of that *goyishe* middle name of his."

"Alden," Jonathan whispered.

"It all made me think of trees."

"You're the reason he never wrote me back."

Twin trails of tears striped her face. "I wrote to him too, when you did, begged him to respond to you. I thought about ghost-writing replies, like the gentiles do for Santa Claus, but I couldn't mislead you . . . and I couldn't tell you the truth either. I just wanted you to let it go. I never dreamed it would take this long."

"Does Dale know?" he asked.

"I didn't tell him. I wouldn't risk it. I didn't know what Dale might say, how Neil might react. And I was ashamed."

"Armstrong never contacted you after Dad died?" Jonathan worried that he had to add another suspect to the list.

"Not a peep. He shrunk back inside himself like a turtle."

"You think he knows anything about Dad, or Schottstenger?"

Jonathan had given his mother a status report after the visit with Naughton and finally convinced her to listen to the recording. She couldn't explain Avi's behavior, but it didn't change her mind about the cause of death. "Neil Armstrong is completely irrelevant, son. Even Cassandra knew he was only good for bait."

"I'm springing the tape on Dale tomorrow, first thing."

"Jonathan, don't get your hopes up, if 'hope' is even the right word. He's not covering up a murder. You know where I stand on that." Eva grasped her son's hands and spoke in a fortified baritone. "Dale probably knew more about the Nazis than he let on. I'm sure they all knew more. Sounded like even your dad maybe knew more. Dale is military to the core. In his mind, soldiers don't air dirty laundry. That's what I think."

Jonathan stood near the window and pressed his hand against Eva's palm print. "That's why Dad needed forgiveness. He chose the future over the past. He put the mission first. He should have said something."

Eva stood behind him and wrapped her arms around his waist. "If he knew, it must have been eating him up inside. He would've spoken out if he had more time. His launch was declared a national holiday in Israel, remember? It was a dark time, and he was a beacon of hope. You can't fault him for that. Would you have done any different?" Jonathan turned to face his mother, his own eyes overflowing.

She drew him closer and whispered, "Now it's your time. You have the chance to go . . . *and* to speak for him."

Noah's shrieks were chilling but short-lived. The *mohel* left with the parents' thanks and a wad of cash in his pocket. The guests plucked cocktails from the bar as they circled the pool. Once color returned to their cheeks, the relieved couple split up to mingle among their guests. Grandma kept Noah inside. After a smooth set of Brubeck and Desmond, the band broke into klezmer. A frenzied clarinet spun intricate, driving melodies, shifting back and forth between major and minor keys, then slowed *subito* for a poignant gypsy motif. Jonathan felt a shudder in his chest. His eyes welled behind mirrored sunglasses. He thought about that long-lost cousin—in his imagination always a petite, gap-toothed girl with long, red-ribboned pigtails—wailing on a licorice stick like her legendary landsman, Artie Shaw (Arthur Jacob Arshawsky).

"It's because we can't forget."

The bittersweet interlude hung on a long-wavering final note as if it were about to fall off a cliff. As the spent clarinet teetered on the brink, the other instruments rescued it with a raucous, full-throttle crescendo to the end. Vigorous applause echoed across the water. Jonathan understood why Armstrong had safeguarded that poem, and why the Jews say *kaddish* at every bar mitzvah.

19

April 25, 2005

8:12AM

Jonathan sat at his desk, exhausted. He'd spent half the night pretending to ice skate while singing "Old McDonald" and "Baby Beluga" to his restless son. The morning sun glinted off gentle ripples wrinkling the bay. A dozen sailboats, anchored at even distances, their sails still furled tight, rocked like bassinets. A lone fishing boat chugged toward deeper waters, its spreading wake like a zipper opening the ocean.

Lunden poked his head into Jonathan's office. "You wanted to see me?" He carried a Fisher-Price airplane play set and a box of cigars.

Jonathan waved him in. "Thanks." He placed the gifts on the credenza.

"Sorry I couldn't make it yesterday. Got in pretty late. Thought you might give the boy his first flying lesson." Lunden stood behind a guest chair, gripping its back with both hands. Dressed in a navy-blue suit and a tightly knotted red tie, he'd apparently skipped his morning workout. Jonathan remained seated, his chin nearly touched his chest, his eyes rolled up.

Lunden picked up a picture from Jonathan's desk—Noah swaddled in a white hospital blanket with blue and pink stripes and topped with a tiny stocking cap, his parents cradling him. "Looks like his momma, thank god." Lunden winked. "The Stein name marches on."

"Have a seat, Dale. I need to tell you something. After my dad died, I started writing letters to Neil Armstrong. I did it for years."

"Did he ever write back?"

"Never. Nothing."

"Why didn't you tell me?"

"I thought you'd be jealous, like your friendship and your support weren't enough. I didn't want to hurt your feelings." Jonathan rolled a twisting rubber band in his fingers as he spoke.

"Heck, I wouldn't have cared. Did your mom know?"

"Yeah, she told me it was a waste of time. 'Armstrong's a shut-in, weirdo,' she'd say." Jonathan intended to safeguard his mother's indiscretion.

"Some astronauts never get over the Moon," Lunden said. He leaned forward, forearms pressed against his thighs. "Neil was one of them. I always kept my distance, which was pretty easy since he was almost never around." Lunden plucked a fountain pen from its marble base and scribbled in the air. "Soon little kids will start writing to you."

Jonathan flashed a copy of the *New York Times*. "A new Pope was just inaugurated."

"Nothing we Lutherans pay much attention to."

"He was in the Hitler Youth, they say."

"I don't think the little German kids had any choice, eh?"

"Just following orders works for children, doesn't it? I want you to listen to something, something I found in the National Archives." Jonathan crossed the room to cue a CD player sitting on a low bookcase beneath the painting of Avi Stein seated at a mock control console. Lunden turned halfway around toward the speakers.

When the interview began, Lunden blanched. "Where did you find it? How'd you—"

Jonathan raised his hand to stop him. "Wait. Just wait. Listen first." His stare soldered Lunden to the chair. When the replay had ended, Jonathan sat next to him.

"Jon, let me explain."

"Stop. Look at this." Jonathan reached for a stack of papers on his desk. He handed Lunden the Dachau experiments list from Nuremberg and explained what it was. "I know exactly what tolerances my father was talking about." Jonathan underlined a name with his finger. "Dr. Schottstenger gave NASA the results of gruesome tests at Dachau, and this country used them to come up with the specs to outfit the Mercury astronauts." He overstated the certainty of his theory, hoping to encourage Lunden to surrender the truth. "That's what my Dad was talking about, that kind of tolerance. And you knew it too, didn't you? Instead of getting justice for my dad or exposing a war criminal at NASA, you did your best Dick Nixon and covered it up. Godspeed. No looking back, right?"

Lunden stared at the list, his head hung low, avoiding eye contact. "Why didn't you come to me sooner? I thought you gave up on that stupid website. For Pete's sake, why didn't you come talk to me?"

"I spoke to the reporter, Naughton. I know you took the tape. Why'd you do it? Why did you say there wasn't anything strange before launch? I asked you for help."

Lunden cleared his throat. "I feel terrible," he whispered. Jonathan felt worse, like he'd passed over the high point on a roller coaster, his stomach floating out of his body. "Avi told me a story about Schottstenger and those goddamned experiments. I didn't listen. I didn't believe it, didn't believe *him*." He handed the list back to Jonathan. "Obviously, I should have."

The confession that Jonathan had hoped for still staggered him. He slumped against the armrest, unable to speak. He had expected Lunden to fight back, to challenge his assertions. The sudden surrender felt like a sucker punch. The room seemed to snap in and out of focus. He counted his breaths—One . . . Two . . . Three . . . Four—to settle down. "Why not, Dale? Didn't believe him, or didn't want any trip-ups on your victory march to the stars?"

Lunden, his eyes glazed and red at the corners, looked at Jonathan. "He wouldn't tell me how he knew. He was so damn squirrelly about it, never wanted to give me any proof. It was personal, he said. Told me not to ask any questions. Then he had the heart attack. There were rumors flying around NASA that he was a spy. Did you know that?"

Jonathan suppressed his own suspicions, fearful that any acknowledgement of the possibility might encourage Lunden to spin a diversionary tale of espionage, a smokescreen to let the truth get away. "It was personal because my grandfather was murdered at Dachau," he said.

"That much I knew," Lunden said, "but Avi never explained how he found out about the doctor. When he told me about this Nazi experiments business, the way he was acting, all hush-hush, cloak-and-dagger, I thought maybe he was a spook. With the good ones, of course, you never know. I told him it all sounded like dive bar scuttlebutt. It did too." Lunden cleared his throat again, said he needed water. He filled a pointed paper cup from a water cooler in the corner of Jonathan's office. As he drank, he stepped in front of the bay-facing windows, a backlit shadow. "You think conspiracy theories are big now, but back then, you have no idea. JFK, Martin Luther King, Malcolm X, Bobby, Watergate. Shit, everybody had one on the tip of his tongue. Fucking D. B. Cooper jumped out of that Northwest Orient flight in 1971 with a parachute and $200,000 in ransom, disappeared into thin air. Nothing was too crazy." Lunden paused to examine Avi's vintage lunar globe. Jonathan assumed he was looking for his old landing spot. "I couldn't get your dad to back it up. Maybe he couldn't. Hell if I know." Lunden shook his head and pointed a bouncing finger at Jonathan. "But you're right, I didn't want to get involved in any international intrigue either."

"Wasn't it your job to be involved?" Jonathan joined him at the windows, facing the bay. "You weren't ordered to keep tabs?"

"You mean counterintelligence?"

"Why not?"

"No, sir. Never happened. I was just a fellow astronaut and a friend."

"What about the tape?" Jonathan spun the moon globe back and forth in semicircles. Outside, the marinas were waking up. A hodge-podge of sailboats, yachts, and trailing kayaks formed an accidental flotilla heading east.

Lunden arched his back, wincing. He rubbed the base of his spine with both hands. "Right before launch, your dad was set on quitting the program, making a big stink in the press." Both men gazed over the water as if trying to see past the horizon. "Imagine that. Weeks from blastoff, he was about to jump in a T-38 and hightail it straight to Woodward and Bernstein. I talked him out of it, told him if he went public without backup he'd end up fucked like Linda Lovelace, and that was the wrong kind of deep throat. That's just what I told him. As the mission got closer, boy I could tell he was about to pop. When it got to that last interview, he could hardly hold it in."

"So you took the tape to protect him?"

"Damn right."

"And to protect yourself."

"To protect Avi and me and the whole program. That tape was a powder keg. He had no right to jeopardize our strategic advantage in space, especially for what seemed like rank gossip. You're too young to remember, but we couldn't afford the luxury of a clean slate back then. Missile silos were going up in cornfields every day, and I can guarantee you there were no moral quandaries in the Kremlin, that's for damn sure. We had to keep pace. Besides, burning books was what Hitler did. Told him that too. Avi promised to bite his tongue until he got back, but he hated it."

"So you're the hero I suppose?"

"Yes, I was trying to save my moon shot too. Who wouldn't? It was the Moon, Jonathan." Lunden put his hand back on the globe. "The Moon was all I ever had." He thumped his chest. "Last of the Lundens."

"That was your choice."

"You think so?"

"What's that supposed to mean?"

Lunden sank into a white leather coach. He scratched the top of his head with his eyes closed. "We all had to give samples of our seed when we started the program. They wanted to see if our swimmers would survive the cosmic rays. I thought all those years I'd been lucky whenever I went diving without a wet suit. Turns out my boys were all DOA. They said it might've been something I was exposed to in Vietnam. The Moon became my only legacy. And now I won't even be the last man." He squinted like he was pulling out a splinter. "Sure I had my own interests—and my country's, but I swear I was trying to protect Avi." Lunden planted an elbow on his knee and rubbed his temples. "I never thought I'd hear that tape again."

"And you turned down the offer to take command of Eighteen?"

Lunden paused to study Jonathan's face before answering. "At first, yes."

Jonathan returned to his stack of papers. "Exhibit C, Dale. I got the memo." It fluttered in his quivering hand. He offered it to Lunden. "You lobbied hard to get Eighteen back. You were the one who twisted arms. You didn't turn down shit."

Lunden scanned the memo and tossed it on the cushion next to him. "What was I supposed to say to you and your mom?" He stood and put his hand, a leathery boxing glove, on Jonathan's shoulder. "Yes, I lied to you. You got me." Lunden held up his hands as if he were turning himself in. "Your dad would have understood why. We were career soldiers. Avi would have done the same damn thing. The mission was more important than any one man. His heart attack was simple bad luck, like stepping on a land mine. Soldiers keep marching. I tried to make it easier on you and your mom, that's all. I asked for my mission back, but I swear on a stack of Bibles I wouldn't have ever killed for it. Jesus, Jonathan. Don't all these years count for anything?"

"Why didn't you trash the interview?" Jonathan returned at his desk and swiveled to face Lunden. "Maybe that tape was your ticket to ride?"

Lunden rolled his eyes and moved in front of Jonathan's desk. "I didn't tell anyone about it, naturally. I stuck the damn thing in Avi's locker. He wouldn't be out of quarantine until after the mission. I planned to play it for him, let him hear how crazy he sounded and explain why I'd done it. Once he passed away, they took all his personal effects. That's the last I knew of it until now." Lunden dropped in the guest chair, cradling his head like he had a hangover.

"It was in an envelope labeled 'classified—top secret,'" Jonathan said.

"Because of what I told that kid reporter. I had to give him some reason why I was taking it. I made up some bullshit about classified information to shut him up. He tell you that?"

"Nobody ever asked you about the tape? How it got in the locker?"

"I was expecting that, but it never happened. No way I was going to ask any questions." Lunden pressed his fist against the armrest, his eyes wide but unfocused. "That bit worried me. That's when I should've said something."

"Why didn't my father just go to the IDF with whatever he'd found?"

"What do you mean?" Lunden said. He glanced over his shoulder at Eva's painting of Avi and turned back to face Jonathan. "Of course he did. He went to them first. He made me drive to some flea-bag motel in Titusville about three weeks before quarantine, said he wanted an untraceable phone. I sat in my 'vette while he screamed into a parking lot pay phone for ten minutes. Don't know what the hell he said to them. *Shalom*'s the only Hebrew I ever knew, and I sure as heck didn't hear that."

Jonathan felt like he'd been zapped by a Taser. He bit his lip while his hands quaked with aftershocks.

"Your dad was on fire back to the Cape, said his superiors ordered him to stick to the mission, keep quiet. They would have been none too pleased if they had heard that interview. You don't have to believe me, Jon, but I thought I was saving your dad's career."

Jonathan had never considered the possibility that Jews had guarded the loathsome secret, but he knew Israel would put strategic considerations first. Survival in a hostile Middle East was three-dimensional chess with no piece moving in a straight line—feints and facades, public denunciations and backroom deals, straw men and sacrificial lambs. Avi once told him that the Israelis had played Kissinger like a violin, threatening the use of nuclear weapons to get tons of military supplies to repel the Egyptian and Syrian attacks of 1973. All warfare was based on deception. Jonathan refused to believe the IDF had killed his father, that would make no sense, but that it had issued a gag order was plausible, even likely. Looking forward, not back. "Did you tell anyone else what my father suspected before he died?"

"*I* didn't."

"Did my dad?"

Lunden leaned forward, grasping his knees. "He did."

"Who? Who'd he tell?"

"After the IDF crammed a lid on it and I talked your pop off the front page of the *Washington Post*, he still wouldn't let it drop. He wanted to go up the chain, here I mean." He pointed to the floor. "I told him 'no' a half-dozen times. It was a terrible idea, but he was desperate. It was almost like he knew his time was short. He could be unbelievably persistent." Lunden peered up at Jonathan. "Your dad knew about my connections to the West Wing, the chief of staff. General Chamberlain was the one who got my ass out of the jungle and into the test pilot program. Nixon was gone, but the general hadn't bugged out yet. Avi thought he could help. I told him not to rock the boat, but your dad wouldn't take no for an answer." Lunden wagged a finger at Jonathan. "It was a bad idea, and I said it, but I finally gave in, set up a meeting."

"Where?"

"At the Cape a few days before quarantine. You can probably check the general's travel logs if you want the exact date."

"Were you there?"

"Where? The archives?"

"No, the Cape, but wait a minute. What about the archives?" Jonathan imagined that Lunden had beaten him to Washington, anxious to see what was left out of the official files, determined to figure out how he might weave an expedient, flattering story that wouldn't conflict with recorded history.

"Why would I go there? You mean recently? No."

"Not worried I might find something? Maybe you're the one who told my dad about Schottstenger? Wanted to be sure you could make yourself look like the good guy?"

Lunden stood up, his stiff arms braced against the front of Jonathan's desk. "If I were a younger man, I would've laid you out on the carpet for a remark like that. After everything I've done? Don't you ever accuse me. I've had enough, Jonathan. Half the guys used to call him 'a greasy kike' behind his back, said vulgar, disgusting things about your mother. I stood up for both of them, even decked a couple of wannabe Klansmen at a bar in Rockledge. Only places I've been in the last six months are commercial shoots, Vancouver, and L.A. Check my damn credit card and phone bills if you like. I'm done with this horseshit, Jonathan. I tried to do right by my friend, best I could. And you too."

Jonathan held his hands, palms down, at his chest in a gesture that meant "settle down." "So what about the meeting at the Cape, my dad and General Chamberlain?"

"Just the two of them. Strictly off the record." Lunden took more water.

"And?"

"Your dad was disappointed. I warned him the general had become a politician. Avi told me Chamberlain had promised to make inquiries about Schottstenger but expressed doubts about the information. Your dad thought he'd been given the brush-off."

"You think the general knew the story was true?"

"We never spoke of it. I wasn't going to open up that can of worms after Avi died. That's where I was wrong. That I should've at least told Eva."

Jonathan returned to the globe. He spun it with a side-swiping slap. One . . . Two . . . Three . . . Four. And let it stop on its own. At the credenza, he picked up the picture from that last fishing trip, tilting it at different angles to watch the play of light on its surface.

"Your dad deserved better. So did you. But I didn't lie when I said Germans didn't kill your father. There's no way they could've. What was the point, after thirty years, of stirring up a controversy because of a godforsaken website? Your dad died of a heart attack. That's what I believe to this day. It's what you should believe."

"But you aren't certain, are you? You're not. I can tell. I know that look in your eye."

Lunden sighed as if too old to keep fighting. "Our government— mind you it's the best we've got in this screwed-up world—is no stranger to *force majeure*. You know the general's reputation." His eyes seemed bigger, piercing. "That possibility, still remote in my mind, has shadowed me for the last thirty years. Why should it haunt you too? You father was gone, and you were on your way to the Moon. There was no point."

"What about the Nazi experiments?"

"I'm sorry about your dad, deeply sorry. It was tragic. But I'm not sorry if we used that data to beat the Russians. I told Avi the same thing. If the Nazis had developed the polio vaccine, would you have tossed it in the incinerator?" He picked up the picture of Noah and showed it to Jonathan. "Let little kids—maybe your little kids—hobble along for the rest of their lives, leaning on principles for crutches? What good would it have done anybody at the bottom of a garbage can? I can only assume the IDF agreed with me. Or maybe they traded that guilt chip in for another airlift of Sidewinder missiles and M60 tanks from Uncle Sam."

Jonathan sat at his desk, his jaw like stone. He rapped his fist on the blotter and then stabbed the air with his finger as he spoke. "I may never be able to prove it was murder, but I intend to make damn sure that Schottstenger's name is taken off of that fucking air force library wall and out of the Space Hall of Fame. And it's going to be very public and very loud. People will know."

"If you want me to resign, I'll go quietly. I'm old enough to cite health reasons to get out of anything."

Jonathan stood up. "No, no need for that. If my father was murdered, it wasn't your fault. You should have said something, a long time ago, about the Nazis, about what my father tried to do. But you're not the only one. You shouldn't have lied to me, especially now, but I'm not going to embarrass you like that, not after everything you've done for me. You understand why I had to press you? What else could I do? I had to look back."

"I do," Lunden said. He checked his watch. "It's forgiven. Like it never even happened."

Jonathan walked around the desk and extended his hand. Lunden paused before shaking it, as if it might be booby-trapped, and pumped harder as soon as it didn't go off. "I've got a meeting tomorrow with NASA," Jonathan said, "to share the results of my investigation. I'd like you to come with me."

"Do I really have a choice?"

"I'm afraid not."

"I guess I'll be there."

20

June 19, 2005

6:53PM

In a darkened media room, Jonathan waited for the broadcast to begin. A supersize flat-screen television reflected fuzzy rows of plush stadium seats. He draped his legs over the padded armrest, balancing a vodka tonic on his stomach.

Susana entered from a side door, baby monitor in hand. "Is your mom even gonna watch?"

"She said she would, but I don't think so. Is he asleep?"

"Finally. My nipples are still so sore. It's got to get better soon. Why wouldn't she come over? She's usually dying to find an excuse to see Noah. I swear she steals something from my bag whenever we visit her just so she can bring it back the next day."

Jonathan shook his head and finished his drink. "It's buried too deep. She didn't even really want to listen when I told her what Dale said. Still believes there's no way it could have been intentional."

"I don't think it was either, Jon."

"Mom did seem pretty pissed at Dale. She even called him 'a self-centered prick.'"

"Did that make you happy?" Susana sat next to him and massaged his shoulders.

"Not happy. It's not Dale's fault, what happened, but yeah, it felt like some kind of validation, or vindication. Like we're not supposed to keep quiet. That I was right." He checked the cable box clock and turned on the television. He had arranged for an exclusive interview on a prominent Sunday evening news program three weeks after meeting with NASA. Though the NASA administrator seemed receptive to his requests and promised immediate action, Jonathan wanted the press and public opinion on the backs of the government bureaucrats.

In a classic voiceover, its scratches and timbre like stones being polished in a rock tumbler, Harry Saffit, the venerated elder statesman of TV journalism, introduced the segment. His script was synchronized to a series of stills and clips from Jonathan's life—his business successes, his political connections, his father, the announcement of the upcoming lunar mission, familiar images from NASA's lunar expeditions, and black-and-white photographs of the emaciated survivors of concentration camps.

"Jonathan Stein is a multimillionaire, an engineering and computer genius, and the CEO of Apollo Aeronautics. An ambitious man, Stein is not satisfied with his impressive earthly accomplishments. He wants to shoot for the Moon. Literally. Stein, the son of an astronaut who never made it to space, is intent on being the first man to set foot on the lunar surface in over thirty years. While that story alone would be worth telling, our report is about something else. He's made a startling discovery about what our government was apparently willing to do to beat the Soviets in the space race. How he uncovered that secret is almost as remarkable as the secret itself. Through a combination of conspiracy theory, a fascination with Neil Armstrong, and some old-fashioned detective work, Stein learned that the National Aeronautics and Space Administration, NASA, likely relied on scientific data obtained through barbaric experiments on prisoners in Nazi death camps. This so-called "blood data," it appears, was brought to the United States by at least one former Third Reich scientist to aid in the design specifications for the protective clothing worn by American astronauts in the early 1960s. The scientist, Horst Schottstenger, was part of something known as Operation Paperclip."

A montage *qua* history lesson followed—newsreel clips of Wernher von Braun and grainy Nazi rocket test footage, accompanied by Saffit's description of the secret government program that brought German scientists and engineers, including several loyal Nazi Party members, to the United States after World War II to work on rocketry and chemical and biological weapons.

"What's more," Saffit continued, "Stein believes that his father may have discovered this startling secret thirty years ago, and that Avi Stein's death two days before launch, officially ruled a heart attack, may have been the result of foul play, an effort to keep that dark secret from seeing the light of day."

"Who's gonna play you in the movie?" Susana asked.

"Yeah, right. Maybe I'll play myself." Jonathan had already imagined Leonardo DiCaprio or Matt Damon in the role.

Saffit interviewed Jonathan in his office. After he described Cassandra's website and his visit to the National Archives, a clip from Avi's interview was played. Jonathan recounted the trip to Armstrong's house, the content of the journals, and the assistance of the research center in Berlin in corroborating his suspicions about Schottstenger. Saffit explained that the network was unable to locate Cassandra despite extensive efforts. The website had been taken down without warning days after the search had begun. Jonathan confirmed his own efforts had likewise been unsuccessful.

An excerpt of Lunden's interview followed. At his request, Saffit interviewed him in front of the Apollo 18 capsule at the Smithsonian's Air and Space Museum in Washington. Lunden, wearing his shiniest medals pinned over his heart, repeated what he'd told Jonathan about his father's discovery, the IDF's response, and the August 1974 meeting between Avi Stein and General Chamberlain. "If the White House and Israel weren't going to do anything about the doctor, who was I to buck the chain of command?" he said. When asked about Avi's death, Lunden stated categorically that it was "natural causes" and that the general was blameless. Saffit quoted a letter to the network from the late general's family condemning "in the strongest terms" the insinuation that he might have engaged in any foul play to silence the Israeli astronaut.

"You think they'll sue?" Susana asked.

"They won't. You can't defame the dead. That's what my lawyer says. Plus, I haven't even accused him. It's not like I think the general went rogue. If something happened, it was bureaucratic, faceless, like a hooded executioner. That's how I explained it to Saffit. Of course, they cut that part out."

A prepared statement from an IDF media liaison scrolled on the screen. Having declined an on-camera appearance, the IDF categorically denied any communication from Avi Stein regarding Dr. Schottstenger or NASA's use of Nazi torture data to design space suits. A thorough and expedited investigation, conducted after Jonathan provided his information to the Israeli ambassador to the United States, revealed no indication that the IDF had ever received any such report from Stein. The statement concluded with a call for the United States to publish a full accounting of the German scientists and engineers brought to the United States after World War II, including an official apology for the harboring of Nazi war criminals.

After a commercial break and a brief recap, the segment cut to an interview of NASA Administrator S.W. Rockwell. A polished politician, Rockwell assured Saffit that NASA had conducted an exhaustive search of its records once Jonathan had brought the Schottstenger journals and the Nuremberg document to its attention. To date, NASA had found nothing about German wartime research on human tolerances, but the administrator acknowledged that Schottstenger was instrumental in early space suit designs.

SAFFIT: Did NASA have any idea that Schottstenger supervised prisoner experiments at Dachau?

ROCKWELL: Harry, we just learned about Mr. Stein's discoveries a few weeks ago. Since then, we have combed through all the personnel records we could find, in every archive available. All we could locate was a record of Schottstenger's various posts as a doctor and scientist for the German government and several of his early academic articles from the 1930s and '40s on the emerging field of aviation medicine. No record nor article that we've uncovered indicates his participation in prisoner experiments during the war.

SAFFIT: You've personally inspected the document from the Nuremberg records, I presume?

ROCKWELL: I have, Harry, and of course, even though it was over sixty years ago, we're deeply concerned. We've launched a full investigation into the matter, and to that end, we've already requested extensive information from the German government. They've promised their full cooperation. We hope to turn up whatever we can.

SAFFIT: And if it's true? There's an air force medical library named after Dr. Schottstenger, isn't there? In Houston? Is this someone we, as a nation, really want to honor?

ROCKWELL: We can't rush to judgment. He's entitled to due process after all. The doctor has a thirty-year history of dedicated work on behalf of the American space program. His contribution was instrumental to our success. And that's the sole basis for the naming honor: his science. We're not celebrating anything about the Third Reich. So how do we balance the value of scientific breakthrough against the imperfections of any man's soul? That's really the question, isn't it? Personally, I believe the doctor does deserve some credit for his decades of valuable service to this country. However, if, after our investigation, we turn up evidence of his complicity in war crimes, names can always be changed.

SAFFIT: So you would at least consider that?

ROCKWELL: Absolutely, we'd consider it, after a careful review of the evidence, if the facts warrant.

SAFFIT: And there's an annual space award named after Schottstenger. What about that?

ROCKWELL: That's given out by a nongovernmental organization. I've got no jurisdiction there.

SAFFIT: So that means?

ROCKWELL: So that means no comment.

SAFFIT: How many Jews have ever won the doctor's award?

ROCKWELL: I have no idea.

SAFFIT: Care to speculate?

ROCKWELL: Nice try, but I'll pass.

SAFFIT: What about the Kurt Debus Award? How many Jews
               have been honorees?

ROCKWELL: Same answer. It's given out by a private club, and I
               haven't got a clue.

SAFFIT: No dispute that former Kennedy Space Center Director
               Debus was in the SS?

ROCKWELL: No dispute. I'm happy to say I've never been nominated
               for it. But if I were Jewish—

SAFFIT: Excuse me. Why does that matter? Do you have to be
               black to hate the KKK?

ROCKWELL: You're right. I'd rather have a congressional medal any-
               way. Who wouldn't?

SAFFIT: With all due respect, sir, you haven't really addressed
               what seems a straightforward question. I'm not asking
               you the perhaps more difficult question of whether our
               government should have employed ex-Nazis in the first
               place. I simply want to know if we should ever have any
               awards, buildings, or institutions named after men who
               once faithfully served our enemies during the war, and
               worse yet, perhaps perpetrated war crimes.

ROCKWELL: I think I've been quite clear about our position based on
               what we currently know. You can ask me to speculate
               all you want, but I'm an engineer, not a philosopher.
               Speculation is not my job. I've gone as far as I'm willing
               to go at this point.

SAFFIT: No more comment then, I presume?

ROCKWELL: That's correct. Let's move on.

SAFFIT: What about Neil Armstrong? He wouldn't respond to
               our requests for an interview. Have you been able to
               talk to him? Learn what he knows?

ROCKWELL: I am in contact with Neil Armstrong. I'm satisfied that he has nothing to add to our investigation.

SAFFIT: Why won't he talk to us?

ROCKWELL: As you know, Harry, Neil Armstrong is a very private man with no love for the media. I selfishly wish he would speak publicly, and not only on this particular matter. But he's lived a very quiet retirement for decades and wants to keep it that way. I think we have to respect that.

SAFFIT: Now I'm going to ask you this, not seeking an official finding, just your opinion. From what you've seen and heard, do you personally believe Schottstenger participated in war crimes and that his particular type of participation—involuntary human experiments on Jews or homosexuals or Slavs or Gypsies, torture really— likely benefitted the early days of NASA's manned space program?

ROCKWELL: Harry, again, I don't want to rush to judgment, but at this point, we have to acknowledge it's highly possible.

SAFFIT: "Highly possible." If it's true, was it OK to use this "blood data"?

ROCKWELL: If NASA knew where it came from?

SAFFIT: If it knew.

ROCKWELL: No. NASA could've eventually developed the technology without what you call "blood data." We should not have knowingly used information, even if valuable, if it came to us as the result of the brutalization of unwilling human subjects.

SAFFIT: What about information we get from Guantanamo Bay detainees? Government officials know exactly where it's coming from, and they also know how it's gotten. The US intelligence community, many would say, uses that kind of "blood data" every day. Should it stop?

ROCKWELL: I'm not a part of the intelligence or military communi-
            ties. I'm a civilian. I can't speak for them. I speak for
            NASA. I'm not about to get into a discussion about what
            our government should or should not do during an
            ongoing war against terrorist enemy combatants who've
            taken up arms against the United States. That's a conver-
            sation you'll have to have with someone at the Defense
            Department.

"He's really good, smooth." Susana said.

"I know. It's so hard to tell with American politicians. All of them,
with a few exceptions like Nixon, are either avuncular or the boy next
door. You know you can't spell 'Rockwell' without 'Orwell.' Why can't
our crooks be easier to spot, like Berlusconi or Putin?"

The administrator—in contrast to his wait-and-see approach regarding the allegations about Schottstenger—denied any possibility that Avi
Stein was murdered, citing the lack of evidence, the restricted access
of prelaunch quarantine, and the thorough postmortem examination.

"He should've been a press secretary, this guy," Jonathan said.

"You can't realistically expect him to say anything else at this
point," Susana said.

The administrator concluded his interview by reaffirming his
promise to Jonathan that, with the assistance of the Defense and
Justice Departments, a full and expeditious inquiry into Schottstenger
and his father's death would be concluded. The segment ended with
a final round of questions for Jonathan.

SAFFIT: I'd like to focus on your allegations against Schottstenger.
            At least at this point, Mr. Stein, you've got no book of
            human tolerances, no record of any specific camp exper-
            iments personally conducted by Schottstenger during
            the war, and no evidence, witnesses, or documents from
            NASA to indicate that his wartime work, whatever it
            was, helped put the Mercury, Gemini, and Apollo astro-
            nauts into space. It's more than a conspiracy theory but
            a theory nonetheless, wouldn't you agree?

STEIN: It's much more than that. Let's look at what we know. Schottstenger was a high-ranking Luftwaffe researcher in the field of aviation medicine who supervised scientists conducting prisoner experiments at Dachau. Incidentally, we've recently learned from the German government that the doctor authorized involuntary experiments on epileptic German children to study hypoxia in a pressure chamber as his research institute. At Dachau, the scientists weren't running any endurance tests on prison guards. I'm quite sure of that, and I have no doubt that the knowledge gained from the freezing and pressure tests, whether written into a book of tolerances or recorded in the dark recesses of the doctor's mind, traveled across the Atlantic Ocean, via American transport, and ended up woven into the fabric, quite literally, of the space program. Obsessed with beating the Soviets, we made the texture of those first space suits more important than our own moral fiber.

SAFFIT: You're going up in outer space yourself. Quite soon.

STEIN: True. About five months.

SAFFIT: Technological development is accretive, building on years of past research, correct?

STEIN: Correct.

SAFFIT: So you will be benefitting, though in a very indirect, attenuated way, from Schottstenger's work. How do you feel about that?

STEIN: That's a complicated question, one I've thought about, a lot. I'm appalled at what Schottstenger did and the Faustian deals our government made with the Nazis. (He raised a closed hand to his mouth and cleared his throat.) And, of course, the possibility a ruthless pragmatism silenced my father—

SAFFIT: And perhaps your grandfather too, who died at Dachau.

STEIN: That too. It's possible, yes. (His head twitched. He cleared his throat again.)

SAFFIT: I know this must be hard to talk about.

STEIN: Sorry, no, it's fine. I can't . . . I can't undo the past—

SAFFIT: And you can't bring them back?

Jonathan looked away from the television screen. "The bastard thinks he's Barbara Walters. He's supposed to be a real journalist. I wasn't gonna let him get me teary-eyed like some misunderstood pop star who just wants to be loved."

STEIN: I can't bring them back, Harry. I can't. I know that. So what do I do now? I can educate. I can strip away the whitewash covering the stained hands of the Operation Paperclip scientists and engineers. I can take them down off of their pedestals and put them in context. And I can go to the Moon. I do no honor to the memory of my father, or his dream, if I stay on the ground in indulgent protest. We must move forward *differently*, *openly*, but we must still move forward as we begin our emigration to the stars.

"That was great, Jon," Susana said. She climbed into his lap and wrapped her arms around him. "I think you're ready to go." She pressed her lips against his forehead.

"Almost," he said.

21

October 13, 2005

10:56AM

A delivery truck rolled down the narrow dirt road lined with mature spruce and fir. After several sharp turns and three stream crossings, it parked in front of a weather-beaten log cabin next to a small Michigan lake. The utility poles had ended miles back.

A man dressed in a brown shirt and pants and matching baseball cap got out of the driver's side of the truck, a thick envelope in hand. The laminated company ID clipped to his breast pocket read "Gene" in big block letters. Another man, "Ray," identically dressed, got out of the passenger side. Both men wore dark sunglasses. Gene was clean-shaven, and Ray had a thick beard. After knocking on the front door a few times and calling "anybody home," they checked the back of the cabin. A long dock extended out from the lakeshore. In a lawn chair at the very end, a man sat fishing. They walked toward the lake down a small hill littered with brown-orange pine needles.

"Maybe you should call out to him," Ray said.

"Not to a man with a fishing pole in his hand," Gene said. "I did that once to my daddy when it was time for supper. Got slapped across the mouth."

They approached the fisherman so as not to startle him nor the fish. As he neared the seated angler, Gene cleared his throat and said, almost whispering, "Excuse me, sir . . . sir . . . ."

The old man turned his head but remained in his chair, rod in hand. "You two must be lost. Turn around and go back three miles, then turn right at the red barn with the old silo and go another two miles to the gas station. They can help you find whatever address you're looking for."

"No, sir," Gene said. "I think we are in the right place. Are you Neil Armstrong?"

"Yes," he said, bushy eyebrows raised.

"I have a package for you."

"What the hell. I never give out this address."

"Sir. I am just the deliveryman. This here is my trainee, Ray. Dispatch gave me the address and directions. We drove an awful long way to get here so I really hope you will sign for it. Otherwise, they are liable to send us right back here again tomorrow."

Armstrong seized the envelope and studied the address label. The return address indicated the package came from a law firm in Miami.

"You're not a process server, are you? How did a lawyer find me? I never told any of my lawyers about this place. Maria doesn't even have the address."

"Sir," Gene said, "them lawyers are real good at finding people. My ex-wife's lawyer hunted me down six times all over the country." Armstrong face scrunched like a prune. "Mr. Armstrong, the dispatcher told me I am supposed to wait for you to open it. Apparently, there might be something to return."

"This is just insane." Armstrong pointed to the sky. "Do I have to go all the way back up there to get away from people?"

Gene shrugged his shoulders and looked intently at Ray, who, after a brief instant of confusion, added his own shrug. Armstrong opened the package and found a letter explaining that a space enthusiast client wanted the astronaut to be the executor of his will. "Executor? I don't even know this guy. And at my age?" The letter further provided that if Armstrong declined he could simply check the box at the bottom of the first page, indicating his refusal, and sign the second page, which was blank except for a line for the date and a signature line with Armstrong's name typed below. The package included a return envelope. Armstrong took the second page and placed it on his tackle box for a writing surface. Ray offered him a pen. Armstrong scribbled his name and handed the letter and the rest of the package back to Gene.

"You don't sound like you're from around here," Armstrong said.

He picked up his rod to make a cast.

"No sir," Gene said. "Like I said, I have had some domestic issues. It keeps me on the go. You have a good day now."

Gene hesitated before heading back to shore.

"Mr. Armstrong, it sure would tickle me and Ray if we could shake your hand."

"Make it quick, and I'm not getting up."

They approached and each did a firm, two-pump handshake.

"Nice to meet you, sir," Ray said. "And thank you."

"For what?"

"For getting us to the Moon. We'll be on our way now."

"That is a really nice tackle box," Gene said. "I do some fishing myself. I used to do more when I was a kid, with my daddy. Here, let me show you. I keep it in my wallet." The deliveryman put the package on the dock and withdrew a torn and heavily creased photograph held together with jaundiced Scotch tape. An aluminum johnboat floated perpendicular to the muddy bank of a small river. "Me and my pops after he got out on the parole. Ran the fastest chop shop in town. Look at the size of that thing." A young boy, shirtless with a missing incisor and a crew cut, stood in the front, holding up a fat, sallow-bellied catfish. His father sat in the back, one hand on the outboard motor, the other clutching a beer can.

Armstrong gave an obligatory glance. "Nice fish," he managed.

"That was a good one. Right, Ray?"

"Good eating," Ray mumbled.

"You got that right," Gene said. "We devoured her that night. Nothing like deep-fried catfish you caught yourself. Would you mind if I took a peek at your lures before I go?"

"Make it fast, and, for God's sake, don't make any noise," Armstrong said, through clenched teeth. "These jittery trout will turn off in a snap if they get startled."

Gene opened the box and lifted the top tray to expose the inventory. "Look at that, I caught a lot of fish on a jig just like this one." He stood to show Armstrong, stepped on the open lid of the tackle box, and spilled its loud contents all over the dock.

"Jesus Christ! That's it. I won't catch a fish all day."

"I am awful sorry, sir," Gene said. "I will pick up everything and put it right back where it was."

"Don't bother. Just go. Please go away."

"No sir, no bother. No trouble at all."

All three men bent over at the same time. Gene leaned to avoid a head butt with Armstrong and knocked off his fishing hat.

"Good lord! Can you please leave me alone? Go. Now."

Gene picked up the fallen hat and held it against his chest. "Sir, I am deeply sorry for the mess. We will get going. I apologize again for the inconvenience. Please do not call my company to complain. I was hoping to keep this job for a while."

"Just go back the way you came, and don't either one of you tell anyone about this place."

"That is a deal, sir. Your secret is safe with us," Gene said. "Right, Ray?"

"Right."

The two men started to retreat, but Armstrong called out, "My hat!"

"I'm so sorry, sir." Gene jogged to the end of the dock. "Here you go."

Inside the truck, Gene started the engine and put on the CD player, "Lonesome Road Blues," a classic rendition by Lester Flatt and Earl Scruggs.

"That was unbelievable, Wyatt." Jonathan laughed as he removed his baseball cap and fake beard. "You missed you're calling. Jesus, you shouldn't be a tow truck driver. You're a freaking natural. Fuck Billy Bob Thornton. I'm dead serious. Un-fucking-believable."

"Mr. Stein, to tell the truth, I did not think it would work at first, but when he saw that envelope from the lawyer, he got real interested."

"And we got just what we came for," Jonathan said.

"Yes, sir," Wyatt replied. "You got your autograph, and I got my hair sample."

"It was brilliant," Jonathan said. "They must have my plane ready to go by now." He yawned. "I really need to get some sleep. I wish you could fly." Jonathan had to get back to Florida for an important lander simulation the next morning. Launch was in three weeks, and six-month-old Noah was still waking up at least three times a night.

"Do not worry, Mr. Stein. You will get plenty of sleep, too much sleep, on your spaceflight . . . just kidding. I think you actually might be the first to walk on the Moon. Forget that two-bit, two-stepping fisherman. He did not even notice I swiped his best lure."

"You didn't?"

"Take a look." Wyatt withdrew the bronzed-back, hand-carved minnow, still in its box, from his pocket.

"Wyatt, wouldn't the government have a problem explaining the lack of leftover Apollo equipment and American flags on the lunar surface when I get there and find nothing?"

"Mr. Stein, you really need to spend more time online. They got that one figured out already. I was reading ASAN-off.net, my new favorite website now that eclipsedtruth.com is gone. Another great name, by the way. You get it? It means NASA is backwards and *off.* Plus, when you say the site name fast, it sort of sounds like Asimov. You see that? It is all science fiction, not science fact."

"Clever," Jonathan said, looking out the window to make sure Armstrong was still on the dock.

"That is how I picked our names, by the way. I made us the berry brothers."

Jonathan kept his eyes on Armstrong. "I don't follow."

"Gene and Ray. Really? Roddenberry and Bradbury. All science fiction."

Jonathan smiled and turned toward Wyatt. "So what's your new friend Isaac have to say?"

"Did NASA have to approve your landing zone?"

"Yes."

"They made it miles away from the alleged Apollo landing sites, correct?"

"True."

"See what I mean?"

"Maybe they're just protecting all the space poop. Ninety-six bags of human waste. Talk about trash to treasure. Online auction sites would be buzzing for forty-year-old Aldrin scat, wouldn't they?"

"Damn, right. My buddy Russell would flip for some real astronaut logs, for sure, but no sir, they are still keeping their secrets." Wyatt pretended to zip his lip. "And they have not turned up any more evidence about that Nazi research or about your dad, right?"

"Nothing so far."

"ASAN-off.net says they are holding you at bay until the last of the old astronauts and flight controllers are all dead."

"I'm sure you're right."

"Glad to hear it," Wyatt said, still tone deaf to sarcasm. "You sure we get to keep these uniforms?"

"That's what Zubin said. I wouldn't ask too many questions when we drop off the truck."

"It will be an awesome disguise when I am out on repos. You promise your wife will run that hair through her lab right away?"

"Absolutely, we'll call you with the results as soon as we get them. Now let's get to the airstrip." As Wyatt shifted into gear to back out of the driveway, Jonathan yelled "Wait!"

"What is it?"

"I almost forgot. I'll be right back." Jonathan leaped out of the truck and ran to the cabin. At the front door, he bent down, resting on his haunches for a moment, popped up, bounded off the porch, and back into his seat.

"What the heck were you doing?"

"Mailing a letter."

"I hope you are not expecting a response. You know how he is."

"I know. That's what I'm counting on."

October 12, 2005

Dear Neil:

This is the last letter I'll ever write to you. After all these years of waiting to hear from you—waiting for your autograph, your advice, your sympathy, your approval, your support, your friendship, I have one last favor to ask. I know you've denied all of my other requests, but this time I think it might be different:

Please don't answer this letter.

I've come to believe that you've been writing me back, in your own eccentric way, for the last year. I don't have categorical proof, no smoking guns, probably couldn't convict you of it in court, but nonetheless I am certain. I came to this conclusion when I saw something in Cassandra's words. After I visited your house, I reread the website pages and the e-mails with a new perspective, and I discovered something—someone—in these writings: me. I was right there, pieces of me scattered among the tirades. You read all of my letters.

I've spent years telling you everything—sharing my triumphs and failings, my most crippling fears and intimate desires, my secret insights and lingering doubts. You knew everything you needed to know to create a customized, irresistible temptress. Who else could've have sent messages so finely tuned for my particular set of ears? You knew about the gym incident in Huntsville. You knew my frustration with NASA's mediocrity. You knew my love of wordplay, numbers, and puzzles. You knew the hoax websites Susana had found. You knew my dislike of Walt Disney. And better than anyone, you knew the hold that my father and Neil Armstrong had on my imagination. You wove all those threads together to draw me in. You knew I'd be coming. I know it was you in the archives.

You should really be an acting coach. Maria's performance was impeccable. Does she even have Tourette's? Maybe you snuck out the back the day we were there. And you knew I'd look for a computer. That IBM relic in the basement was like those worn-out duck decoys on the shelves, wasn't it? I don't know why you could only communicate through masquerade, but I know it was you behind the screen.

So why do I ask you, after all this time, to stay silent? Because faith doesn't require a response. Because I believe that the truth mattered to you, that justice mattered to you, that I mattered to you. Because I believe that you tried, as best you could, to do something good, something right. So I forgive the reclusion, the eccentricity, the manipulation—I forgive all of it.

Even God, if he exists, needs our forgiveness.

I believe you are Cassandra. So don't tell me that you're not. I wouldn't believe your denials anyway.

If I come across your footprints up there, I promise I won't step in them.

Infinitely yours,
Jonathan

EPILOGUE

November 3, 2005

23:23:56UTC

"Mission Control, do you copy?"

"Copy Commander Stein."

"We're firing thrusters to decelerate."

"Copy. Commence final landing sequence."

"Touchdown in . . . four . . . three . . . two . . . one . . . Noah's Ark has landed!" Jonathan cried. "The return of humanity to the Moon, after thirty years."

The copilot and mission specialists ran systems checks while Jonathan prepared himself.

"All systems nominal," the copilot said.

"Copy Noah's Ark. Commander, you are go for EVA."

Jonathan checked his space suit one last time, running his gloved hands over the synthetic fabrics that would protect him from the inhospitable environment. He grabbed a metallic pouch, opened the airlock, and stared out at what Aldrin had aptly described as "magnificent desolation." With only traces of gas in the diaphanous atmosphere, the Moon's vistas were razor sharp. The barren pockmarked plains and chalky mountains glowed radiant white. Only his glare shield protected him from the lunar equivalent of snow blindness. As he descended the ladder, he thought about what he'd planned. He hopped away from the lander, floating in slow motion above the surface between each step, and looked back at the Earth, a pale blue dot against a backdrop of an engulfing, infinite blackness, a glistening drop of water in an immense galactic desert. The sight was startling, glorious, heartbreaking.

He understood what Neil Armstrong had felt.

After checking the audio link with his crew and receiving confirmation that he stood within the sights of the lander's camera, he spoke to a worldwide audience.

"No one promised us this land. We've come here without covenant, entitlement, or assurance, to make our own way, guided by our mistakes as much as by our breakthroughs, seeking knowledge and meaning and survival. We may not have enough time. We may not find the answers we seek. The distances may be too great. But we come nonetheless. We come for the challenge, for the discovery, but we also come because it is a chance to start over, a chance to right wrongs, a chance to do better. We come, most of all, because every adventure—like every escape—begins with hope."

As soon as he finished his remarks, he cut the audio feed and moved away from the camera. He dropped to his knees and unzipped the pouch. He took out a titanium plaque and placed it on a flat section of ancient, blue-gray lava. The raised letters on the plaque's surface included Avi's full name, dates of birth and death, and a different quotation from the Book of Psalms, its citation a final variation on the numerals identifying the passage engraved on his tombstone. This time Psalms 9:19:

> Arise, Lord, do not let mortals triumph;
> Let the nations be judged in your presence.

Jonathan picked up two stones to take home. A pair of teardrops, untouchable under his visor, crawled down his cheeks as he stood up. With his head covered, multiple times, he pulled out a well-worn piece of blue and white cloth, his father's *tallit*, and draped it over his shoulders. *Yonatan ben Avraham* faced Jerusalem, which for the first time in his life was as simple as facing the Earth, and began to say *kaddish*:

Yisgadal v'yiskadash sh'mei rabba . . .

AUTHOR'S NOTE

During World War II, Wernher von Braun (1912–1977) was instrumental in the development of the German V-2 rocket. ("V" for *vergeltungswaffe*—"vengeance weapon.") In violation of international law, prisoners of war, thousands of whom died from malnourishment, disease, and beatings, were forced to work in rocket production facilities. Von Braun joined the Nazi Party in 1938 and the SS in 1940. In 1944, Hitler awarded him the Knight's Cross of the War Service Cross. Von Braun directed NASA's Marshall Space Flight Center from 1960 to 1970. He visited Brazil and Argentina in 1963. He also proposed the creation of space camp. An obituary in the *New York Times* referred to him as a "nominal" Nazi Party member. Psalms 19:1 is cited on his tombstone.

Kurt Debus (1908–1983) worked on von Braun's V-2 rocket team. He was also a member of the Nazi Party, joining the SA in 1933 and the SS in 1939. Debus proudly wore his SS uniform to work and once denounced a colleague to the Gestapo for anti-Hitler remarks. He directed NASA's Kennedy Space Center from 1962 to 1974. Each year, the National Space Club, Florida Committee, presents the "Debus Award" to a person who has made "significant contributions to the space industry." At the Kennedy Space Center Visitors Complex in Orlando, Florida, the Kurt H. Debus Conference Facility includes a "full-service kitchen staffed by an award-winning chef."

Hubertus Strughold (1898–1986) was a senior aeromedical researcher for the Luftwaffe from 1935 until the end of the war. He was not a member of the Nazi Party. In 1942, he attended a conference where results from experiments on prisoners at Dachau were presented. The extent of his involvement in, or authorization for, those experiments remains undetermined. In 1943, German children with epilepsy were taken from a euthanasia center to his Institute of Aviation Medicine and put into a vacuum chamber to induce seizures for the study of high-altitude sickness. After the war, he became a professor at the US Air Force's School of Aviation Medicine. He played an important role in the development of astronaut life support systems. According to a 1976 *New York Times* article, "[a] war-crimes inquiry focusing on him was ended after a call on his behalf from the chief counsel to the Senate Armed Services Committee." As a result of protests from the Anti-Defamation League, his name was removed, decades later, from the aeromedical library at Brooks Air Force Base in San Antonio, Texas, and in 2006, he was removed from the International Space Hall of Fame in Alamogordo, New Mexico. Prior to the war, during a Rockefeller fellowship in the United States, Strughold performed oxygen-deprivation and electric shock experiments on dogs imported from Canada because the Humane Society of the United States had prevented him from conducting tests on American dogs. The Space Medicine Association retired its annual Strughold Award in 2013.

In 1963, NASA acquired the Beach House as part of an expansion of the Kennedy Space Center at Cape Canaveral. It was the site of several mission celebrations in the 1960s and 1970s. More recently, the Beach House served as the place where shuttle crews said goodbye to their families before launch. It has a liquor cabinet displaying empty bottles signed by NASA astronauts to commemorate their missions.

Neil Alden Armstrong (1930–2012) often refused to sign autographs, particularly in the later years of his life. In 2005, he threatened to sue his barber for the return of his hair clippings, which had been sold to a collector for $3,000.

Ilan Ramon, the first Israeli astronaut, died on February 1, 2003, when the space shuttle *Columbia* exploded upon reentry. In honor of his mother, an Auschwitz survivor, Ramon had carried into space a copy of *Moon Landscape,* a 1942 drawing by Petr Ginz, a fourteen-year-old boy who was murdered at Auschwitz. The name "Ilan" means "tree" in Hebrew. After the *Columbia* tragedy, the entire crew was posthumously awarded the 2003 Strughold Award.

ACKNOWLEDGMENTS

The Astronaut's Son would not have become what it is without the guidance, encouragement, criticism, and love of so many people. While a mere written acknowledgment is insufficient to express my profound appreciation, here at least, in print, is a record of my sincere gratitude. Records help us remember and remembering is good.

A big thank you to the gang at Woodhall Press for their interest in my manuscript, their eager collaboration and professionalism, and their desire to share this story with the world. Thanks especially to Chris Madden, my astute and inspiring editor.

I had little more than a stack of unkempt papers with a jumble of words when I began my MFA studies, but with the enthusiastic and trenchant criticism of my terrific mentors—Hollis Seamon, Eugenia Kim, Howard Norman, and Rachel Basch—I graduated with a thesis that would eventually become this novel. I am deeply grateful for their commitment to the craft of writing and for their friendship.

Throughout this process I have learned that a novel is never really done until you think it is done at least three times. My wonderful developmental editor, Arielle Eckstut, not only helped me to see that the finish line was not as close as it first appeared but also plotted a course for me to reach it.

I am also grateful to my early readers—Baron Wormser, Jessy Sullivan, Nick Bourtin, Gena Cobrin, M.D., Kathryn Mayer, and Bill "Z.Z. Boone" Bozzone—for their honest reactions and insightful suggestions.

As little more than an amateur historian and space enthusiast, I could not have written this book without the background and context provided by real professionals. Among the books I lived with while writing this novel were: Eric Lichtblau's *The Nazis Next Door:*

How America Became a Safe Haven for Hitler's Men; Annie Jacobsen's *Operation Paperclip: The Secret Intelligence Program That Brought Nazi Scientists to America*; Michael Neufeld's *Von Braun: Dreamer of Space, Engineer of War*; Al Worden's *Falling to Earth*; and Gene Kranz's *Failure Is Not an Option*.

The biggest thanks, of course, go to my family. Without the love and support of my wife, Helene, and our two amazing daughters, I would never have been able to begin this journey and certainly would never have finished it. I love you all to the moon and back.